A Murder in Springtime

Also by Martin Walker

THE DORDOGNE MYSTERIES

Death in the Dordogne
(previously published as *Bruno, Chief of Police*)
Dark Vineyard
Black Diamond
The Crowded Grave
The Devil's Cave
The Resistance Man
Death Undercover
(previously published as *Children of War*)
The Dying Season
Fatal Pursuit
The Templars' Last Secret
A Taste for Vengeance
The Body in the Castle Well
A Shooting at Chateau Rock
The Coldest Case
To Kill a Troubadour
A Chateau Under Siege
A Grave in the Woods
An Enemy in the Village

SHORT STORIES

Bruno's Challenge & Other Stories

Martin
WALKER

with Kate Walker

A Murder in Springtime

QUERCUS

First published in Great Britain in 2026 by Quercus

Part of John Murray Group

1

A CIP catalogue record for this book is available from the British Library

HB ISBN 978 1 52944 865 8
TPB ISBN 978 1 52944 866 5
EBOOK ISBN 978 1 52944 867 2

Typeset in Swift by CC Book Production

Printed and bound in Great Britain by Clays Ltd, Elcograf S.p.A.

FSC www.fsc.org MIX Paper | Supporting responsible forestry FSC® C104740

Papers used by Quercus are from well-managed forests and other responsible sources.

Quercus
Carmelite House
50 Victoria Embankment
London EC4Y 0DZ

John Murray Group
Part of Hodder & Stoughton Limited
An Hachette UK company

The authorised representative in the EEA is Hachette Ireland,
8 Castlecourt Centre, Dublin 15, D15 XTP3, Ireland (email: info@hbgi.ie)

In loving memory of Fabien Mills-Marchez

a
MAP OF
BRUNO'S
PERIGORD
FRANCE
PERIGUEUX
CENDRIEUX
SAINTE-ALVERE
château de tiregand
ST DENIS
BERGERAC
LALINDE
DORDOGNE RIVER
LIMEUIL
BERGERAC
AIRPORT
château de monbazillac

château de hautefort
O R D
VEZERE RIVER
LASCAUX
(CAVES)
CAP BLANC
(ROCK SHELTER)
château de commarque
LES EYZIES
SARLAT
BEYNAC
N
château castelnaud la chapelle

The young boy's thin arms started to tremble under the strain. He gritted his teeth, tears forming in the corners of his eyes, and summoned every ounce of his remaining strength to keep his arms out straight, to stop the heavy books from falling on the floor. His shoulders shook and his elbows began to buckle.

'Attention!' *Madame shouted as he felt himself start to sway, his field of vision narrowing to blurry grey pinpricks. He closed his eyes and breathed in deeply through his nose, concentrating on the feeling of the air entering his lungs, of his ribcage expanding to let the outside in. In the fresh air he found untapped reserves of strength, the trembling in his limbs subsiding as he rounded his lips and slowly exhaled, his belly button drawing back into his spine as he focused on becoming solid, immutable.*

'Non!' *Her voice was muffled, far away, his ears felt like they were clouded with water, or cotton wool. 'Eyes open!' A sharp slap across the cheek. He bit his lip and tasted blood but managed to avoid flinching. But it was all for nought – his hard-won equilibrium had been shattered. Almost simultaneously, the two heavy tomes tumbled to the floor.*

That was the last thing Matthieu heard before his knees gave way, his skull hitting the old stone floor with a heavy thunk. He didn't hear Madame's horrified screams, nor the wailing sirens, not the clicking of the police's crime scene photographer's cameras, nor the swoosh of the wet mop as it wiped what was left of his blood from the flagstones.

1

Bruno Courrèges, chief of police of the Vézère Valley in the *département* of France officially named the Dordogne but which the locals stubbornly continue to call the Périgord, was engaged in one of his favourite pursuits. He was in the kitchen of his house on a Saturday evening in winter, cooking, with a glass of wine at his elbow. This was not unusual, since he loved to feast his friends, but on this particular evening he was cooking for two, which was rather less common. And he was doing so with a touch of romance in his heart, and a sense of occasion that had ensured that the carpets had been vacuumed, the sheets and towels changed, and the windows scrubbed till they sparkled.

His wine had been freshly poured from a bottle chilling on the steps outside the kitchen door, a locally grown Chardonnay from Château les Brandeaux. A bottle of Château Mondazur from the Pécharmant had been opened and awaited decanting. He had cooked a new batch of his own dog biscuits, not just for his basset hound, Balzac, but to be shared with an elegant young female of the same species who was also expected for dinner. She was named after the defiantly liberated novelist George Sand, who had shocked nineteenth-century France by wearing trousers and smoking in public while conducting flamboyant affairs with Chopin, de Musset and Prosper Mérimée, among others. It had been Bruno's recognition of the dog's name, and his appreciation of her looks, style and pedigree, that had alerted him to the special attractions of George Sand's owner, Laura Segret, who was to be his guest that evening.

They had met in unhappy circumstances, connected by the suicide of Laura's friend and business partner, Monique Duhamel. Bruno had found the body, in her own car, parked near a spot of Monique's happy childhood memories, and had brought to Laura a farewell letter addressed to her from her friend. The legal complications surrounding Monique's death had brought Bruno and Laura repeatedly together, and mutual admiration for each other's dogs soon turned into mutual attraction between their owners.

Cooking for a lover was special, Bruno thought, an act of love in itself. There was the planning of the setting; should lovers sit face to face? But the magic of touch would be much easier if one sat at the head of the table and the other alongside. It would also facilitate one of the special pleasures of lovers dining together, to offer choice forkfuls to the beloved. And then there was the choosing of the menu – nothing too heavy – and then of the wines, to be enjoyed in moderation.

Soup was not a good idea, and Bruno had decided to present as a first course a little smoked salmon. It was to be accompanied by two thin slices of toasted wholemeal bread, generously smeared with avocado, and a touch of black pepper. He had already prepared the dessert, a light syllabub of lemon juice, double cream and two wine glasses of Rosette, the sweet but light white wine that was unique to the Bergerac. Bruno had experimented with the dessert wine of the region, Monbazillac, but found it tended to dominate. These two dishes had been already prepared and were cooling in the fridge.

For the main course, he had decided on duck legs, picked up the previous day from his friends at the Lac Noir farm, who sold so many breasts to restaurants for *magrets* that they always had plenty of legs to spare. He swapped four legs and four of the tender *aiguillettes* in exchange for one of his own truffles. He recalled cooking *aiguillettes* with a sauce Montmorency, of sour cherries with orange juice, sweet cherries and kirsch, but that had been back in summer when cherries were ripe, so he'd thought of using honey and mustard to sauté them. But then he had a sudden mental image of himself and Laura each with a duck leg in hand, chewing happily together like some modern version of his favourite king Henri Quatre with his mistress Gabrielle d'Estrées. The memory of several jars of blackcurrant jelly made the previous summer confirmed his choice.

Bruno had chopped four cloves of garlic together with a handful of dried rosemary leaves and rubbed the mixture into the flesh and under the skin of four fat duck legs before laying them flat in a roasting pan, dusting them with five-spice powder and letting them marinate for an hour while he brought in sufficient wood to keep the stove going through the night.

Then he set the oven and put the roasting pan with the duck legs in for an hour and carried on with his cleaning. When the hour had passed he poured out the cupful of fat that had been sweated from the legs and added a quarter-litre of his home-made chicken stock and a glass of red wine, returned the pan into the oven and lowered the heat for another thirty minutes.

As Bruno checked his watch he saw it was almost eight – Laura seemed to be running late. He checked his phone, but she hadn't messaged. After thirty minutes had passed he checked on the duck and there was still a little stock not yet evaporated, so he lowered the heat further and gave it another twenty minutes. By this time he was getting nervous. She had planned to arrive by 19:30, and given it was Saturday she should have left the office hours ago. Strictly speaking, she shouldn't have been there at all.

This was now a dilemma: wait for her arrival and then serve the first course at once, or forget the first course and let her sit down and catch her breath so they could enjoy a drink together. He decided to do the latter and began peeling the potatoes, setting them to parboil before moving on to the garlic and mushrooms. There was still no word from Laura and it was almost nine. A call to her mobile went straight to voicemail; he hoped that meant she was driving. He would only need ten or fifteen minutes at most to slice the half-boiled potatoes and put them with the mushrooms, garlic and some parsley into a frying pan. He would also have to heat the remaining wine and the blackcurrant jelly and blend them into a gentle simmer, stirring constantly until it was ready to pour over the duck legs for their final twenty minutes in the oven.

At 21:15 he called the desk at the gendarmerie to ask if there was any trouble on the roads from Périgueux or Bergerac and was assured that all was well. Bruno now pondered his options. He could put the wine jelly mix over the duck legs and roast them for another twenty minutes and they would be perfect. Or he could stop everything, wait another half hour and know that he could have a hot meal on the table at ten, which Laura would find welcome after an evidently busy and perhaps difficult evening.

Bruno was aware that the transition of her company after Monique's death had not been going as planned. Laura had wanted to move the headquarters from the market town of Sarlat, whose tourist-trap status made movement almost impossible throughout the summer, to be closer to Bergerac and its airport. Many of their clients arrived by private plane, or by flights from London, Berlin or Amsterdam; she had assumed that the remaining clientele, who had long complained of the difficulties of reaching Sarlat, would fall in with her plans. But although she was by far the longest-serving member of the company's directors, she was not Monique, and she did not carry Monique's authority.

It was an unusual business that Monique had invented and slowly built with Laura's help, selling a package deal to clients who liked the idea of owning a small French chateau but could hardly justify the expense and the heavy insurance costs. Monique had realized that if the chateau were rented out by the week year round, and thus constantly inhabited, the insurance costs would plummet. They now had thirty such chateaux on their books, with owners who spent July, August and Christmas in their chateau, which for the rest of the year was rented out to holidaymakers, companies holding seminars or conferences, for fashion or commercial shoots and film-makers. They even had a package deal with a local dentistry to offer cosmetic treatments to international clients for a fraction of the cost back home, with recuperation in a French chateau thrown in.

Laura had been startled to learn that the two women who

worked out of Périgueux and managed the properties in the north of the Périgord did not want to move to a common base in Bergerac, and nor did the ones based in Sarlat. The two Bergerac-based staff did not want to move to the farmhouse near the airport that Laura had thought would have been perfect as their new HQ. Now her colleagues were suggesting that perhaps the company should be broken up into separate parts. The whole affair had been complicated by Monique's will, which had left Laura as the largest single shareholder in the company. But Laura could easily be outvoted by the other women. Three of them had been on board for not much more than a year while Laura could boast a decade's service.

Bruno had no voice in the matter, but he knew that in Sarlat, Laura's house and business were barely thirty minutes from his home outside St Denis. The Bergerac farmhouse would be an hour away, differences in commuting time that would not be helpful for a love affair, let alone a more enduring relationship. Laura now had the worst of both worlds with half her fellow partners in revolt against her move of the business office to the old farmhouse she had rented beside Bergerac airport. The two in Perigueux and another partner in Sarlat had refused to accept the change. And Bruno was not even sure whether Laura was officially living at her old address in Sarlat or at the Bergerac farmhouse. But he was unhappily aware that she was all too seldom seeing him.

Finally, his phone rang.

'I'm so sorry, *chéri*, but I only just got away. In fact I walked out, because otherwise you might have been arresting me for the murder of that greedy bitch from Périgueux.'

'Sorry you've had such a grim time,' he replied, trying to sound understanding and supportive and dampening down his own sense of frustration. 'Where are you now? I'm sure you must be hungry.'

'I'm still in Bergerac, and I'm too tired and too angry to drive. I'll crash at Sylvie's place tonight and see you tomorrow. Will your dinner keep?'

'Yes, of course, don't worry about it,' he said. 'We don't need to eat. But it sounds as though you do need comfort. Shall I drive over and pick you up?'

'You're so sweet, Bruno, but I'm not fit company. I'll probably be stalking the floor in a not-so-quiet rage. And I'll make sure to be on time tomorrow.'

With a heavy heart Bruno set about finishing his dinner preparations, a romantic supper *pour deux* now two sad meals for one. He made a plate for himself and wrapped up the second portion to reheat for a quick supper later in the week. Despite his careful attentions in the kitchen Bruno ate without pleasure, his mind on the unique challenge of pursuing a relationship with a woman clearly dedicated to her career. He had been down a version of this road before, he thought. Was Laura becoming Isabelle mark two? He quickly shook his head to dislodge that notion. Laura and Isabelle were two very different women, and he couldn't let his baggage from one affect the potential of happiness with the other.

Despite waking up alone, the pans from last night's attempt at a romantic dinner mocking him on the draining board while he made his coffee, Bruno had to admit that it was a beautiful

Sunday morning in the Périgord, the first day of the year that really felt like spring. It had been an endless winter, the Vézère Valley draped in an uncharacteristically thick blanket of grey cloud from All Saints' all the way through to Shrove Tuesday. For the first time in his many years in the Dordogne, Bruno had come to understand his friend Pamela's occasional sense of claustrophobia from the high hills and thick forests that surrounded them.

But this morning was different – fresh, vibrant. Bruno recalled the opening line of one of the many novels Pamela had pressed upon him over the years: 'It was a bright cold day in April, and the clocks were striking thirteen . . .' As if cued, a distant bell tower struck the hour – a perfectly normal nine.

Reaching his Land Rover with a spring in his step and a smile on his face, Bruno rolled down both windows before putting his keys in the ignition. He turned right down the main street, following the new one-way system through the centre of St Denis at the twenty kilometres per hour crawl now mandated by law. One advantage of this new system, though, was how much it encouraged interaction – scarcely a shopkeeper allowed his vehicle to pass by without a wave, a smile, or a *bonjour*.

To his left was the Moroccan *boulangerie* whose hearty olive loaves had become something of a bad habit before his once-daily indulgence had been cut back to weekly. On the other side of the road, Florence was dunking a croissant into her café crème in the courtyard of the Café de Paris, her nose so deep in *Le Figaro* that she failed to notice Bruno call and wave as he passed on his way out of town. Her twins, Dora and Daniel, were rather more alert and blew kisses at Balzac.

Today he was a man on a mission – St Denis was undergoing a slump, and Bruno had decided that he was going to be the man to bring his beloved town back to life. It had been St Denis that had restored him after the horrors of his time in the Balkans all those years ago, and as a man of honour it was on him to return the favour.

Bruno drove in the direction of St Christophe de la Domaine, on the other side of Les Eyzies. Similar in size to St Denis, in recent years St Christophe had positioned itself as the most desirable village in the Périgord, attracting a seemingly endless stream of high-rollers after the town had been chosen as the location for a Netflix series that had done for it what Inspector Montalbano did for Sicily, every bed and every table booked solid from New Year's Day to Christmas Eve.

The drive took him along winding roads lined with thick rows of chestnut trees. Where pockets of sunlight made it through the dense foliage they landed on the green buds just now beginning to spring from the bushes, the scent of greenery filling the cab and bringing with it a vitality, an energy, that can only come from the newness of spring. Bruno inhaled deeply. 'Ah, what a beautiful day,' he said to Balzac, who seemed to snuffle his agreement.

As he drove, familiarity making easy work of the sweeping corners that rolled up and down the gentlest of hills, the thick forest eventually making way for open fields that in the summer would be given over to maize and sunflowers, Bruno turned his mind to the meeting ahead. As luck would have it, the mayor of St Christophe was an old friend from St Denis – everyone in the Périgord was an old friend from St Denis, it seemed sometimes – and he looked forward to a weekend morning spent both reminiscing and brainstorming.

Rounding the final bend, the forest gave way to the valley below, layers of green falling over themselves into the slowly moving river, less springtime swollen than usual after an atypically mild – if grey – winter. After the damaging floods of the previous autumn, very little rain had fallen – a relief for those whose homes had been at risk from the deluge, but yet another challenge for the *vignerons* and farmers whose livelihoods depended on a more reliable climate.

Spanning the banks on both sides was the town of St Christophe, neat rows of townhouses in the honey-hued stone so characteristic of the *département*. Bruno's eye was drawn to the church spire, which peered above the trees, and for a moment he fancied he could smell the waxy magnolias that dominated the market square with their discarded petals in late summer.

It was a picture-perfect scene, and a far cry from the soulless modern building on the outskirts of town that had been built to accommodate the ever-growing number of public officials needed to service the Dordogne. Bruno paused at the entrance to the car park and called a greeting to Agnès, the eldest daughter of his nearest neighbour in the hills above St Denis. A recent graduate of the local school and also of Bruno's rugby programme, Agnès had stepped straight into an admin role at the local council. It was a perfect fit for an efficient and dedicated young woman, he thought.

Taking care to park his Land Rover in the shade, Bruno took out his phone to call Laura. 'Did you make it in on time today?'

'I did. I'm sorry about last night, but I needed the sleep more than anything.'

Bruno felt mildly aggrieved but understood. 'Not a problem. I was able to rescue the dinner.' He heard Laura draw breath down the phone and felt he might be treading on dangerous ground. 'And I look forward to seeing you tonight, of course.'

'I don't think tonight will be possible, I'm afraid.'

'No?'

'I can't promise it won't turn out like yesterday, and I don't want to let you down again.'

'Another late one? What about the rest of the team? Isn't there someone you can delegate to?'

Bruno thought it was an innocent question, but the response was cool. 'I am perfectly capable of doing my job.'

'Of course you are. It's why Monique left you the lion's share. I'm just worried about all these long hours you're keeping – it can't be good for you.'

'Then you won't mind me ringing off so I can get on with my work.'

The answering 'I miss you' landed on dead air, and Bruno felt dejected as he crossed the car park. He had scarcely made himself known at reception before a clattering of footsteps on the stairs heralded the arrival of Jérôme, an outstanding performer at the St Denis tennis club – and breaker of a few hearts – before finding his *métier* in the world of local politics on the other side of the Périgord Noir.

'*Mon brave!*' Jérôme approached Bruno with his bear-like paw extended, wrapping a hairy hand around Bruno's own and drawing the policeman into a tight embrace before squatting down to lavish attention on Balzac. 'It has been far, far too long.'

Bruno pulled back, a smile on his face. 'St Denis misses you, my friend. You should try and make the drive.'

Jérôme shook his head. 'It's all work and no play, the life of a mayor.'

'I'm sure you hardly have a moment to yourself these days. I'm grateful you've made the time for me, especially on a Sunday.'

'For Bruno Courrèges? Anything.' He pointed a thumb over his shoulder at the stairs. 'Would you like to head up to the office, or shall we go for a coffee?'

Bruno cocked his head to one side, thinking. 'How about a walk along the river? It would be a shame to waste such a day.' Jérôme nodded, and the two men walked in lockstep through the automatic doors and turned as one towards the riverside promenade, recently rebuilt thanks to a generous interpretation of EU community funding grants.

They chatted companionably, Bruno taking in the extent of the work done while Balzac sniffed for updates from the local canine population. Where once the riverbank had been a resting place for abandoned stolen bicycles and the soda cans and beer bottles left behind by recalcitrant teens, now there were raised square flower beds dotted with the sprigs of new growth, surrounded on all sides with bench seating. As they drew closer to the historic centre, the wide flagstones were taken up with café tables, each and every one occupied. It was a far cry from the sorry state of affairs in St Denis, Bruno thought.

'This is looking fantastic,' he said, turning to his friend. 'I can't believe what a difference it's made.'

Jérôme nodded. 'It's changed the character completely. Instead of kids hiding from their parents, we've got the whole town using it to meet.'

'And to work.' Bruno waved his hand at a cluster of pulled together tables occupied by a group of men and women in their twenties and thirties, all of them sitting at laptops and barking into headsets.

'Netflix. They're here to scout locations for season four.'

Bruno pursed his lips and whistled slowly. 'Season four? That's impressive, I didn't realize it had been running so long. And how is it with the tourists? A busy summer ahead?'

Jérôme shook his head, but the look on his face was of astonishment, not denial. 'Even busier than you can imagine, *mon ami*. It's what, April? And we have maybe four beds available for the rest of the summer. Campsites, hotels, *gîtes*, you name it – we're like Bethlehem on Christmas Eve.'

Bruno laughed. 'Not a bad problem to have. And, in fact, not unrelated to my purpose in coming to see you.'

'You mean it wasn't for my good looks and scintillating company? Bruno, I'm offended!' Jérôme laughed as he punched his friend in the bicep.

'And so you should be! No, this time I'm here for your brains.'

'That's more like it,' Jérôme interrupted before being silenced with a look.

'Jokes aside, I'm here for your counsel. St Denis is struggling these days, and I'd like your advice on how we can put ourselves back on the map.'

Jérôme stopped walking and turned to look at Bruno, concern etched on his face. 'Struggling how? We're not even at Easter.'

'Struggling however you can imagine. When was the last time

you came to the market?' Jérôme paused to think and Bruno carried on. 'It's telling that you even have to think about it. Ten years ago and Tuesdays in St Denis were like the Galeries Lafayette during the sales – you couldn't move!'

'And now?'

'And now we're not even seeing the same number of locals. Le Croiseau moved their market to a Tuesday morning and ever since we've been, what do you call those rolling balls from the Westerns? Ah yes, tumbleweeds. We have been tumbleweeds. Pierre-Olivier is considering not renewing his permit when it expires, says he's not covering his costs any more. And he's not alone.'

Jérôme shook his head as Bruno went on. 'It's like dominoes. When a lynchpin like Pierre-Olivier goes, others will follow. If enough leave, the market dies. And what's a market town without a market?' Jérôme made to interject, but Bruno held out a hand to stop him.

'Rhetorical question. The market is our heart. It's where our old folks shop, where they stop and chat, where they keep a foot in the community. It's where our farmers, our producers, our artisans make their living. Without the market, how long would the café stay open? The Maison de la Presse? The *boulangeries*? Our market is our magnet and we can't afford to lose it.'

Turning his back on the river, Bruno leaned his elbows on the railings and met his friend's worried gaze. 'I need another brain on this project and I'd like your advice.' With a raised arm he indicated the revitalized riverside. 'Look at what you've managed to pull off here.'

*

Bruno was reflective on the drive back to St Denis, so lost in thought that he failed to notice the chorus line of wildflowers beginning their dance on the verges. The flashing of his phone's screen as it rang in its holder was harder to ignore, and a quick glance showed it was Pamela. He would ring her back the minute he parked. How productive his expedition would turn out to be remained to be seen, but if nothing else Jérôme had left him feeling confident that change was possible. If there was one thing he'd learned from his years in St Denis, it was that its population was capable of springing more than the odd surprise when push came to shove.

Pamela's call was entirely forgotten by the time he pulled into the parking lot next to the Hôtel de Ville that housed the Mairie. Bruno was chuckling at one of his earliest St Denis memories, more than a decade old now, of chasing an escaped camel through the backstreets after an over-ambitious nativity scene went awry. Dozens of his fellow townspeople had joined in the chase, which concluded with one captured camel and a rather drunken Christmas singalong in the very square in which he was now parking. This was a town that had embraced him as a son, and as a son its rescue was on his shoulders, he felt.

Bruno reached into the back seat, where his work clothes were freshly pressed and sitting tidy in a suit bag, ready for his afternoon rounds. Ducking into the Mairie, he tossed a quick *bonjour* at Claudette on the front desk before making his way to the bathroom in the lobby for a quick change.

'From Clark Kent to Superman!' Claudette laughed when he re-emerged. 'Did you have a good morning off?'

'I went to St Christophe, had a coffee with Jérôme. He asked me to send you his love, tell you to stay out of trouble.' Claudette blushed and Bruno smiled to himself; the receptionist's crush on her former colleague was the stuff of town legend.

Suited and booted, Bruno quickly assessed his reflection in the glass doors as he headed out and found that he looked properly professional. Waiting to cross the road by the bridge, he took the opportunity to look down at St Denis's dilapidated riverside, shrouded in a thick tangle of climbing plants pockmarked with discarded rubbish. Little was left of the town bandstand and the remains of an ancient nunnery after October's floods, which had left their mark on the town. Happily, the loss of life had been minimal, the only two confirmed deaths a cybercriminal and his brother.

Under the carpet of greenery had once been a handsome brick path; he half-remembered a fleur-de-lis pattern surrounded by a Greek key in a darker stone. In his mind's eye he stripped back the foliage and littered the path with café tables and sun umbrellas, sun-kissed laughing couples stopping for *un petit apéro* on their way to dinner, families having coffees as small children clattered between the tables, shouting for ice cream. Shaking his head of the vision, Bruno took a deep breath and turned around to begin his beat.

Officially far too senior for foot patrol, Bruno had no time for policemen of any stripe who found the task beneath them. To Bruno, to know the job was to know the people, and besides hosting groaning town feasts whenever the opportunity arose, as far as he was concerned there was no better way to know the people than to know their gossip, know their lives. He had always been of the mind that a village policeman did his best work through community involvement, by making his presence more familiar and reassuring than threatening. For as long as he'd been in St Denis Bruno had invested his free time in the local community, getting to know the local children through sport and other activities. Now that he was chief of police for the entire Vézère Valley it was a little trickier to get to know all his charges, but his approach remained the same.

He suddenly remembered, he must ring Pamela. There were now two missed calls from her number. His own call rang out, and he left a message. 'Sorry to have missed you, meetings and driving. But I'm back now, so do call me when you get this. *Bisous.*'

He decided to head for the *tabac* on the roundabout, where Marcel was sure to bear a fresh grudge or six. Tourists parking in his spot, an increase in the price of fuel, someone ahead of him in line at the post office; somehow Marcel managed to find a new enemy with every passing day. It was hard to believe that this was the same grouch who dressed up as Père Noël every Christmas, driving all the way to his childhood home in Avignon to hand out gifts and entertain the kids spending the festive season at the local hospital.

'Marcel, how are you today?' As had been the case ever since they changed the smoking laws, Marcel was leaning in his narrow doorway, cigarette hanging from the corner of his mouth like an extra in *À Bout de Souffle*.

'Very well, Bruno! And you?'

He shrugged. 'You know how it is.'

Marcel nodded and tossed his cigarette to the ground. Bruno coughed and looked at it.

'Would you like to pick that up or should I write you a ticket for littering?'

Marcel rolled his eyes but bent over and picked up the butt before stepping back into the shop, waving for Bruno to follow. 'A coffee?'

Bruno shook his head. 'I've had enough coffee for the moment, thank you. Perhaps a sparkling water?'

While pouring Bruno's drink Marcel spoke under his breath, softly enough that the policeman had to strain to hear. 'As far as I can tell the defectors are up to six now.'

Bruno raised an eyebrow. '*Six?* You're joking.' His phone rang, and he answered without looking at the screen. '*Allô bonjour?*'

'Bruno!' Pamela's voice was breathier than usual, as if she'd been running. 'I'm so glad to have finally caught you. I'm just off the phone with the gendarmerie; I seem to have come home to a murder.'

2

Bruno's Land Rover joined a convoy of police cars and fire engines heading to Pamela's. The property was at zero risk of conflagration, but the pompiers were also trained emergency medical technicians, and someone needed to be at the scene before the medical examiner could make it out from Périgueux. When he pulled up, Pamela was standing on the edge of her front lawn, a grey woollen blanket wrapped around her shoulders despite the warm spring air. There was a look of utter horror etched upon her face, and from a distance Bruno could tell that the officer she was with wasn't bringing much comfort. 'Pamela!' He strode towards her. 'I got here as soon as I could. Tell me what happened.'

Bruno saw his Scottish friend blanch and swallow before inhaling deeply through her nose and setting her back and shoulders straight. It was a pose he knew well. 'God, it was awful, just awful.' She shook her head. 'I'd just headed out to the *boulangerie* to pick up some bread for dinner, and when I came back, there she was on the patio, bleeding out onto the stone.' Pamela shuddered, and Bruno gave her arm what he hoped was a reassuring squeeze.

'And so you called me?'

'What?' She shook her head, whether to indicate no or to clear her mind of a sight that would never be unseen Bruno couldn't tell. 'Oh no, I called 112, asked for an ambulance. But you know how long they take to get here, so I asked for the *pompiers* too. It was only then that I called you. I didn't go anywhere near the body. I didn't want to disturb anything.'

Bruno nodded. 'You did the right thing. So this woman, the victim. Do you know her?'

'She's my lodger, I'm sure I told you about her. Josette, Josette Quirit.' Pamela shook her head. 'She seemed like such a lovely woman, who on earth would want to hurt her?'

Bruno shrugged. 'I'll have to notify any next of kin, her employers . . . Did you make a copy of her ID when she rented the room?'

Pamela reached into the pocket of her trousers. 'I did actually, there'll be a photo of it on here somewhere.' She quickly scrolled through what looked to be a thousand photos of horses and wildflowers on her phone, interspersed with shots of children he assumed were the nieces and nephews she sometimes spoke of. She held the phone out to Bruno. 'Here you go. If you need anything more than that they'll probably have more information at the old folks' home. They must have done a background check before they hired her.'

He copied all of the information from Josette Quirit's ID card into his little notebook. 'Yes, but without a warrant for that information it's guarded by data privacy laws.'

'I think if you tell them she's been murdered they'll be more than happy to put you in touch with her family.' Under the blanket Pamela shivered, and she wrapped it more tightly around her, gulping as she did so. 'So, what happens now? Do you need me to give you a statement? Am I a suspect?'

'At the moment I would say you are helping the police with their inquiries,' Bruno said. 'I'll have to get someone to take a formal statement from you; you are the person who found the body after all. But once you've done that you'll be free to go, although we'll need you to tell us if you're planning on leaving the *département* for the duration of our inquiries.'

'Really? That feels serious.' Pamela bit her lower lip, a nervous habit with which Bruno was familiar. 'And what about the house? Can I stay here, or is it a crime scene?'

'It's an active crime scene, I'm afraid. Is there anyone else you can stay with? I'd offer my place but given the investigation it simply isn't possible for me to host a potential witness. Sorry.'

'No need to apologize – I understand entirely. I'll start making some calls. But what about the riding school? And Jack and Miranda's houses? Will the whole place be on lockdown?'

Both Jack Crimson and his daughter Miranda were close friends of Bruno's and had been for almost as many years as he'd known Pamela. Miranda was Pamela's partner in the riding school, and lived with her children in a small cottage on site, a hundred or so metres away from Pamela's house. Next door lived her father Jack, a retired diplomat with a background in British intelligence, who had helped Bruno with several cases.

'I can't answer those questions until we've assessed the scene, I'm afraid. But even if I assume the worst, we'll make sure the animals are taken care of. Where are Jack and Miranda? Are they not here?'

Pamela shook her head. 'They're both away for the week, a

father–daughter trip to Biarritz with the children. Félix has been staying at Miranda's while they're gone, but I've not seen him since last night; he went into town to meet up with his friends.'

Bruno nodded. 'At least that reduces the number of people on site. You make those calls. I'll go and assess the scene.'

Bruno made his way around the side of the house and onto the back patio overlooking the swimming pool, a spot where he had enjoyed countless glasses of wine and simple shared suppers over the years, as both a lover and a friend. What had been a peaceful place from which to watch the sunset now told of horrors, with blood staining the pale flagstones and globules of blood and thicker matter splashed up the open shutters and the glass of the closed French windows.

At the centre of the atrocity was the wiry body of a slim but strong woman who Bruno guessed to be older than himself. Her hair had been recently coloured an unusual mix of reds and greys and was cropped fairly short, in that uneven style Bruno knew to be popular among local women of a certain age. It wouldn't take a coroner to identify the cause of death (although one was of course required by law); the hefty, bloodied stone and the concave skull together told most of the story.

Where a specialist would be required was to determine the number of blows. From the amount of blood that surrounded the victim Bruno could tell that it had been a particularly ferocious attack, and he guessed that multiple strikes would have been inflicted post-mortem, usually an indicator of a close personal relationship between victim and killer, a vendetta of sorts. Still, his job was to keep an open mind, not let assumptions cloud his judgement. He spotted Annette Fournet, a young officer whom he had always found to be highly capable, making notes in the corner and walked towards her. 'Who's running this investigation? Has it been assigned yet?'

Annette looked confused. 'I assumed it would be you, chief.'

Bruno shook his head. 'I have to recuse myself. The woman who owns this house is a friend.' The junior officer raised her eyebrows but said nothing. 'When they name a lead can you send him or her my way? I might be able to help with some background.'

From the cab in his Land Rover Bruno began to make calls. First on his list was J-J, or Jean-Jacques Jalipeau, his friend and the closest thing he had to a boss at the Police Nationale – with whom he collaborated but was not employed, French national policing structures being rather complex.

The phone was answered almost the instant Bruno heard the burr of the ringtone on the line. 'Bruno, my man, how are you?'

'Not bad, J-J, I'm okay. Has anyone from my Préfecture been in touch?'

'Not a soul. Why?'

'There's been a murder in St Denis, and I'm going to have to recuse myself from the investigation.'

'Really?'

'The murder was on Pamela's property.' J-J let out a long slow whistle. 'Exactly,' Bruno replied.

'The blessing and the curse of policing in a small town, eh?'

'The ties that bind. I've had a preliminary chat with Pamela, just to get a sense of the timeline before the coroner can give us an approximate time of death, and I've asked her to come in and make an official statement, but we're going to need one of your officers from the *police judiciaire* to be sent over on secondment.'

'But of course, Bruno, of course. Send me an email detailing the request and I'll get the wheels in motion.'

Bruno could hear the creaking wood as J-J leaned back in his chair. 'Watch you don't tip over, my friend.'

J-J laughed. 'Detective Bruno, never off the case.'

'Except this time. I'll send you that request, but if you could get someone here by morning—'

'I'll have someone on their way to you within the hour.'

Bruno looked at his watch and judged that the officer from the *police judiciaire* he'd requested would be arriving in St Denis around sunset. 'I'll book a hotel room as soon as we're off the phone and text you the details. Should I charge it through the Mairie, or can I bill the Police Nationale?'

'Make it two rooms and charge it to us. I'm long overdue a visit to St Denis.'

No sooner was Bruno off the phone with J-J than his mobile began to buzz again in his hand. It was Pamela.

'Bruno? I just wanted to let you know that I've found somewhere to stay. Florence has agreed to put me up tonight, and from tomorrow the Guyonnets have offered me, Jack, Miranda and the children the use of one of their bigger *gîtes* for as long as we need it. Gilles and Fabiola's *gîtes* are all full with Abby's Americans.'

Bruno smiled with relief; that was one small problem he didn't have to worry about. 'Excellent. Are you at Florence's now?'

'I'm about to arrive. One of your gendarmes, Mademoiselle Fournet, is giving me a lift.'

Bruno nodded approvingly, satisfied the team were being both professional and thoughtful, although they technically weren't 'his' gendarmes. 'Let me know if you need me to bring anything over for you.'

'I'm sure Florence will be able to lend me anything I might need but thank you. Tomorrow I can always head into town and buy enough bits and bobs to see me through the week.'

'J-J is sending us someone to manage the investigation; I've got to get off the phone and book them a hotel. But with any luck we'll have you back in your place before too long.'

'Don't let me keep you! I just wanted to let you know I was all taken care of, I know what you're like for worrying.'

Bruno smiled. 'Give my love to Florence when you get there.'

After Pamela rang off Bruno organized two rooms at the Hôtel St Denis for the visiting police officers, and texted J-J with the details. Seconds later, he received a reply: 'Merci. On our way. Breakfast tomorrow 8am. J-J'. Tapping a quick thumbs up in reply, Bruno was about to put his car into gear and set off for the Mairie, where there was still work to be done, when he paused, phone still in his hand. Opening up the web browser, he Googled "Josette Quirit". Dozens of pages of search results appeared, social media accounts, photo libraries and the like.

Bruno navigated to Facebook and completed the same search; the list was sizeable. "Josette Quirit" and "France" scarcely narrowed it down at all, "Josette Quirit" and "St Denis" returned zero results, and "Josette Quirit" and "Dordogne" brought things to a more manageable figure. Of the half-dozen profiles that hadn't been set to private, none featured a woman of the right age. A handful of private accounts with visible profile pictures didn't help eliminate anyone; the photos were a mix of pets and infants and famous world landmarks.

He sighed. There was no guarantee a woman of her age would have been on social media, so there was no low-hanging fruit to be found here at first glance. Bruno saw a long stretch of screen time ahead, and he didn't relish the prospect one bit.

'Bruno! To what do I owe this pleasure?' He found himself clasped firmly by the Mayor, who planted a kiss on each cheek.

'It is good to see you again, Monsieur le Maire. Thank you for making time on a Sunday. I hope you enjoyed your holiday?'

'Wonderful. But the relaxing effect has worn off already, I'm sure you know what it's like. Sit down.' The Mayor led Bruno over to a pair of armchairs near a small coffee table, on which was sitting a cafetière and two cups. 'I assume you'll have a coffee?'

Bruno nodded and perched on the edge of his chair while he waited for the drink to be poured. As the Mayor busied himself with the cups, Bruno surveyed the room, which had hardly changed since his first visit years before, the final stage of interviews for his new life in St Denis. His first impressions had been of a warm and jovial individual, and while the two men had butted heads over the years their relationship had yet to give him a reason to change his mind. If anything, they had grown ever closer, and Bruno tended to think of Gérard Mangin as the father figure he'd never had. While their methods might differ, the two had long been united in their desire to serve St Denis to the best of their abilities. Which, given his purpose in setting up this meeting, was exactly what Bruno was counting on.

'*Alors*, Bruno.' The two men settled back in their respective armchairs, coffee cups and saucers balanced precariously on knees.

With a shake of his head, Bruno refused the proffered splash of Armagnac, and smiled at the not insignificant dose of liquid fire Gérard added to his own cup. 'It's not like you to request a formal meeting out of hours – how can I help you today?'

'Has anyone notified you of the murder up at the riding school?'

The Mayor shook his head. 'I'm shocked to hear it, but isn't that your responsibility?'

'It would be, if I were the investigating officer, but as the crime has taken place on Pamela's property I can't be involved until she's no longer a suspect.'

Gérard nodded. 'Of course. So who's taking over?'

'J-J is bringing up one of his officers from Périgueux today, that's all I know for the moment. I'll make sure that he keeps you in the loop. All I can tell you is that the victim was new to the area, an older woman working at the care home.'

'Very sad news. And is Pamela okay?'

'Shocked, but unharmed. She was the one who found the body, and it was a violent death.'

'What is the world coming to, nurses being killed in cold blood on a beautiful spring day?' The Mayor shook his head. 'And was there something else you wanted to talk about?'

Bruno leaned forward. 'There was. I have a few ideas for St Denis, and none of them will be possible without your support.' Across the table, Gérard nodded for him to continue. 'To be frank, I'm worried. Worried about St Denis. I know that small towns across Europe are struggling, but we seem to be suffering more than most. Not a month goes by without another "to let" sign going up in town, businesses are closing all the time. And now the market is suffering; ever since Le Croiseau—' At this the Mayor groaned.

'Don't talk to me about Le Croiseau,' he growled. 'Jacqueline won't stop complaining that we're losing all our best stalls to them.'

Bruno nodded. 'Precisely. And the market is like the canary in the gold mine. The health of the market dictates the health of the town. And while I'm no doctor I'd say that both patients are in need of intensive care.'

'You're not wrong there. So what do you propose?'

'Pamela was telling me about some projects that are being tried out in the north of England, attempts to regenerate old industrial towns with little to no employment, youth brain drain, that sort of thing. One thing they're trying is to fight the death of the shopping precincts by using closed businesses as launchpads for the young.' Bruno paused to take a sip of his coffee.

'It used to be that the local councils would give what they call "charity shops" – like our Emmaus – free rent, lower business rates. But in recent years, the towns have become overrun with second-hand and discount shops and so a few towns are offering "pop-ups" for new businesses, six months of free rent for enterprises started by young people born in the area. After six months, either the business is successful enough that rents and proper payments are possible, or the site is turned over to the next entrepreneur to give them a chance.'

Bruno paused, gratified to see that the Mayor was leaning towards him as though trying to get closer to the concept. 'And you think we should look at doing something similar in St Denis?'

'I do. If the premises are sitting empty anyway, what have

we got to lose? The new occupants will at least tidy things up, sweep away the cobwebs and add a lick or two of paint, and if they're successful? We could have a bustling centre of enterprise on our hands.'

The Mayor was nodding slowly, and Bruno waited. He pursed his lips a few times, chewing on his thought. 'I like the concept, I really do. Low risk, low cost, and the possibility of real success. But I have to think about this like a politician, you know that.' Bruno nodded assent; he could anticipate the Mayor's objection and already had the answer waiting up his sleeve. 'What about the businesses already operating? They're going to be livid if we ship in a bunch of competition without costs to pay, and who can blame them?'

'They won't be a problem.'

'Really? How so?'

'Marcel from the *tabac* has been keeping his eyes and ears open at the bar, listening to all the gossip from the market. Once the stallholders started dropping out, the likes of Jules and Bernadette started to fear for their own stability, and by the time the Mesniers closed the ironmongery everyone on the rue de Paris started calculating how long they thought they could afford to stay open.' Bruno leaned forward to refresh his cup. 'As long as we can guarantee that none of the new businesses will be in direct competition, and that we stick to the six-month rent-free trial, almost the entire street is on board.'

'It certainly seems like you've got all your ducks in a row.' Gérard smiled. 'You've got no immediate objections from me. But something like this will have to go through the council, get proper approvals, you know how it is.'

'I do. And I know it could take time. But there are some things that we can do quickly, again with no cost, and all the authority we would need is right here in this building.'

'Tell me more.'

'It's the market. We've now got six empty spots on a Tuesday, and that's on top of the stalls we've lost to non-renewals over the past eighteen months. While we wait for the council to discuss my shops idea, why don't we give over some stalls – gratis – to local businesses? We'd have to avoid anything edible or deal with the hassle of licences, but local artisans, crafters? Let's hold a lottery for one of ten free tables at the Tuesday market, May to September, open to anyone who lives in the Dordogne.'

Gérard threw his head back and laughed. 'My word, you have been busy, haven't you?' He nodded. 'I like it, I like it a lot.'

Bruno gestured to stop. 'The market plan hasn't been given the Marcel treatment, I'm afraid – I have no idea how many objections there might be.'

'We can overcome them, it's not impossible. Make it one month and have three tables available. Instead of ten competitors for five months, they can deal with fifteen for a month apiece. We can turn it into some sort of competition, see if we can get some media interest.' The Mayor made an expansive sweep of his hands. '"Find St Denis's Next Market Hero", I can see it now. Perfect silly season material for Gilles to sell to *Paris Match*. We'll be overrun with tourists!'

Bruno chuckled. 'Never let it be said that you lack ambition.'

3

Bruno awoke bright and early the following morning, roused by the dawn chorus outside his open window. This early in the spring there was still a damp chill in the air before the sun crested the hills, but the benefit of breathing fresh air in the night was worth any minor discomfort as he padded from bedroom to bathroom in his bare feet, the tiles cold beneath his toes.

Despite having formally recused himself from the murder at Pamela's, Bruno found himself infused with the energy of an ongoing investigation, endless checklists forming in his head before he remembered – once, twice, thirty times! – that the responsibility for keeping the show on the road wasn't his at all. Checking his watch he saw it was still too early to round up J-J and the mystery investigating officer for breakfast, but there was plenty of time to attend to his beloved garden and have his morning run. Before stepping outside he rang Laura on the off-chance he'd reach her before she left for the office. The call rang out, so she was either asleep or driving, and he tapped out a text. 'Thinking of you, missing you.'

With his phone in his hand he decided to take another shot at finding out something about Josette Quirit. His initial forays on Facebook hadn't proved productive, but there had to be something out there – very few people managed to live without leaving traces of themselves somewhere on the internet. Were he officially on the case he'd be able to search the police computers, cross-referencing the victim's known addresses and employment history with records of any police stops, tax violations, contact with government officials of every stripe. As things stood, he'd have to rely on what he could Google, and which small town bureaucracies had both digitized their records and made them accessible to the public.

He took out his notebook, and went back to the page containing the ID info he'd copied at Pamela's. "Josette Quirit" and "Menton" went into Google. There were a couple of links on the *Nice Matin* site, and he navigated to two human interest pieces about fundraising events at the care home in Menton. In one, Josette Quirit was photographed escorting an elderly resident along the Promenade du Soleil, and named in the caption. In the other, she was quoted as saying how much the residents enjoyed their annual outing to the Fête du Citron each winter, so nothing of any use beyond confirming that she had worked at the home as claimed. Bruno then tried "Josette Quirit" and "debt", "Josette Quirit" and "divorce", "Josette Quirit" and "foreclosure", and "Josette Quirit" and "police", and in each case there were too many potential results to be useful. Adding Menton to the search terms didn't help, and he didn't know where else she'd lived. Yet. Refusing to be disheartened, he stepped out into his garden.

Springtime in the Périgord was a glorious time to be alive, Bruno thought, as he surveyed his potager, neat rows of beans-to-be lined up on their vines like regimental soldiers, tiny green shoots beginning to unfurl as they reached for the heavens in search of sunlight. There were long lines of humped soil where he had planted a variety of lettuces, chard, artichokes and radishes, all of which would bear fruit in a month or so. The tomatoes were beginning their lives in the small greenhouse he used as a nursery; it was at least several weeks too early for them to brave the vagaries of life outdoors.

With a whistle on his lips Bruno busied himself tending to the garden, bending down to pluck the odd weed and checking his green shoots for signs of progress. With the hose on its gentlest spray-setting he doused his plants, briefly distracted by the miniature rainbows that shimmered out from the collision between droplet and sunlight.

Once he was satisfied that his garden would live to grow another day, Bruno turned back to the house, where Balzac was sniffing around the baseboards in the kitchen, his keen nose seeking out errant crumbs. He tossed a heel of old baguette down for the dog and started heating water for his coffee, then jogged up the stairs to the bedroom, where he pulled on a pair of running shorts and his trainers in readiness for his morning run. Returning to the kitchen, he poured a strong cup of coffee and tossed it back before calling to Balzac to join him.

Curious to take another look at the crime scene, and mindful of the fact that the horses at the riding school would need their water and oats refreshed, Bruno put Balzac in the Land Rover and drove in the direction of the riding school. When they reached a small farm track around two kilometres short of the gates he parked up, lowered Balzac from the car, and performed a few stretches. He then turned in the direction of Pamela's and broke into a gentle jog that increased in tempo step by step, Balzac following along at his heels. When he got to the riding school, in a light coating of sweat yet hardly out of breath (the same could not be said for the heavily panting basset, who was built more for endurance than for speed), Bruno made for Hector's stall, where the horse was happily snuffling around the big pile of straw in the corner.

'*Bonjour, mon ami.*' Hector stopped his snuffling and came to the door in the hopes of an apple, a carrot, or maybe even a sugar lump. Bruno did not disappoint; as he rubbed the horse's forelock with one hand, the other reaching into the pocket of his running shorts and pulling out a bruised apple he had retrieved from Pamela's basket of windfalls. 'A small morsel for you.' As Hector crunched away loudly, Bruno spoke to the creature, who he was convinced understood the essence of his words, if not the actual meaning. 'No riding this morning, my friend. But I'll try and make it up to you this evening, we'll go for a proper trek if we're allowed.' Hector whinnied what Bruno presumed was his approval, and turned back to his snuffling.

Hector taken care of, Bruno went from stall to stall, mucking out the overnight leavings and giving each animal a fresh pile of oats and hay. After checking that every trough had sufficient water, he sent a quick text to Pamela to let her know the horses had been taken care of, and then walked up to the house, where the crime scene tape that cordoned off the patio was fluttering in a gentle breeze.

From this angle, roughly fifty metres away, he could see his reflection clearly in the glass of the French windows. Had Quirit's killer reached the murder scene from a similar angle while the nurse was seated at the table, it simply wasn't possible that the victim could have missed their approach. Did this mean that Mlle Quirit knew her killer, or had she been elsewhere when the killer arrived, then lured to the patio somehow? *Merde*, Bruno thought, if only I had access to the reports. He made a mental note to pass on his observations to the lead officer at breakfast later.

As he drew nearer, Yveline exited a police car that was parked around the side of the house. She had recently been promoted to the task of overseeing all of the gendarmes of St Denis, and Bruno was gratified to note that the security of the scene had been placed in such capable hands.

'Bruno, *bonjour*. What are you doing here this morning?'

'Just checking on the horses, Yveline. With Miranda still away and I wasn't sure about Félix, I wanted to make sure their needs had been attended to.'

'Of course, of course. I'm so sorry, chief, but I have to ask you to leave. The stables are one thing, but this house is still an active crime scene, and as you've been recused from the case . . .' She blushed, and Bruno could see how uncomfortable his presence was making her.

'Say no more.' He raised his hands in apology, and backed away, remembering full well the inherent awkwardness in having to remind one's higher-ups of protocol. Bruno Chef de Police might be off the case, but there was nothing preventing Bruno Courrèges from doing some discreet digging of his own in the background, as long as it stayed discreet. 'The horses all have food and fresh water, so I'll be off. Is someone coming to relieve you?'

*

Bruno wasn't quite sure what to make of the officer J-J had assigned to the murder inquiry. He had no doubt of the young man's competence – the *officiers de la police judiciaire* were all exceptionally well-qualified – but he was unsure whether the more conservatively minded inhabitants of St Denis would take to this particular gentleman.

The officer at J-J's side had an unusual haircut for a policeman. So black that it was almost blue, and very thick, his hair was somehow both floppy and spiky, and on the edge of what Bruno would consider professional. The young man exuded confidence as he introduced himself to Bruno with a firm handshake and a warm grin.

'*Bonjour, monsieur*. I'm Fabien Panton.'

Entering the breakfast room at the Hôtel St Denis the trio of policemen turned heads. Bruno felt the attention had rather less to do with the sight of three policemen than it did the bizarre hairstyle sported by the younger man. He couldn't quite put his finger on who or what the officer brought to mind. But then it came to him, courtesy of a small child sitting at one of the tables they passed, tucked away in the furthest corner.

'Look, *Maman*! It's Sonic the Hedgehog!' The child's mother hushed her charge, pulling an apologetic face at the three men.

The incomer dropped into a crouch so that his face was level with the boy's, a wide grin making him seem impossibly youthful to be a policeman. 'It's me, Sonic! Do you know where I can find coins to catch?'

With a single remark, the officer had won Bruno's approval. He clapped the spiky-haired young man on the shoulder, beaming. 'I think you'll fit in very well here.'

J-J nodded his affirmation. 'Why do you think I chose Fabien to lead this investigation? I'm surprised you two haven't met before.'

The three men busied themselves passing baskets of bread and croissants around the table, pouring their coffees and helping themselves to generous servings of the butter from Stéphane's dairy and home-made jams that were the Hôtel St Denis's pride and joy. Breakfasts assembled, Bruno asked, 'So where are you from, Fabien? Do I detect a Périgord accent?'

'You do,' the younger man replied. 'Lalinde, born and not quite raised.'

J-J broke off a piece of his croissant and heaped it with apricot jam. 'I do like Lalinde. It's a beautiful town.'

'It is.' Fabien turned to Bruno. 'Do you know the butcher who makes the duck salami?'

'Do I? I think I might be their best customer!' Bruno laughed. 'I must have bought twenty kilos last year alone.' He patted an imaginary pot belly.

'They're my parents.' Fabien smiled with pride.

'No!' Bruno was agog. 'How do I not know you?'

Fabien kept a smile on his face but Bruno watched as it disappeared from his eyes. 'I was sent away to school, so I didn't spend as much time in Lalinde as I would have liked.'

'Where did you go?' Bruno fancied he saw a slight tightening of the man's jaw, but he blinked and it was gone.

'A small Catholic boarding school just outside Bandol, I'm sure you wouldn't have heard of it.'

'Ah, Bandol!' Oblivious to the young man's tension, so focused was he on his breakfast, J-J leaned forward, a grin on his face.

'The stories I could tell you about Bandol, *mes amis*. My university girlfriend came from just near Le Castellet; they were endless summers of *vin rosé* and towers of the freshest shellfish, *mon dieu*!' He kissed his fingers and beamed at his companions.

'Your youth was evidently richer than mine, sir,' Fabien said, a dry tone to his voice. 'We were only allowed off school grounds for Mass on high holidays.'

Bruno shook his head. 'Sounds like prison or the army to me. So you went to school in the Var, but you kept the *sud-ouest* accent?'

'Of course I did!' Fabien shrugged, but he had sounded affronted. 'You can take the child out of the Périgord, but you can't take the Périgord out of the child.'

J-J signalled to the waitress for another round of coffees. '*Alors*, gentlemen. Social hour is over, it's time for us to get down to business.' He reached across the table and took the last *pain au chocolat* from the basket without offering it around, putting it on his plate and wiping his fingers on his napkin before taking a pen and a small notepad from the inside pocket of the blazer hanging on the back of his chair. 'So, Bruno – what do you know?'

Bruno wiped his mouth with his napkin and sat back in his chair. 'I myself know only the basics. Yesterday afternoon Pamela returned home to find her new lodger dead on the patio with massive injuries to her head. The murder weapon is almost certainly the rock found near the body, but of course we have to wait for the official verdict from the coroner. We can pinpoint the time of death to within a forty-minute window; Pamela and the victim were together on the patio till just before two, when she left for the *boulangerie*, returning a little after half past to find the body.'

Fabien tapped his pen on the edge of his notepad. 'And this Pamela, she is a reliable witness?'

Bruno and J-J shared a look. 'This is where you come in, Fabien,' J-J said. 'Pamela is a dear friend of Bruno's, and a woman I deeply admire. We have no reason to doubt her, but your impartiality will be essential to solving this case.'

Fabien nodded. 'And what do we know of the victim?'

J-J turned to Bruno, who took up the baton. 'Not a lot yet. I was supposed to be having dinner with her and Pamela this weekend. But she was a recent arrival in St Denis, from where I can't remember.' The white lie made him uncomfortable, but he didn't want to reveal the extent of his own investigations. 'I believe she was a nurse by training? Pamela said she'd moved up here to work at the retirement home.'

Fabien made a note to visit the managers of the home as early as possible. 'If she's on the register of nurses that will make it a lot easier to find out who she is and where she's come from. And if the retirement home has their records in order she'll have had to submit herself for a series of background checks.' He tapped away on his phone for a few moments, eyes on the screen. 'I'm requesting the records now.' He looked up. 'Do you know where she moved from?'

Bruno shook his head and spoke a second untruth. 'The south somewhere, but it could be anywhere from Montpellier to Monaco for all that I can remember.' The breakfast room had begun emptying over the course of their meal, and now that they were alone the three men could speak freely. Bruno continued. 'I can tell you that my first impression of the scene was that the victim knew her killer.'

'Why so?' J-J asked.

'There were several factors. First, the violence of the attack. I'm confident that the coroner's report will reveal that many of the blows were struck post-mortem, which to me suggests that the killing was the deliberate targeting of a victim, and not a burglary gone wrong.'

'There was no sign of attempted entry to the property?'

Bruno shook his head. 'None that I could see, although I removed myself from the scene once I'd spoken to Pamela, made sure she was all right. After breakfast I'll take you to the station and introduce you to the crime scene team, and they'll have more information for you. But when I spoke with Pamela – and remember she was very much in shock – she didn't mention anything except the body. I do remember that the patio doors were closed; the external panes of glass were spattered with blood and tissue.' He pulled a face, the crumb-studded smear of cherry jam across his plate now looking rather less appealing.

'And what of the victim? Was she wearing any jewellery, a watch, something that will allow us to rule out an opportunistic burglar?'

Bruno ran last night's scene through his head. 'Nothing obvious; no flashy rings or designer watch. But I didn't get the sense she was wealthy, this is a woman in her sixties who had just uprooted her life and moved across the country in search of work.' Fabien and J-J nodded their understanding and Bruno went on. 'I think she was wearing a locket or pendant on a gold chain, a simple piece. And there was a small crucifix, also in gold.'

J-J shrugged. 'So far, so typical. Presumably the investigating team have identified and informed any next of kin?'

'I assume they'll be following standard procedures, but you'll have to ask them yourselves when we get to the station – I'm on traffic patrol until this murder is solved.'

J-J laughed. 'Chin up, Bruno – I'm sure you'll find an assassination attempt to scupper before too long. Action seems to have a way of finding you.'

Bruno gestured for the bill and attempted to put on a brave face for his colleagues. 'Don't you worry about me. I have plenty of work to keep me busy. To be honest with you, this recusal couldn't have come at a more convenient time.' Not only would the town revitalization project keep him occupied, he thought, but it could also provide him with useful cover for his parallel enquiries.

4

The declining interest in St Denis market had one small advantage, Bruno decided, as he lingered over the spring greens sold by Lorraine at her organic stall under the arches. Two years ago he would have been jostled from his front row position by a sea of warring elbows. Now, with no other customers in sight, he had plenty of time to grill the farmer about the best ways to cook her produce.

'Do you ever treat them like spinach, adding a little cream?' Bruno ran his thumb over some vibrant but unfamiliar leaves.

Lorraine shook her head so hard it was a wonder it remained attached to her neck. 'Never! These are far too tender. A little bit of steam, a touch of garlic and butter, simple.' She beamed at him, more teeth absent than present in her wizened gums. 'The Chinese eat them with ginger and soy, but . . .' She finished her sentence with a grimace.

'Have you ever even tried them like that?' Bruno laughed. 'I'm sure Pamela's stir-fry would change your mind.'

'*L'Ecosse?* In the kitchen?' Lorraine laughed at the idea of a British woman making Asian food. 'I'll stick with the Périgord recipes my grandmother taught me, and which her grandmother taught her, thank you very much.'

Bruno bid the old woman adieu and carried on with his list. Last week's burst of spring had become a full flourish, St Denis's teenaged population doing away with their sleeves en masse, girls and boys alike soaking up the weak sunshine as they lingered over coffees and sodas after school, delaying homework till the light began to fade behind the hills. Just as full of life were the explosions of spring flowers the Mairie had arranged to have planted throughout the town, a veritable riot of fragrance and colour.

It looked magical, Bruno thought as he looked around with a smile. But it also looked worryingly quiet. Stéphane hadn't turned up this week, which was a shame, as Bruno had hoped to buy a few of his younger *cabécous* for a goats' cheese salad. There were always other options, but Stéphane was the best and had been for years, a canny operator both in the dairy and in the marketplace. His had also been the first name on Marcel's list.

Looking at his watch, Bruno saw it was only just ten o'clock, plenty of time to get over to his ancient Land Rover and make the drive to Le Croiseau before midday.

To drive through the Périgord during the advent of spring with Balzac beside him, windows rolled down and lungs full of air infused with damp earth, new leaves, and the scent of wildflowers was to be given a gift from the gods, and Bruno intended to enjoy every second of it. Mindfulness, he thought the young people were calling it these days. 'Living in the moment'. Bruno chuckled to himself, for when else were we meant to live? He supposed it was different these days, all that connecting with screens. They never took their shoes off to paddle in the river any more, no teenagers skulking home with tell-tale grass stains on their clothes from heavy-petting sessions on the playing fields after hours.

It would take a madman to want to relive one's youth, Bruno mused, but it must be particularly hard these days, social pressures living in your pocket, relentlessly beeping and buzzing and notifying from dawn to dusk and long into the night.

Despite his best intentions to appreciate the drive, so lost in thought was he that Bruno came to with a start when he was still a good eight hundred metres outside Le Croiseau. The road was jammed on either side with parked cars, presumably there for the market. He checked in his mirrors; there was no one behind and he made short work of reversing his machine back to the end of the line of parked vehicles, where he pulled in as tidily as possible. It was only April and Le Croiseau already appeared to have more visitors than St Denis had pulled in at the height of the previous summer.

Bruno took his sunglasses down from behind the driver's shade, grabbed his basket from the passenger seat, and made his way to the market square, Balzac trotting beside him.

In the ten minutes it took him to walk past the line of parked cars and up to the outer edges of the market Bruno recognized at least half a dozen vehicles owned by St Denis residents, not to mention several owned by producers who had been regulars at his market for longer than he'd been alive. It was beginning to look like the hunch Bruno had developed off the back of Marcel's intel was correct: Le Croiseau wasn't just poaching St Denis's customers, but also their vendors.

Before he could set about his mission, Bruno found himself accosted by Agnès, whom he had seen the previous week in St

Christophe. 'Bruno, *salut!*' The young woman kissed him on each cheek before giving him a teasing look with raised eyebrow. 'I never thought I'd see you shopping here on a Tuesday.'

Bruno shrugged. 'If Mohammed won't come to the mountain . . . But what of you, Agnès? I missed you in the market this morning.'

The young woman coloured slightly. 'I can't get everything I need in St Denis any more, and if I'm going to have to come here anyway . . .' She tailed off and wouldn't meet his eye. Bruno patted her on the shoulder.

'Don't worry. We'll have St Denis back to its old strength sooner than you know.'

Agnès looked at him from under knitted eyebrows, her head cocked to the side. 'Don't think I lack faith in you, Bruno, because that's not the case. But we have to face facts. Ever since the Mesniers shut up shop, the centre of town has been dying. How many shuttered windows do we have on the rue de Paris these days? How are you going to bring a town back to life when it has no businesses, no job prospects?'

'I'm still working on the details. But what St Denis does have is community, loyalty, spirit. That little town overcame the Nazis in the Second World War, I don't think there's much they can't face.'

Agnès grinned. 'I don't think there's anyone who believes in St Denis as much as you do, Bruno. Have you ever considered running for mayor? You could give your friend Jérôme a run for his money in local politics, I'm certain.'

'I don't think it's a job for me, but if I ever do run, I promise to make you my campaign manager.' Bruno smiled. 'I must be off. Give my love to your mother.' Two kisses farewell and Bruno was back on his original mission – seeking out those denizens of St Denis who had dared come shopping in the rival town.

To his great surprise, the next person he ran into was Fabiola, who turned beetroot when she spotted him. 'Bruno? I didn't expect to see you here!'

'Not my usual stomping grounds, you're right. I suppose you could call this a scouting party. I am simply doing reconnaissance. And a little bit of shopping.' At this he raised his basket, which contained nothing more than the greens he'd bought from Lorraine in St Denis. 'What are you doing here, if I may be so bold to ask?'

'My shopping. It's so hard to get everything I want in St Denis now, and if I'm getting in the car anyway, I'd much rather do just the one trip.'

Bruno nodded. 'You're the second person to say as much in the last ten minutes. Three if you count myself.'

Fabiola aped a shocked face. 'You? Bruno Courrèges – Monsieur St Denis of all people! – shopping in Le Croiseau? Will wonders never cease?'

'Stéphane wasn't in the market today, and I needed some *cabécou*.'

'Is that all? Or is it *cabécou* and information you're after?'

Bruno leaned over to place a kiss on his friend's cheek. 'A gentleman never kisses and tells.' With that he smiled, turned to walk further into the market before Fabiola's voice brought him to a halt.

'I was going to ring you later, ask how Pamela was doing. I assume you've seen her?'

Bruno nodded. 'She was very shaken on Sunday, but you know what she's like, won't let anything get her down for long.'

Fabiola raised her eyebrows. 'Finding a body can be a very traumatic experience, especially with a violent death. We'll all have to keep an eye on her, although we can't let her know we're doing it.'

'Can you imagine?' Bruno laughed.

By the time the clock tower struck noon, Bruno was weighed down, both literally and metaphorically. His basket was heavy with pieces of cheese, bushels of seasonal greens – he must remember to use the *mâche* tonight – and more than one mini boulder of the famous local wild boar salami studded with walnuts.

Heavier still was the burden of responsibility now sitting on Bruno's shoulders. His chats with the defecting stallholders had left him feeling downbeat; some of the market's most influential providers had told him that they had effectively lost faith in St Denis after two lean years and were now backing a different horse. All six of them.

On the return journey to St Denis Bruno was too preoccupied to pay close attention to the cowslips and daisies that peppered the verges, their gently bobbing petals ushering him home. Instead, he cursed his ageing vehicle, which had as much hope of managing a hands-free call as he did of befriending a woolly mammoth.

By the time the Land Rover had rumbled over the bridge and turned into the empty market square, Bruno felt a tiny shoot of optimism take root inside his gut. He had a solid plan, he had

Gérard's backing. Now all they needed to do was convince the shopkeepers it was the right way to go.

For now, Bruno's main priority was to finalize his dinner plans. Picking up his shopping from the back seat, Bruno turned to face the *tabac* on the corner opposite. As expected, Marcel was leaning in the doorway, veiled in a cloud of thick blue smoke. Bruno lifted his basket and called across the road. 'Dinner tonight? My place at eight?' A thumbs up appeared from behind the fog. Satisfied, Bruno turned around and headed inside the Hôtel de Ville with his basket of Le Croiseau spoils.

On the other side of the glass double doors Claudette greeted him with a smile, her coiffure as immaculate as ever. 'Good afternoon, Bruno. A productive morning?'

'In some ways.' Bruno rummaged around in his basket. 'Here, I have something for you.' He produced one of the salamis he had bought at Le Croiseau. '*Aux noix*, as you like it.'

'*Merci,* Bruno*!* I have missed these. It was a sad day when Guillaume decided not to renew his permit.'

Bruno nodded, solemnly. 'A sad day indeed. But I am optimistic that we'll get him back. We were once the biggest market in the entire *sud-ouest*, and God willing we will be again.' Claudette crossed herself and the reflexiveness of it made Bruno smile; he didn't think he'd seen her at a single church service, not even the children singing songs at Christmas time.

Once back at home, Bruno emptied the contents of his shopping basket onto his long wooden countertop. The cheeses he put to one side; he'd lay them out on a board when the time came for it, but for now they would do perfectly well reaching room temperature where he left them. The *mâche* he left in its paper bag while he dug around in the cupboard looking for the salad spinner, which always conspired to be at the bottom of an inconvenient pile no matter where he remembered putting it. Balzac's attentions only made the job more difficult, the basset winding his way between Bruno's feet like a cat in seduction mode.

Salad spinner found and order somewhat restored to the domestic chaos lurking behind his cupboard doors, Bruno checked the time on his watch before running the lettuce under the cold tap and popping it in the spinner. Marcel would be along any minute, and with him all the latest from the market traders and shopkeepers. A canny businessman, the *tabac* owner opened at five a.m. on market days – sometimes even beating Fauquet – selling cigarettes and legendarily bad coffee to the stallholders while most of St Denis was still tucked up in bed. As a consequence, little of note in the town escaped Marcel's notice.

While he waited for his friend's trademark knock – a rat-a-tat-tat affair the tobacconist had lifted from a Cold War spy film during his youth – Bruno prepared his vinaigrette, measuring his ingredients by eye and instinct into a Bonne Maman jam jar saved and washed for this very purpose. Shaking his mixture hard to emulsify the oil and vinegar, Bruno opened the lid, dipped the very tip of his little finger into the salad dressing, and shook his head. Putting the jar down he reached across the stove for the *vinaigre de noix* that was his secret weapon, and shook in three generous drops. Glugs, Pamela might say. Another taste. Perfect.

There was little else to do but grab plates, cutlery and glasses, and stack them on the kitchen counter. For a meal composed of salad, salami, bread and cheese there would be no standing on ceremony, but there would be good wine. There was always good wine. Bruno stretched onto his toes to reach a pair of carafes down from the high shelf over the lintel. He filled one with water straight from the tap – as good as or better than any mineral water one could buy, he always thought – and the other with an excellent Pécharmant his neighbour, the father of Agnès, secured for less than two euros per litre from a friend with a few rows of vines.

No sooner had he finished wiping an errant fingerprint or six from his wine glasses than he heard the rat-a-tat-tat he'd been waiting for, accompanied by a series of joyful bays from his basset. Bruno threw the dishcloth across his shoulder like a waiter in a downmarket bistro and opened the kitchen door with his arms spread open for an embrace. 'Marcel! Come in!'

Marcel stepped forward to clasp him with one arm, the other carefully holding a brown paper bag that Bruno could see held a patisserie box. 'I know you say never to bring anything, but I thought you might make an exception for a few small slivers of *tarte aux pommes*.'

Bruno patted his still flat (ish) stomach and turned his side profile onto his friend. 'What do you think, *mon ami*? Can I spare the calories?'

Marcel laughed and made his way over to the stack of cheese and charcuterie waiting on the countertop. 'If it's calories you're worried about I think you might want to reassess tonight's menu.'

'Bah!' Bruno flapped his arms at his friend. 'Essential brain food, and with a salad besides.' He turned to the sink and busied himself with the salad spinner. 'I'll be two minutes finishing it up, why don't you lay out our plates and pour yourself a glass of that wine?'

Forty minutes later, elbows resting on the crumb-strewn table, smears of cheese residue and oil from the salad dressing still decorating the plates in front of them, Marcel and Bruno turned their attention to the purpose of their dinner. Balzac slept at their feet, having devoured all the dropped morsels. Taking his cigarettes from his shirt pocket, Marcel started to tap the packet on the countertop, rotating the cardboard box ninety degrees after every third tap. Bruno shook his head. 'Outside.'

'Oh – I'm not about to smoke one. I'm just fidgeting.' Bruno raised an eyebrow. 'So, Le Croiseau. I take it from our *cabécou* that you found at least one of our friends there.'

Bruno nodded. 'I found all of them. Each and every name on your list.'

'You make it sound so dramatic! I gave you six names, not sixty.'

'Every flood starts with a single drop of water.'

Marcel laughed. 'Listen to you, *monsieur le philosophe*! If I know you, you have the beginnings of a plan?'

'That I do. But if it's going to work, I'm going to need your support, Marcel – you and all of your colleagues on the rue de Paris.'

Marcel took a single cigarette from his pack and began to play with it, rolling it back and forth across the countertop. 'I'm all ears.'

5

When Bruno threw open the shutters the following morning it was to a bright blue cloudless sky. In the front garden, small fuzzes of baby bird could be seen lining up along the branches of the big plane tree, ready for a flying lesson. The air smelled fresh and sweet, as if it had rained overnight, and Bruno felt his heart lift. His little corner of paradise was coming back to life after its winter sleep, and after last night's dinner with Marcel he felt confident that where his garden led, St Denis could surely follow. He checked his phone for a message from Laura, and seeing there was none felt his spirits plummet. But he had no time to dwell on it.

'Balzac? *Allons-y!*' He clicked his fingers and the basset hound lifted his sleep-filled head from between his front paws before leaping to his feet and following Bruno along the hall, expecting their usual morning run.

In the kitchen, Bruno set about preparing his morning coffee, foregoing his usual cafetière and instead reaching for the moka pot Fabiola and Gilles had brought back as a gift from a recent Italian holiday. He was in two minds about the quality of the coffee it produced – his cups always seemed to taste slightly scorched – but there was something undeniably soothing about the gentle burbling followed by the hiss of steam that announced its readiness. At his feet, Balzac looked up with beseeching eyes but to no avail.

'No toast for me this morning, which means no toast for you.' Balzac harrumphed in response, and made his way to the kitchen door, making the throat noises Bruno knew were a demand to be let out. Bruno followed the dog outside, coffee in hand, and breathed in the fresh spring air. While the basset made his morning rounds of the garden, Bruno made his own investigations, checking the growing vegetables for signs of animal invasion. Plucking a few slugs from the lettuce leaves that were just beginning to burst through the soil, he was gratified to note that the troublesome bindweed he'd been battling for years seemed to be at least temporarily at bay.

Bruno left his coffee cup in the kitchen sink to be dealt with later and picked up his car keys. 'Balzac, come along.' The dog trotted along behind him to the Land Rover that was significantly older than the pair of them combined. The drive to the Mairie was one he could do with his eyes closed, but both man and dog had their eyes wide open – Balzac's ears flapping in the breeze as he stuck his head out of the passenger-side window – as they drank in the beauty of the early spring morning.

Balzac was on best behaviour as he clambered up the steps to the Hôtel de Ville, on a leash and smartly to heel. Bruno and Mademoiselle Cantagnac had eventually declared a truce over the notion of dogs in the office, thanks in no small part to Balzac's particular charms, but the detente depended on the basset remaining on the executive assistant's good side. So far, so good – just last month *mam'selle* had come in with a set of sleigh bells and hung them from the doorknob, so that Balzac could ring when he wanted to be let out.

The bells tinkled as Bruno opened the door. '*Bonjour, mademoiselle!*' Ceasefire or no ceasefire, Bruno felt safest taking recourse in formality, although he and Colette had exchanged first names several months earlier.

'*Bonjour, chef!*' Mademoiselle Cantagnac shot him a wide smile before dropping her gaze. 'And Balzac.' As if in response, the basset headed over to the dog bed in the corner of the office, where he set about tugging the cushion this way and that with his teeth, stepping back to assess his work before rearranging it further.

Bruno could see the pile of overnight reports ready and waiting on his desk. St Denis might be a small town, but every morning started with a rundown of the crimes committed in the past twenty-four hours: the *bons vivants* caught over the limit on their way back from dinner, teenagers trespassing on the local farms, noise complaints from the houses bordering the holiday park. And now that he was responsible for the entire Vézère Valley, the list of minor misdemeanours had increased tenfold, if not more.

Rolling his shoulders a few times and stretching out his back, Bruno made for his state-mandated ergonomic office chair and made himself as comfortable as the hated object would allow, ready to crack on with his paperwork. The pile of papers was almost processed when something struck him.

Bruno nudged the torture chair to one side with his foot, and leaned on his desk to make his calls, his gaze drawn to the Vézère as it burbled below his open window. The flow was still lower than normal for this time of year, but the water rushed bright and clear over the pebbles below, a much more charming sight than the mud-filled torrent that had hurled tree after tree at the town's historic stone bridges the previous October.

The phone had yet to make a noise before it was answered by the Mayor. 'Bruno.'

'Monsieur le Maire. I've had more thoughts and I wanted to run them past you.'

Bruno detailed his plan, more an expansion of their existing concept than it was anything new.

'So how soon do you think you can put this into place? One week? Two?'

Bruno thought for a second. 'In practical terms, we could do it tomorrow. But if we really want to promote it, I think we should go for two weeks' time. We can put notices up, tell the schools, maybe even get a mention in the local press, on *France Bleu Périgord*. I'm sure Laura will promote it to the *conciergerie*'s clients, and we can get the word out to everyone in the region who rents out holiday homes.'

'Sounds sensible to me. Consider this your go-ahead and let me know what you need from my office. I'll make sure that Claire knows that any paperwork has my pre-authorization.'

'Thank you, sir.' Bruno was about to sign off the call, but the Mayor went on,

'While I have you on the line, any update on this murder? It's hardly the sort of publicity we want when we're trying to drum up tourism, put ourselves back on the map.'

'It's not,' Bruno agreed. 'But I'm afraid I don't know much more about the case than you do. J-J's brought a young officer down from Périgueux to serve as lead. Fabien, a local boy. You might know him; he was born in Lalinde.'

'Fabien? You don't mean the butcher's son?' Gérard's voice softened. 'I remember him when he was just a slip of a thing, scared of his own shadow. So he's an officer now?'

'Not just an officer, an *officier de la police judiciaire*, no less. And only in his late twenties, I would guess.'

'I would expect nothing less from a son of Lalinde.' Down the line, Bruno could hear a second voice enter the room. 'I'm off, Bruno. You and Market Mark Two have my full support.'

Bruno was feeling restless. He had every confidence in Fabien but he wanted to be solving crimes, not helping to manage the traffic flows on market day.

Luckily, he had his revitalization project to occupy both his time and his brain cells, and to provide cover for his own inquiries into the Quirit murder. After speaking with the Mayor, he'd headed out for a series of conversations with the local merchants only to find that the vast majority had elected to shut up shop for the afternoon, handwritten signs on the door stating they'd be back in the morning. Well, now it was morning. Bruno stood up with a sense of purpose and placed his *képi* firmly on his head.

He decided to start at the far end of the rue de Paris and work his way back down to the square, one shop at a time. The last bar before the edge of town was Le Cromlech, named for the Cro-Magnon archaeological sites the region was known for. It was an awkward location, despite the passing traffic, and the premises had changed hands half a dozen times in the years since Bruno had moved to St Denis. The current owner, an Italian giant appropriately named Massimo, he knew to be a fan of the local rugby team.

The bar was empty when Bruno pushed open the door, its

dark wooden interior and low lighting giving the narrow room a cave-like feel. 'Bruno, *ciao!*' Massimo raised his bear-like paw in a wave; it was speckled in soap suds. 'You'll have to forgive me, I'm a little short-staffed at the moment.'

'Not to worry, *mon ami*. How's business?'

Massimo heaved a sigh and began to dry his hands on the dishcloth hanging over his shoulder. 'Not great. Hence being short-staffed – I can't even afford to pay myself this month.'

Bruno shook his head. 'I'm sorry to hear it. But I have an idea that I hope will help bring customers back to St Denis, and I'm doing the rounds trying to get you all on board.'

'Would this be anything to do with the shopping precinct idea Marcel was on about the other week?'

'It's not quite a shopping precinct, but yes. I believe that if we combine forces, we can once again make St Denis the premier market town in the region, bring the rue de Paris back to life.'

'Music to my ears. But a nice idea won't pay my bills. What's your plan?'

Bruno smiled. 'Consider it a three-pronged attack.' He outlined the concept he and the Mayor had devised to promote local artisans with a free market stall, using the competition to publicize St Denis as a whole, Massimo nodding all the while. 'But we also want to help you shopkeepers. Once we've got extra foot traffic in the market, we want to keep them in St Denis. So the plan is that on market day we pedestrianize the rue de Paris.'

Massimo frowned. 'But it is pedestrianized on market day.'

'Only in the mornings. The Mayor and I thought that if we kept the road closed to cars throughout the afternoon, people might linger, have lunch. You can throw a few tables outside on the pavement, and your customers won't have to worry about choking on traffic fumes.'

'And what about the permits? I can't afford to apply for more space.'

Bruno waved his hand. 'All taken care of. The Mayor has pre-authorized any licences I need to make this happen for the good of the town.'

'I like it. So what's the third prong?'

'Well, this is where we need your cooperation. We thought of creating a St Denis loyalty card, given to any customer who spends twenty euros in a single transaction on the rue de Paris. After ten such spends, they get a twenty-euro discount on purchase eleven. Participating businesses can put a sign in the window, and people will be encouraged to do their shopping here and not drive out to Sarlat or Périgueux.'

'It's not a bad concept. I'm not sure how many of the others will go for it, but you can count on my backing.' He proffered his giant mitt for Bruno to shake. 'Have you spoken with Franc yet?'

'Marinet?' Bruno shook his head. 'I hadn't thought to, why?'

'He has more than a bit of money to spare. Maybe he could sponsor some shuttles, bring in shoppers from the neighbouring villages? How much could it cost to rent a bunch of minibuses for one morning each week? Old Lespinasse at the garage will know someone, I'm sure.'

'That's a great idea. Maybe charge a token euro for the round trip, give some of the more independent pensioners a low-cost day out.'

'And that canny mayor of ours could probably drum up some EU funding if he called it a community public transport scheme.' Massimo laughed, a sonorous bass that rolled up from his Pavarotti belly.

'You're probably right there. Anyway, Massimo, I must be off. Thanks for your time – I can only hope that your fellow business owners are half as helpful.'

Bruno continued his rounds of the local businesses and was unsurprised to discover that the Quirit murder was the hot topic on everyone's lips. Not once had he needed to bring up the woman's name: every threshold he crossed, he was given an update on the latest gossip surrounding the case. Some of it was fantastical – the owner of the shoe shop was convinced the victim was a mob witness failed by the witness protection programme, while at the hair salon the junior stylist had heard she'd been killed over unpaid drug debts.

Bruno listened to their stories with a smile, solicited – with varying degrees of success – support for the loyalty card scheme, and moved on to the next business, and the next, and the next. Two of his stops were potentially fruitful: Mademoiselle Quirit had been in the habit of visiting the *maison de la presse* each morning for a newspaper, and over the course of her short stay in St Denis had built up something of a friendly relationship with the proprietress, Murielle.

'Josette?' She shook her head. 'What a tragedy, that poor woman. To travel across the country, rebuild your life, and then lose it so suddenly? Sad, sad times.'

'Rebuild her life? What do you mean?'

Murielle shrugged. 'She told me she'd been recently widowed, that the finances weren't what she'd been led to believe, and that she was forced out of retirement and back into work.' She shook her head. 'It's terrible what some women suffer. You'll never catch me letting some man hold the purse strings.'

At the butcher, Bruno found Guillaume Mazillier behind the counter, a young man of about seventeen or eighteen with whom he'd played many rounds of tennis over the years.

'Guillaume, *ça va?* How are you finding the new job?' Guillaume had always been socially awkward but fearsome behind the net, and Bruno had a feeling that being forced further out of his comfort zone would only do the young lad good.

He received a shy smile in return. 'I like the work, and I'm learning a lot, but I'm still getting used to the customer service side of things.' He cleared his throat and stood a little straighter in his white overall. 'How can I help you today?'

Rather than waste time talking town revitalization with a trainee, Bruno decided to take advantage of their relationship to do a little light prying. 'I'd like to buy some of your bones for Balzac, please – have you got any going out back?'

'The boss already asked me to put a particularly good one to the side for you.' He smiled. 'No charge.'

While Guillaume set about wrapping the treat in butchers' paper, Bruno tested the waters. 'I bet you hear all the gossip, working here. All the women chatting while they wait, all the farmers dropping off news with their deliveries.'

The young boy laughed. 'You can say that again. Some of the theories flying around after that murder were ridiculous. Mademoiselle Josette would never have been involved in the mob, can you even imagine?'

Bruno's ears perked up. 'Mademoiselle Josette? You knew her well?'

'Not well.' He turned his head back down to the task at hand and Bruno saw the tips of his ears turn red. 'But she often came in to pick up things for the nursing home, and we'd talk while I prepared the order. She'd ask me where the best place was for a *pain de campagne*, or which local market had the best fish, that sort of thing. Once she brought me a jar of wildflower honey she'd bought near Brive-la-Gaillarde, said the taste reminded her of home.' He blushed. 'She was a sweet lady, recently widowed. I think she was lonely.'

Back at the Mairie, the Mayor's mobile went straight to voicemail, and Claire said that he was out of the office, so Bruno left a message with each requesting a callback. His conversations with the owners on the rue de Paris had been largely fruitful, although one or two of the longest-established businesses had expressed reservations about the loyalty card system, thinking it '*un peu déclassé*'. It would be their loss, Bruno felt. He was certain that by the end of the summer local businesses would be clamouring to expand the scheme beyond the rue de Paris.

He took a pen from the pot on Mademoiselle Cantagnac's desk and pulled his notebook from his breast pocket to prepare a list. Pending the Mayor's approval he would talk with Franc Marinet about the prospect of financing some shuttle buses. There was no point wasting any time trying to convince the recalcitrant owners, Bruno decided; they would come around of their own accord when the plan proved itself to be a success. For the moment, his highest priority would be to spread the word about No Traffic Tuesdays, make sure that the whole of the Dordogne knew that Tuesdays in St Denis were the place to be.

6

'Bruno, *bonsoir!* And Balzac! I'm glad you could make it.' Florence beamed when she opened the door. She'd phoned in the morning to invite him to supper, saying there was something she wanted to discuss with him. 'Come on in.' He followed as she turned on her heel and made for the kitchen.

Bruno rubbed his palms together as he entered the kitchen to be greeted by the scent of onions slowly softening in butter. 'It smells glorious in here, what are you making? And where are the twins?'

'They're at Rouffillac, having a sleepover with Patsy. Those three have been thick as thieves since last summer; I'm so glad you introduced them.' Florence was already back at her chopping board, the frying pan on a hob set to the lowest possible heat for caramelizing onions. 'Dinner is nothing special, just a simple tart. You know how it is, you look away for a minute and half of your vegetables have conspired to collapse.'

'That's when I usually turn to soup.'

'Not me, not in this weather. I just grab a box of puff pastry and empty the fridge onto it. Twenty-five minutes on a low heat, make a quick salad, and that's both tonight's supper and lunch tomorrow.'

Bruno smiled. 'Sounds delicious.'

Florence continued her chopping. 'Pamela was here last night.'

Bruno nodded. 'How was she?'

'In shock, as is only to be expected. But you know Pamela. She might not be English, but she has the famous stiff upper lip.'

'Keep calm and carry on.' Bruno's attempt at Received Pronunciation was beyond atrocious.

'Exactly. She was clearly shaken, but she didn't want to dwell on it. But how ghastly – to find a violent death in your own home. I shudder to think.'

'Did she eat?'

Florence laughed. 'You and food. I offered her a small supper, but she wasn't hungry. We shared a couple of brandies and then she took herself off for a bath and what she called a *nap*. When I left for the school in the morning she was still out like a light.'

While Bruno wondered why he had been summoned, Florence set about preparing the tart, scoring a border around the edge of the pastry and aerating the centre with the tines of a fork. She spread the base with the last scrapings of a pot of *aillou*, scattered that with a layer of the caramelized onions, and arranged a selection of vegetables on top – Bruno spotted broccoli, cauliflower and leeks, as well as some sagging green leaves well past their peak – and topped the whole thing with a drizzle of olive oil. She put it in the oven and checked her watch. 'I'll take a look in twenty minutes, but it will probably be closer to thirty.'

'Can I help with the salad?'

Florence pulled out a chair and sank into it, swinging her feet up onto the next seat, and shook her head. 'The salad will take me less than two seconds. If you really want to help, you can fetch me a glass of wine.' She gestured at a cardboard box in the corner. 'I bought a mixed dozen from Julien de Savignac just the other day – take your pick.'

Wine glass in hand Florence took a deep breath, and Bruno braced himself, now having an inkling of what was to come. Balzac, sensing a change in atmosphere, walked over to Florence and resettled himself next to her chair, his velvety head within reach.

'I wanted to have a word with you, on our own.' She reached down and started to toy with one of the basset's ears.

'Go on.'

She took a deep breath. 'I wanted to apologize, really.'

'Apologize? For what?'

'Just listen. I've been doing a lot of thinking recently, and what it all boils down to is this: I don't want to throw the baby out with the bathwater.' Bruno knew the expression, he'd heard it before from Pamela, but he wasn't sure how it applied in this context. He stayed silent, to let Florence say her piece. 'We both know I have feelings for you. But I've also come to realize that you don't share those feelings, that your love for me is purely platonic. Laura was something of a nail in that particular coffin.'

Bruno shifted uncomfortably in his seat. 'And I also know that our friends haven't been making things easy for you. They want to pair us off, and they're not all that concerned about your feelings in the matter, not even with Laura in the picture.' She winced.

'So what I wanted to say to you is this.' Another deep breath. 'I love you deeply, dear Bruno, and my life is richer for having you in it. But I don't want my feelings to jeopardize our friendship, nor your relationship with my children.' Florence reached behind her for her glass, and took a gulp, holding up her hand to silence him. 'My feelings for you might be beyond my control, but my behaviour towards you is. So I am going to enjoy our friendship, our dinners, our chats, but I am going to stop building castles in the air and try my best to get on with just being your friend.' She held out a hand. 'Deal?'

Bruno was almost overcome. After a few beats he said softly, 'Deal. And thank you. I know that can't have been easy. You're an incredibly brave woman, and I can't tell you what a pleasure it is to call you my dear friend.'

Bruno left Florence's apartment feeling as though a weight had been lifted from his shoulders. The imbalance in their feelings for each other had been bothering him for many months, and interventions from the likes of Jack and the Baron had only made things worse. Bruno had been beating himself up with the thought he'd given Florence the wrong impression, and as far as he was concerned her brave speech was the beginning of a new chapter in what he was sure would be a lifelong friendship.

He was now feeling restored in a way he hadn't known he'd needed. It was a real privilege to spend time with people who knew you, who listened to you, he thought as he strapped Balzac into the Land Rover. He hadn't said anything specific – at least, he didn't think he had – but Florence had sniffed out that he was feeling at sea and had done her utmost to restore him to an even keel. She was a remarkable woman.

The fridge-clearing tart had been exceptional, an easy addition to any repertoire, and Bruno had enjoyed his glass of Château de la Jaubertie's latest red, a twist on their award-winning Cuvée Colombier, so much that he'd taken a photo of the label so he could pick up a few bottles of his own.

The clock on the dashboard told him it was earlier than he'd thought, the dark nights of winter not yet entirely behind them. Bruno navigated his car around the sharp bends that led from St Denis to his home, the twilight locals called *le crepuscule* casting shadows in the undergrowth. Above him, the moon was growing close to full in a cloudless sky. It would be a cold night, he thought as he indicated to turn down the unmarked road that led to his property.

Before heading for bed, Bruno and Balzac made their rounds of the garden, Balzac sniffing the perimeter for news updates left by the wildlife with which they shared the hillside. The thought of animals made Bruno think of Hector which in turn made him think of Pamela, without whom he would never have admitted Hector into his life. He decided to check in on his old friend, and moments later heard her soft Scottish tones.

'Bruno, how nice to hear from you. I wasn't sure if I was allowed to call you.'

'My apologies for not ringing before – I wanted to check in, see how you were.'

'I'm fine, I'm fine. At least, I will be when I'm allowed to get back into my house.'

'Have they given you any indication of when that might be?'

'By the end of the weekend, I hope. But I can't complain – the Guyonnets have been incredibly generous; they've put us up in an absolute palace.'

'Are Jack and Miranda back from Biarritz then?'

'Not yet. But they've cut their trip short and will be driving back tomorrow to look after me.' Pamela snorted, and Bruno smiled, knowing full well how much his friend resented the notion of being looked after.

'I'm sure you'll be glad of the company. Where are you staying, exactly?'

'Do you know the old road just past Le Cygne? We're about ten minutes' drive up the hill, spectacular views of the valley.'

'So, no claustrophobia?'

'None whatsoever.' There was a pause and Bruno could feel the weight of the air change down the phone line. 'It's awful, Bruno, just awful. But I can't sit and think about what happened to that poor woman or I'd never be able to feel at peace in my own home again.'

Bruno started to make reassuring noises but Pamela hushed him. 'I know what you're going to say. That there's no reason to feel unsafe, that there weren't any signs of attempted entry, nothing to suggest I might be a target. But it's not about that, Bruno. It's about sitting down on the patio to enjoy the sunset and catching a shadow out of the corner of my eye that looks like blood – or worse. I need to find a way of blocking out those images, no matter how hard that's going to be when there's a murder investigation going on around me.' She sighed.

'Of course. It's very hard. I was going to ask, how did it go at the station?'

Bruno heard air whistling between her teeth before she replied. 'Given that I was being interviewed by the police, I'd say about as well as can be expected. Don't get me wrong – they were perfectly kind, if a little young, but a police interview has never been an item on my bucket list.

'I'm not sure how much help I was, to be honest,' Pamela continued. 'Other than the approximate time of death I don't think I told them anything they didn't already know.'

Despite the many questions swirling around his head – *What did she tell you about her life? Why did she move up here? Did she ever mention enemies or grudges?* – Bruno suppressed his policeman's instinct to ask. 'I'm sure you were more useful than you think. The devil is usually in the detail, and often we need to have it pulled out of us. The detective's job is to take those details and find a solution.'

'You're itching to be involved, you poor thing. I can hear it in your voice.'

Bruno sighed. 'I am. It's not that I don't trust them to do a good job without me, more that this is my team, my patch, my people.'

Pamela let out a throaty chuckle. 'If I know you like I think I do, I'd say it wasn't impossible that you'd taken on' – she coughed – 'an *inactive* role. That you might have your ear to the ground in search of jungle drums, as it were.'

'You know I would never admit to such a thing. But perhaps I pick up a few things on my rounds here and there, perhaps not.'

After depositing Balzac in his office – the empty coat hanger told him that Mademoiselle Cantagnac had yet to arrive – Bruno made for the gendarmerie, where he sought out the office that had been assigned to Fabien for the duration of the investigation. As he raised his fist to knock on the closed door it opened, and the

Sonic-haired policeman looked startled to find someone standing on the other side. He broke into a grin.

'This is good timing, Bruno – I was just coming to find you.'

'Really? Why?'

'More pleasure than business, although I suppose it's a bit of both. But you were about to knock on my door – is there anything I can help you with?'

'I just wanted to see what the situation was with Pamela's house, if you still thought she could be home by the end of the weekend.'

Fabien nodded. 'She might even be back in by tomorrow, but I don't want to get her hopes up. But we've done everything we can there for the moment, so unless anything new comes to light . . .'

'I understand. Don't worry, I won't raise her expectations. You said you were on your way to look for me?'

'I was. Like I said, it's a mix of business and pleasure. Your business, anyway. The word around the station is that you're working on a project to bring more shoppers to St Denis, restore the market to its former glories.' Fabien took out his phone and opened Instagram, tapping away at the search box. 'One of my friends in Paris does social media for the flea market his neighbourhood runs every month.' He held the phone out to Bruno. 'Look. Twelve months ago there were a dozen sad stalls, now it's huge.'

Bruno scrolled through a series of pictures, attractive young families and groups of friends shopping in a bustling flea market. He spied food trucks, furniture, clothes stalls and crafts; the stream of photos was endless. 'Impressive.' He handed the phone back. 'But I'm not sure how it relates?'

Fabien smiled. 'Look, I know we're not Paris, there aren't the numbers locally to draw these sorts of crowds. But my friend has said he'll happily set up a few social media accounts for St Denis across a range of platforms, give us a few volunteer hours each week.'

'That's very kind of him – and you. What will your friend need from me, from St Denis, to make this work?'

'Content, mostly.' Bruno looked puzzled, and Fabien went on. 'Pictures, video, material to publish. You know everyone in this town, aren't the teenagers always doing photo shoots or making movies with their phones?'

'Only around ninety per cent of them.' Bruno shook his head. 'Claudine Jaboullier is probably the most reliable, and she's always been a great help volunteering at Florence's computer club. How should I brief her?'

'Bring her along to meet me. We can video chat with my friend, he'll be able to tell her exactly the sort of things to shoot to really drive traffic to the feed. We'll also need to get as many locals following it as possible; if we can have ten thousand followers within a week of launch we'll start attracting new ones like bees to honey.'

'I'm not sure I understood a word you said after that first sentence,' Bruno laughed. 'Why don't we meet Monday afternoon, around four thirty at Fauquet? That gives me time to speak with Claudine's parents, get their approval to bring her on board.'

'Perfect.'

Fabien returned to his temporary office and Bruno decided to walk to the computer store on the main road heading out of town in the direction of Le Buisson, where he hoped to cross off the next item on his list. It was yet another beautiful spring day. Next weekend would be Easter, and Bruno resolved to buy chocolate eggs for Pamela and Florence to mark the occasion, and perhaps some bunnies for Dora and Daniel. He would get them at Fauquet when he met with Fabien and Claudine, he decided; he kept hearing good things about the new chocolatier they'd brought on board.

The bell above the door announced his arrival in the small shop, formerly an internet café and now the place St Denis residents relied upon to fix their technical gremlins, buy reconditioned old-model iPhones, and repair smashed screens. It was this last service that was the store's most profitable, and by no small margin, although the owner was always trying out new income streams, from the taking of passport and ID photos to the sending of electronic postcards whose purpose eluded Bruno given the existence of both text messages and email.

'Bruno! What can I do for you?'

'*Salut*, Gaston, you're looking very well. Are you in love?'

'Aren't I always?'

The two men chuckled, then Bruno got to the purpose of his visit. 'I need some help designing and printing some promotional materials. Leaflets, posters, that sort of thing.'

Gaston waved at the wall behind him, listing the services offered. 'You've come to the right place. What are you promoting?'

A little over an hour later, Bruno was on his way back into town, a dozen posters and five hundred leaflets under his arm. Gaston would be delivering the rest of Bruno's order to the Hôtel de Ville when it was ready, but he had enough copies to make a start on his promotional duties. The two men had come up with a simple but effective design, a bare footprint outline with all the relevant information printed in easy-to-read capitals inside the border. At the top of the page a red banner headline screamed *NEW! NO TRAFFIC TUESDAYS!*

On his way back to the market square Bruno stopped in at the supermarket and *boulangerie* as he passed, hanging a poster on the public information board in the former and leaving a few dozen leaflets with the latter. He turned off the main road and took a detour that would enable him to drop off more posters at both the primary and secondary schools before passing by the vet's surgery with a handful of leaflets. At every stop his scheme was warmly welcomed, and Bruno continued his circuitous route back to the office with growing confidence.

'Busy morning?' Mademoiselle Cantagnac looked pointedly at the clock when Bruno stepped into the room.

'Very.' Bruno beamed at his assistant. 'But also productive. I hope Balzac didn't inconvenience you?'

'We're growing accustomed to one another.' Colette melted as she turned to look at the dog, who was lying on his back, legs akimbo, proudly displaying his undercarriage to the skies. Her face was decidedly less soft when she turned back to look at Bruno. 'I've had Claire on the phone half the morning. Apparently you're causing her no end of trouble.'

Bruno looked abashed. 'I suppose I am making her process rather a lot of paperwork. But it's all in a good cause.'

'There's no harm in bringing a little good into the world,' Colette agreed. 'There's just so much misery.' She gestured at the newspaper on her desk, the headline yet another in a long series decrying the abuses by the Catholic church in the United States, in Australia, in Ireland . . . With every passing month the list grew longer, the sense that abuse was endemic within the institution more pervasive.

'To think the church is supposed to offer sanctuary to those in need.' The two sat in silence for a moment, the air heavy between them.

'Those poor children. I can hardly bear to think about it.' Colette shook her head and got to her feet. 'Is there anything I can be helping you with? I've not got much on my plate with you recused from the murder investigation, and all the systems in the Hôtel de Ville up to date at long last.'

'You could help me distribute leaflets this afternoon, if you're at a loose end.' He held up the bundle he had yet to get rid of. 'Gaston will be dropping more boxes off in the next hour or two; I've ordered ten thousand leaflets and two hundred and fifty posters.'

'Not all for distribution today, I hope!' Mademoiselle Cantagnac laughed. 'You can count me in, we'll divide the town in half.'

Driving home, Balzac by his side, Bruno reflected on a successful afternoon's collaboration with Mademoiselle Cantagnac, something he would never have guessed possible after their first disastrous meeting. Luckily their relationship had since evolved from grudging acceptance to tolerance and even to friendship – a relief to Bruno who was unaccustomed to being at odds with people.

Their leafleting had been rather more strategic than simply splitting the town in half. They'd brainstormed a list of places people went to most, and left piles of promotional material with the bank, the post office, the schools, the doctor and the vet; the butcher and baker and candlestick maker. Locals taken care of, they targeted the tourist hotspots of the museum, the canoe rentals, the campsites, the aquarium . . . Within a few hours they'd handed out over three thousand leaflets and put up more than fifty posters. Tomorrow they'd agreed to split up, repeating the process in the neighbouring towns and villages until they ran out of material.

7

Many hours, more than three thousand leaflets, and goodness knows how many kilometres later, Bruno was back in St Denis, his Land Rover trundling slowly over the bridge by the market square. Indicating right, he pulled into his usual parking space in the shade. When Balzac was safely at ground level Bruno locked the car and the pair of them crossed the road to the *tabac*, where Marcel was slouched as usual in the doorway.

Spotting their approach, he set about opening the umbrella over the table nearest the door. 'Sit yourself down, I'll bring a bowl for Balzac.' Marcel returned a minute later, holding a large plastic ashtray, water sloshing over the rim. 'And what can I get you, my friend?'

'Just a coffee, please.'

When he returned with the coffee – and a second one for himself – Marcel pulled out a chair and joined Bruno at the table, an unlit cigarette dangling from the corner of his mouth while he patted himself down for a lighter. 'Looks like our plan is coming together.' He leaned back in his chair, lighter in hand, and took the cigarette from his mouth. 'Lots of chatter in the local market this morning about the car-free Tuesdays.'

'Good, I hope.'

'Mostly.' Marcel shrugged. 'You know what some of the old bastards can be like. While most of the stallholders see the value in trying something new to draw a crowd, more than a few of them have been ranting about the injustice of lottery-winning upstarts getting spaces for free.' He sighed. 'They'll come around in time.'

'I hope so, but we've got to attract enough customers to make it work, otherwise all we're doing is giving the old guard new competition.' Bruno's shoulders sagged. 'Have you met the new investigating officer they've brought in, Fabien, the guy with the strange haircut?'

'Officer Sonic? Of course, he's in bright and early every morning for a coffee. What about him?'

'Apparently one of his friends in Paris is one of those technical types, a wizard with social media. He's offered us a few hours of his time each week to help with promotion.'

'That's generous of him.'

Bruno nodded. 'He's said to have done wonders with his neighbourhood flea market, turned it into some sort of hipster hotspot via the magic of Instagram.'

Marcel choked on his cigarette. 'Not words I ever thought I'd hear from your mouth. Do you even know what Instagram is?'

'I'm not a Luddite, you know. Even I have a Facebook.'

'Facebook! You do sound like an old man.'

'Are you saying I'm not hip? Not cool?' Bruno pretended to look wounded.

'Bruno, you're the village policeman! It's against the law for you to be cool.' Marcel laughed, but there was kindness in it. 'Besides, people love you because you're generous, reliable. We want Bruno Courrèges, not Eddie Murphy, Beverly Hills Cop.'

After leaving Marcel's, Bruno and Balzac went for a short stroll over the bridge, from where they could reach the riverside path that cut through a mid-sized field that was part recreational ground, part public campsite. When Balzac found a particularly interesting patch of soil to investigate, Bruno took advantage of the opportunity to call Gaston for an update on the next round of posters and leaflets, which he was pleased to learn would be ready early the next day. That left around three weeks for people to apply for and prepare a May stall, quite tight but not impossible.

He rang Mademoiselle Cantagnac, but there was no reply. Bruno assumed that the hours spent leafleting had tired her as much as it had him. Just then, he saw Fabien walking down the footpath towards them, the young man's distinctive hairdo shouting his identity from a great distance. It was lucky the officer didn't want to work undercover, Bruno thought to himself. There would be no disguising that hair.

'*Bonsoir,* Fabien.'

'Bruno!' He crouched down and won a few more points of Bruno's esteem. 'Balzac, *comment vas-tu?* Are you enjoying your walk?' The dog's tail wagged in response, and Fabien remained close to the ground, scratching Balzac behind his long velvet ears.

'You've met Balzac?' Bruno couldn't remember the two meeting, and Fabien shook his head.

'Not met him, no. But he's something of a celebrity in the police station, I've heard all the stories.'

'How's the investigation going?' Bruno asked. 'In general, I mean,' he added, not wanting to make it look like he was breathing down Fabien's neck. 'I hope you're finding the team easy to work with, that you're making progress.'

Fabien stood up with the ease of a man in his twenties, and Bruno's forty-something knees ached with envy. 'The guys are great to work with, no worries at all there. As for progress, who knows? We're at that point of having assembled a lot of information but not yet knowing how it all fits together. If it all fits together.'

Bruno nodded. 'Hence the walk?'

'Hence the walk. I just needed to clear my head of all the noise, try and unwind.'

'Is there anything I could do to help?'

'Help?'

'You could tell me what you've got so far, what leads you're currently pursuing. Sometimes simply knowing the key players is all it takes to solve a crime in a town of this size.'

'Like Agatha Christie, Miss Marple!' Fabien laughed. 'Are we in St Denis or St Mary Mead?'

'You may laugh, but Madame Christie was right about one thing – people are people wherever they happen to be in the world, and their motives are usually pretty similar. Sex, money, power, revenge. Why else do people kill?'

'Why else indeed?' There was a heaviness to the young man's pause. 'I've noticed your chats with local businesses have quite a remarkable crossover with the interviews my team have been conducting for the murder investigation. How does the nursing home fit into the market revitalization scheme exactly?'

Bruno was taken aback, but before he could open his mouth Fabien smiled and continued. 'I trust you'll brief me on anything you unearth?'

'Of course. And I didn't mean to step on your toes.'

Fabien shook his head. 'The thought didn't cross my mind. This is your patch, these are your people. But I don't think you want your inquiries getting back to J-J, and if I've spotted what you're doing there's a very good chance the likes of Jules and Yveline have too.'

Bruno sighed, he should have known better than to underestimate his colleagues. Sergeant Jules was one of his most reliable officers, the pair of them had worked together on more cases than either of them could remember. 'And there I was thinking it was my job to keep half an eye on you. Thanks for the friendly advice, I really mean that. See you at Fauquet on Monday, if I don't run into you before.' Fabien nodded and cut right, walking through the long grass towards the bright lights of the main road, the supermarket and the petrol station glowing like beacons in the early dusk.

Turning back in the direction from which he'd come, tugging lightly on the leash for Balzac to follow, Bruno took his mobile from his pocket and checked in on Pamela. 'How's it going? Have they let you back into your house yet?'

'They have indeed. And what a state they've left it in, fingerprint dust on every surface. It's going to take me hours to knock it all back into shape, you can't imagine. Well, I suppose *you* can.' She laughed; it was deep and throaty, and after assuring Bruno that yes she was absolutely fine, and of course finding the body like that was a shock, but no, absolutely not in any way did she want counselling for her 'trauma', Pamela returned to her scrubbing.

Before slipping his phone back into his pocket he tried Laura's number, but his call was rejected. Seconds later, a message popped up. 'So sorry mon amour, in a meeting. Will ring you asap. Bisous!' His shoulders slumped as he trudged slowly home.

By the time Sunday morning arrived, Bruno felt the same sense of restlessness that had been dogging him ever since his recusal from the case. A policeman without any policing to do was the very definition of redundant, even if his days were kept full with his attempts to bring St Denis back to life. He decided to call J-J; there had to be some way he could be of use to the investigation, especially now that Pamela was back in her house and didn't appear to be a person of interest. But the screen on his phone told him it was only just gone seven in the morning, definitely not the right time to make a Sunday call and expect a warm response.

His phone also told him that Laura hadn't tried to get in touch. He would head into town after his run, he decided. Pick up a newspaper, and while away the first half of the morning in Fauquet's, with a large café crème and a croissant to dip into it. The mornings were getting warmer as April continued its inexorable march towards Easter, and a spot of spring sunshine and a drop or two of St Denis gossip would be the perfect way to kill time before he could reasonably expect to get J-J on the phone.

Decision made, Bruno threw back his covers and swung his feet to the floor, spreading his arms wide and giving his shoulders a big stretch. At his feet, Balzac responded with a perfect demonstration of a yoga downward dog.

'What a big stretch.' Balzac looked up, unamused. 'Are you ready for your breakfast?' In response, the basset hound padded across the floor and waited at the closed bedroom door for

Bruno. Still clad in his pyjamas, Bruno led the way, Balzac's nails click-clacking behind him. He opened the kitchen door, and the basset made his way outside and started the hedgerow snuffling that marked the beginning of his morning routine. Dog taken care of, Bruno jumped into the shower, where he used a quick blast of cold water to ready himself for his morning's exercise.

Clad only in a pair of running shorts and trainers that were older than Balzac, Bruno stretched out his calves on the low wall surrounding the potager before using the same wall to perform a series of elevated press-ups, only a little stiffness around the shoulder to remind him of breaking it the previous summer. Once he could feel the blood start to course through his veins he whistled for Balzac to follow him and trotted down the path to the main road, the dog hot on his heels. While the run was ostensibly part of his fitness regime, Bruno found the exercise to be even better for his brain than it was for his body, helping to get his thoughts in order while his feet pounded out the kilometres.

Soon he was turning away from St Denis and running up the hills and into the forest where he foraged for wild mushrooms in season. In the autumn, the air would ricochet with the sound of distant gunfire, and Bruno would never risk such a run when *la chasse* was in play. But now he and Balzac appeared to have the woods to themselves, although both man and basset alike knew that the undergrowth was full of wildlife keeping their distance from the hunting dog, who stopped occasionally with a lifted paw, his tracker's nose scenting new life and potential new friends.

After three kilometres or so, Bruno turned around and retraced his steps, continuing his jog all the way home and into a second brief shower, where he relished the pounding of the hot water on his aching muscles. Once man and basset were ready to face the day, Bruno lifted Balzac into the cab of his Land Rover and rolled down both windows to let the fragrant spring fill the car. According to his phone it was already more than twenty degrees outside, and barely eight a.m. If the spring carried on like this, Bruno thought, they'd be in for a scorching summer, hosepipe bans for the third consecutive year. He made a mental note to check his water butt that evening, see how much rainwater he had collected to feed his garden.

The drive passed in minutes, Bruno deftly navigating the sharp turns that led down the hill and along to the main road that would take him into town. Indicating to turn into the market square, Bruno was mildly annoyed to find his usual shady spot was occupied by an unfamiliar large and lightly scuffed people carrier with tinted windows and a 75 number plate, revealing that the vehicle was registered in Paris. Leaving his car in the sun and helping Balzac back down to ground level he decided to leave the windows down in the hope it might alleviate some of the heat that was already beginning to build inside the Land Rover.

Together the pair crossed the market square and found a table on Fauquet's terrace half-shaded by the wall of the building. Balzac settled under the table, Bruno went inside to place their order but there was a throng of people between him and the counter, a youngish group of men and women who looked familiar. It took a minute before he placed them at a cluster of tables on Le Croiseau riverbank the week before: the Netflix team. Over the shoulders of the crowd Bruno signalled at the owner for his usual and returned to his seat on the terrace.

Balzac had made himself comfortable under the table when

the Netflix crew burst through the door onto the terrace, thirty conversations somehow taking place in a group of six or seven. Bruno raised a hand to acknowledge the group, and one of the women broke away. 'Is this your dog?' She crouched down and held out her hand for Balzac to sniff. 'He's beautiful.'

Bruno smiled. 'His name is Balzac.'

'*Bonjour,* Balzac, *enchanté.*' She scratched the dog behind his ears and turned to Bruno. 'In my family we always had bassets growing up, they're the best dogs in the world.'

'I couldn't agree more. Stubborn creatures, but wonderful.'

The young woman smiled, a warm and wide toothy beam that brought to mind a young Julia Roberts. 'I'm not sure I could respect an animal that didn't know its own mind.' She extended a hand for Bruno to shake. 'Marion. Marion Perrin.'

Marion's handshake was surprisingly firm for a slight-looking woman, but the network of prominent veins on her hands and forearms betrayed an addiction to the gym. 'It is a pleasure to meet you, Marion. My name is Benoît Courrèges, but everyone calls me Bruno. So what brings you to this little corner of paradise? Are you scouting locations?'

The young woman coloured slightly. 'You know who we are?'

Bruno smiled. 'Not to worry, *mademoiselle*. I saw you and your Netflix colleagues in Le Croiseau last week; the Mayor pointed you out to me while you were working on the riverside.' He nodded his head over to where the rest of her group were setting up their laptops. 'We don't see many people working remotely in the Périgord; you do stand out.'

'As long as we're not earning a reputation for chaos!'

'Not in the slightest. Are you considering using St Denis for any of the episodes in your next series? There's nowhere in this town I don't know; perhaps I could be of some use?'

Marion shook her head. 'We actually came here for a bit of peace and quiet, to be honest with you. Everyone in Le Croiseau knows who we are, and we can't get anything done with all the interruptions.' She put on a series of voices, none of them flattering. '"My niece is an actress, perhaps you can audition her? Do you need any extras? Why did you choose Madame Pompadour's garden when my roses are so much more vibrant?"' She sighed. 'It's relentless, and that's before I even get into the kids trying to film our meetings for TikTok clout.'

'TikTok I know, but clout?'

'Don't get me started. Anyway, the guys were looking for somewhere out of the way, somewhere we wouldn't be disturbed, and I suggested we come here. It's been lovely to meet you, Bruno. I should be getting back to work.' She dropped back into a squat and gave Balzac a fuss, earning Bruno's approval in the process, although the basset seemed unimpressed with the attention. 'I do hope I run into you and Balzac again.'

No sooner had Marion returned to her colleagues than Fauquet arrived bearing Bruno's order, a grand café crème and a croissant. 'Another lovely young woman falling for the charms of Bruno Courrèges! You'll have to tell me your secret.'

'I think she was falling for the charms of Balzac, if I'm honest with you.' At the mention of his name the dog raised his head, but when no treats or scratches were forthcoming he returned to his dozing.

Needing something to read, Bruno asked, 'Do you happen to have a copy of *L'Equipe* inside?'

'Not today's, it hasn't been delivered yet. But I can bring you yesterday's? There was lots of rugby coverage, Top Fourteen finals coming up.'

'Perfect!'

The next hour or so passed by in a happy blur of caffeine and newsprint, Bruno almost hypnotized by the warmth of the sun, the rattle of cups and conversation from the Netflix group on the other side of the terrace, and the background burbling of the river flowing below. When a shadow fell over his newspaper he was startled for a second, and then smiled to see who it was standing above him.

'Florence! What a lovely surprise. Will you join me?' He folded his newspaper and cleared some space on the tabletop, waving through the window for someone to come and take her order.

'Why not?' She sat down at the table, and Balzac shuffled himself around under it so that all of his weight was resting on her feet. '*Salut, mon petit*,' she said as she bent down to ruffle his ears. 'Are you happy down there in the shade?'

They proceeded to chatter about everything and nothing, hardly noticing the time pass until they were shocked back to reality by shouts across the terrace.

'You idiot! What have you done?' Next to where Marion was sitting, a young man with a shaved head and oversized hexagonal spectacles had jumped to his feet, a wet stain spreading quickly across his crotch. It took a second or two before Bruno realized the young man was more worried about the health of his water-soaked technology than he was the potential embarrassment of what looked to be a bladder accident. 'I swear to God, if this laptop is broken you're the one who's paying for it.'

On the other side of the table a meek-looking woman with mousy brown hair and the most prominent cheekbones Bruno could ever recall seeing looked as though she wanted to crawl under her chair and die. '*Désolée, désolée*, I'm so sorry.'

'Sorry? Sorry? Odelie, you shouldn't be allowed near technology, especially with liquids. I don't even know why you're here.' The young man spat his derision. 'Haven't you got some invoices you should be paying? Timesheets to fill in? Maybe try and leave the creative work to the actual creatives?' Just as Bruno had made up his mind to go over and intervene, the young man sat down again.

Florence pulled a face at Bruno. 'Glad I'm not with them.'

'As if working on such a beautiful Sunday wasn't bad enough. Give me a peaceful life in St Denis any day.'

Florence grinned. 'As if your life here has been peaceful! That collarbone of yours still giving you trouble?'

Reflexively, Bruno reached up to give his shoulder a rub. He'd seen his collarbone smashed in a gunfight the previous summer, and suffered laborious surgery and physio in the aftermath.

'The older we get, the longer it takes to recover. But I'm fine, I promise.'

'Your face is telling a different story.' She gave him a long look, one eyebrow raised in expectation. 'I'm sure a massage wouldn't hurt.'

'Are you offering?' Bruno smiled, and Florence laughed.

'You'd do much better in the hands of a professional.' The two sat and chatted in the sunshine. St Denis was springing to life around them and the clock on the church tower slowly clicked from nine and around to ten. When Balzac began to fuss at their feet Bruno looked at his watch.

'I'd better get going, I have some calls to make.' Bruno got up. There was sadness in Florence's eyes and it hurt him to see it.

'It was lovely seeing you, Bruno, it always is.' With a swift kiss to each of Florence's cheeks Bruno was off, trundling down the road with Balzac in the direction of the Hôtel St Denis.

Bruno waited for Balzac's first extended sniff stop before getting out his phone to call J-J. It was just past ten, a perfectly acceptable time for a Sunday morning. His friend answered on the first ring.

'Bruno! What can I do for you this fine morning?'

Bruno laughed. 'Almost exactly the opening to this call I was hoping for, my friend. I want you to let me back on the case. Now that Pamela is officially off the list of potential suspects, and you have her witness statement, I don't see why I can't be involved in some capacity.'

As J-J cleared his throat, Bruno thought he could anticipate the likely objections, and ploughed on. 'I have no desire to usurp Fabien; I think he deserves this chance to prove himself as a senior investigating officer. But I do think that I can be of use on his team – no one knows St Denis like I do.'

'And you think you can play second fiddle to a man almost half your age?'

Bruno was almost offended. 'Do I think I can be professional and support an investigation? Certainly. Do I think I can be a useful addition to the team? J-J, I know it. And I know that you know it too. So tell me – what are your real objections?'

J-J sighed. 'No shooting the messenger?'

'How often have you known me to use my firearm?'

'Literal, or metaphorical? Because those are two very different answers.' Bruno laughed at that, and J-J went on, sounding relieved. 'Listen to me, Bruno. There have been mutterings among the higher-ups that you're becoming too much of a local celebrity, that you're bigger than your uniform after all your high-profile cases. In the Police Nationale we need to be the invisible mandarins, the unseen grease that keeps the cogs turning. In the Périgord you've become something of a star, and the brass don't like it.'

'Then this is perfect.'

'Perfect how?'

'Because this is an opportunity for me to act as support on a case, not to take the lead. I can give the investigating team the benefit of my experience, of my local knowledge, and let them bask in any attention that results from their success.' Bruno didn't want to beg, he wasn't that sort of man. 'You know I'm not motivated by ego. Let me demonstrate that to these "higher-ups" who clearly think so well of me.'

The line went silent, but Bruno could hear enough background noises to know that his friend was thinking, that the call hadn't been terminated.

'I'll have to speak with Fabien, make sure he's happy to have you on board. But I don't see why we can't allow you to work as a consultant on this investigation, if nothing else. Get you to sit in on the briefings, assess the interviews already conducted, that sort of thing. I'll get back to you.'

Bruno ended the call and bent down to fuss Balzac, stroking his forefinger along the ridges of wrinkles that slumped along the basset's brow. From a short distance away he could hear a mobile start to ring; his ears pricked up when he heard the words 'J-J? What can I do for you?'

On the other side of the road Fabien stood on the steps of the Hôtel St Denis, a mobile phone clasped to his ear. Bruno waved, and the younger man held his hand up in response, bidding Bruno to wait for him.

The phone call had taken less time than Bruno had expected, and it was only a few minutes later that he and Fabien were dragging chairs across to one of the shady tables in the empty open courtyard in front of the hotel. The Hôtel St Denis was a popular meeting spot on market days on both Tuesdays and Saturdays, and as a consequence the locals of St Denis tended to give the place a wide berth on Sundays – in a small town it was important to spread one's custom, to leave no business neglected.

Fabien went inside with their drinks orders and came back bearing a bowl of water and a handful of dog biscuits. 'When I said I needed some water for Balzac Christophe insisted that I bring him these as well. Apparently they're freshly baked to your recipe?'

At the sound of his name – and the smell of the biscuits – Balzac sidled over to Fabien, planting a heavy paw on the young officer's foot. He looked up, mournfully, decades of deprivation in his deep brown eyes. Fabien crumbled, as Balzac knew he would, and seconds later the dog was contentedly munching away.

'So, business,' said Fabien. The young man was direct, and Bruno liked him all the more for it. 'J-J tells me you're keen to get involved in the investigation. Or should I say *officially* involved?' Bruno had the good grace to grin ruefully. 'And that you're more interested in being of use than being in charge? Sorry, that sounds rude.'

Bruno laughed. 'Not rude, more to the point! Yes, I want to help. It's been driving me crazy not being able to get my hands dirty.' Fabien nodded.

Their conversation was briefly interrupted by Christophe bringing out their coffees, and a brief flurry of greetings and gossip followed before the hotelier began grilling Bruno on his thoughts about the local rugby team's prospects in their next match, an exchange Bruno headed off at the pass lest it occupy hours. With a final scratch behind Balzac's ears and a few morsels of leftover breakfast sausage for the dog, Christophe headed back inside his bar and Fabien returned to the object of their meeting.

'Obviously we've done the preliminaries – autopsy, coroner's report, witness statements, crime scene investigation, all of that. There's not really much left in the way of early stage legwork. What have you found out on your own?'

Bruno looked to the sky, collecting his thoughts. 'It's odd. Obviously I've been limited by town gossip and what's on public record, but the picture I've been drawing of the woman just doesn't make sense. At the butcher and the newsagent's she'd been recently widowed. Colleagues at the nursing home say she was a life-long spinster. And on Google, there doesn't seem to be any trace of her much older than a decade.'

Fabien nodded. 'So what do you think?'

'That she had some reason for wanting to obfuscate her personal history?' Bruno took a sip of his coffee. 'I'm sure of it. But why? What have the official records thrown up?'

Fabien raised an eyebrow. 'Not much more than Google, it sounds like.'

'*Merde.*' Bruno shook his head. 'Who do you have looking into Quirit's original identity?'

'At this point? Half the team. Why?'

'You should contact Gabrielle Teyssier, the IT expert at Périgueux. You must know her?'

Fabien shook his head. 'Never heard of her.'

'If only the left hand would tell the right hand what it was doing, *mon Dieu*. J-J should have put you in touch with her immediately; she was a great help with that crypto case last autumn that saw hacking attempts on my police phone and laptop. I'm not sure there's anyone more internet-savvy in the whole of the Dordogne. Not even the security experts at Domme.'

Fabien took out his phone and made a note of the name. 'I'll contact her first thing, thank you.' He returned his phone to his pocket. 'I think it's pretty clear that I'm really happy to have you on my team, Bruno. Why don't we head down to the station once we've finished these coffees; the team and I can take you through everything we've established so far.'

8

Despite it being a Sunday morning, the gendarmerie was a hubbub of activity when the trio arrived. Bruno would have expected nothing less in the middle of a murder investigation, but still found himself gratified to note that the team he'd assembled over a period of years had been running like a well-oiled machine in his absence. To be a police officer in a small town presented its own challenges – there was none of the anonymity of office afforded to gendarmes working in a big city. Investigations tended to centre on one's friends, one's neighbours, and familiarity could never cross the line into bias.

As he and Balzac made their way through the station and towards the room that had been devoted to the Quirit investigation their progress was impeded by a series of friendly faces, each of whom had an ear scratch or a belly rub for the basset. His team were happier to see Balzac back in the gendarmerie than they were him, Bruno thought to himself with a smile, and he didn't mind in the slightest. It showed they had their priorities in proper order.

Once the three of them had passed through the receiving line and were ensconced in Fabien's temporary office with Sergeant

Jules, Bruno took a seat and brought out his notebook. 'What have I missed?'

Jules looked at Fabien. 'If I may?' The younger officer nodded, and Jules cleared his throat. 'The autopsy confirmed that the murder took place in the forty-minute absence the property owner described on Sunday afternoon, with time of death estimated as between two p.m. and two thirty p.m. Pamela Nelson says she returned from the bakery around two thirty, having left a little before two, and spotted the body through the doors to the patio as she entered the kitchen.

'The murder weapon has been confirmed to be the bloodied rock we found adjacent to the body; there were no prints on the stone and all of the blood, skin and hair on it has been matched to the victim. We have yet to find any DNA that might lead us to the killer.'

Bruno raised a hand. 'Do you have anything to work with?'

Jules nodded. 'We're still going through all the CCTV footage we've brought in, but you know how big a job that can be. As for the coroner's report, there's a very high probability that the killer was left-handed. If that proves to be the case, we can eliminate about ninety per cent of the planet.'

'And what do we know about the victim?' asked Bruno. 'Have you been able to contact friends and family? I know she was new to the area, but there has to be a reason she came here, some sort of link.'

Fabien cleared his throat. 'We're trying to track down living relatives, but so far it's been dead end after dead end. There has been one anomaly, though. While Mademoiselle Quirit came to St Denis with glowing references from her most recent employer, we can find no record of her existence before arriving in Menton. Like you, we're operating under the assumption that she changed her name but have yet to be able to find any records that confirm it.'

'The Menton retirement home, what notes do they have on her?'

Fabien shook his head. 'We've been furnished with details of her impeccable employment record at the facility, but it appears that proper procedure was not followed when she was hired – there's no *casier judiciaire* in her files.'

Bruno let out a long slow whistle. 'That's illegal. You can't work with vulnerable people without a full background check.'

'It is,' Jules chipped in. 'Luckily, Annette Fournet is a cousin of Suzette, who works at the home, and she convinced her to do some digging.'

'What has she found out?' asked Bruno.

'Apparently, Mademoiselle Quirit started working at the Menton home as a volunteer, vouched for by one of their long-standing employees, and by the time they took her on as a staff member she was so much a part of the furniture that the need for a *casier judiciaire* fell through the cracks.' Jules's phone rang and he checked the screen. 'Excuse me, I need to take this in private.'

'This long-standing employee who vouched for her, I assume you've interviewed her?'

Fabien shook his head. 'She died a few years ago. Nothing suspicious about it, it was a heart attack and she was in her seventies.'

'Could we review the coroner's report together? I formed my own impressions of the crime scene, and I'd like to see how they compare with the official verdict.'

'Of course. Can I bring it up on screen, or would you rather look at a hard copy?'

'Screen, please. Electronic images are easier to work with.' Bruno saw Fabien's Adam's apple bob in his throat as the younger man swallowed, evidently yet to develop the iron stomach that being a policeman required. It would come in time, he knew.

'Of course, I'll just open it.' While Fabien entered his password and navigated through a series of menu options, Bruno pulled up his chair alongside and got his notebook out from the pocket of his blazer. A second password was required to open the file. 'Here we go, it's loading now. What was it you wanted to look at?'

'Cause of death, please.'

'You can't possibly have any doubts about the blunt force trauma? We've matched the matter on the rock to the victim, there is absolutely no question that Quirit was struck repeatedly by the stone you saw next to her body.'

'No, no, none at all. But the coroner will also have recorded her observations about the killer. Left-handed, we believe, yes?' Fabien nodded. 'Taller or shorter than the victim? Come to that, how tall was the woman we know as Josette Quirit?' While Bruno spoke, Fabien scrolled through the pages on screen, stopping before he reached the appendix of photos inserted into the official report as high-resolution JPEGs.

'Here you go, cause of death.' Fabien pushed his chair back from the desk, giving Bruno space to work the mouse and peer closely at the technical jargon on the screen.

Bruno read through the report, occasionally pausing to make a note. After about five minutes he sat up straight and turned to face his colleague, the 360-degree range of movement the only benefit of the hated ergonomic chairs the entire force had been lumbered with.

'There's something bothering me.' He tapped his pen on the notepad. 'Josette Quirit, whoever she turns out to be, was of above average height for a French woman, but not excessively so, at a little over one-seventy centimetres.'

'Okay. Where are you going with this?'

'It says here,' Bruno tapped his pen on the monitor, 'that the angle of blows suggests that our victim was killed by someone her own height or shorter.'

Fabien nodded. 'Yes, I remember reading that. So?'

'The average man in this country is one-seventy-five centimetres tall, meaning that we're either looking for a male killer of below average height, or a woman.'

'Again, all of this I've seen in the report. I'm not sure where you're going with it?'

Bruno scrolled down a few paragraphs and began to read.

'"The force of the blows suggests that the attack was carried out by a male perpetrator, although we cannot discount the possibility that the assailant was a female with unusual upper body strength. The angle of the blows indicate that the perpetrator was left-handed; given the force involved it is statistically impossible that the attack was carried out by any person, male or female, not using their dominant side. The overall violence of the attack, with more than two dozen strikes incurred post-mortem, implies but does not confirm a personal relationship between victim and assailant."'

He turned to Fabien. 'You see?'

'I'm afraid I don't.'

Bruno thought it was obvious, but he didn't want Fabien to feel patronized. 'Okay. Let me tell you how I see it. We know that our killer is left-handed.'

Fabien nodded. 'As Jules said before.'

'If I may continue?' Bruno raised his eyebrows. 'We can be reasonably sure that our killer knew the victim – I have my own theories there, which I'll get to in a minute.' Another nod. 'Which is why we have to find out who Josette Quirit really was, and who might have had good reason to keep beating her skull with a rock after she was dead. Even at the scene the force of violence suggested to me a personal connection.'

'Not to be rude, Bruno,' Fabien in interjected, 'but so far you've not told me anything we didn't know already. The team have all read this report backwards and come to the same conclusion.'

'And what was that conclusion? That you're most likely looking for a left-handed male of below average height?'

'Exactly.'

'And that's where I think you're wrong. I think we have to keep our minds open to the possibility that the killer was female. I think it's highly likely that we're looking for a left-handed woman, physically fit, and perhaps one who is a little taller than most, but not by much.'

'But that hinges on the assumption that the killer was French.' Fabien took out his phone and behind the thick curtain of hair Bruno saw the Google logo appear. After a few taps on the screen, Fabien looked up. 'The average Mexican male is one-seventy centimetres, same with El Salvador and Panama. Who's to say we're not looking for a Latin American man? A Saudi? An Omani? A Mongolian?' He showed the screen to Bruno, and there were indeed many nationalities where one-seventy centimetres was the average height for a male.

'Of course we could be. But is it likely? Here in deepest France, when we're dealing with international criminals they tend to have more profitable targets than a nurse in an old folks' home. Unless we can connect our victim to international crime, it's far more likely that we're looking for a French killer – or at least a European one – than it is someone from Latin America.' He smiled. 'Although we must, of course, keep our minds open to all possibilities.'

Fabien nodded. 'I'm still not convinced about the woman angle. It was such a violent attack.'

'True, the attack was particularly violent – an act that required the killer to get very close to their victim. When men kill, even when they kill themselves, there's usually a degree of certainty in the act – using a gun or knife to ensure success. Women, on the other hand, are statistically less likely to use weapons and more likely to use items close at hand. The rock was almost certainly an object found nearby, rather than a weapon brought along for the purpose.

'Which brings me to my next point. The nature of the attack tells us that the victim came face-to-face with her killer. If she was facing the view, she would have seen her killer coming around the corner. If she had her back to the view, she would have seen them reflected in the glass doors. Either way, it seems to me that when our victim saw the killer approach, she didn't feel a sense of alarm. And that, to me, implies that our killer was female.'

Fabien nodded. 'Or someone she knew and was comfortable with.'

'Why not both?' Bruno asked.

9

On Monday morning Bruno bounded into the Mairie, excited to face the week to come. Beside him, Balzac appeared to share his master's enthusiasm for the working week, his tail thumping excitedly. Mademoiselle Cantagnac was already at her desk, tapping away at her keyboard with frightening speed. 'Bruno! I didn't expect to see you here this morning; I thought you'd be heading straight to the gendarmerie.'

'So you've heard the good news then?'

Colette raised an eyebrow in disapproval. 'I'm not sure I'd call a murder investigation good news exactly.'

'No, you're absolutely right. But I'm happy to be back in action.'

'Then I'm happy for you. But what does this mean for your St Denis revitalization project? Are we putting it on the back burner until the case has been solved?'

'Of course not.' Bruno would never have admitted it, but the project had slipped his mind somewhat in the hours since he'd been brought officially up to speed on the Quirit murder. 'I'm going to be dividing my time between here and the gendarmerie; I'm only acting as support on the investigation and I will still have plenty of time to devote to our cause.'

'I'm glad to hear it.' Mademoiselle Cantagnac reached into her desk drawer and pulled out a notebook. 'We've had thirty applications already for the May market slot, and I think we should do our draw soon. We need to give the winners time to prepare themselves, and May is less than three weeks away.'

'*Merde*, you're right. That's not much time at all.'

She winced at the mild profanity. 'I know you want to run this as a proper raffle, and for the rest of the summer I think we can do so. But if we're going to give the May winners any chance of success I think we're going to need to bend the rules a little this month.'

'Bend the rules how, exactly?'

Mademoiselle Cantagnac turned to her notebook. 'I've taken the liberty of Googling the names that have applied so far. Of the thirty-odd who've put their names down, a dozen have existing Etsy or eBay operations, which to my mind means they're in a better position to have stock ready to sell than anyone who might need to start from scratch. I think we should do our draw from those twelve names only, and put the others into the lotteries for June through September.'

'That sounds good. Any unsuccessful names should be automatically entered into the next month's draw, don't you think? Give people as many chances as possible?'

Colette beamed. 'You and I are on the same page, boss. Should we do the draw now?'

'Why not?' Bruno reached for his *képi*, which was hanging on the same coat stand that held Mademoiselle Cantagnac's blazer, and placed it on her desk. 'Write down all the names on scraps of paper and put them in here. I'll do the draw and you can film it for our first social media post.'

'Give me a few minutes to get the papers ready, and I'll be with you.' Bruno nodded and made to enter his office before Colette's voice had him pausing in the doorway. 'We should film the draw outside, don't you think, in the market square? It's a more telegenic backdrop than the inside of an office, especially on a sunny day like this one.'

'Very good point. How about on the steps of the Hôtel de Ville? Claudette can disable the automatic doors for a few minutes, stop anyone from wandering into the shot.' Mademoiselle Cantagnac nodded her approval. 'I'll head down now and speak to her. See you out front when you've prepared the papers?'

'*Bien sûr.* I'll bring your hat with me.'

Ten minutes later Bruno found himself standing on the steps of the handsome seventeenth-century building, upturned *képi* filled with scraps of paper in his hand. Behind him, the modern automatic doors to the Hôtel de Ville had been electronically locked by Claudette, who was standing guard at the bottom of the internal stairs, preventing anyone from an accidental walk-in role in their video.

At the foot of the steps, Mademoiselle Cantagnac stood with Bruno's smartphone in her hands, ready to film the event. 'I think you should say a few words before doing the draw, explain the purpose of what we're doing.' Bruno nodded. 'Are you ready to go? I'll count down from five, and you can start speaking when I reach zero.'

Bruno straightened his shoulders and looked into the camera with a smile. '*Bonjour, messieurs-dames.* Welcome to St Denis market's search for new local talent. We've invited local young creators to apply for a free slot at our Tuesday market. There'll be three winners, all given one month in which to promote their businesses and sell their wares. Now, let me pick the May winners.'

Bruno reached into the hat he was holding in his left hand and pulled out a piece of paper with his right, fumbling to open it single-handedly. 'The first stall will go to Marianne Mentier, from La Terrasse. Congratulations, Marianne.' He shook the hat and reached for a second slip. 'The second to Javier Arnoux, from Journiac, and a star prop forward on our local rugby team.' A final shake of the hat and one last name. 'Our final May winner is Aurélie Marcelin, from right here in St Denis. Congratulations to all three winners!

'Those of you who were unsuccessful this month, never fear – your names will be automatically entered into our draws every month for the rest of the summer. And if you missed your chance to enter the May draw, please put your name down at my office in the Hôtel de Ville. I wish you the very best of luck for June and beyond. You can find our winners every Tuesday at the St Denis market, the oldest in the region. Come and support our winners, and our local businesses, and take advantage of our No Traffic Tuesdays, when the streets of St Denis will be free of cars so that you can shop and socialize at your leisure. Thank you, and till next time!'

Bruno paused for a second for Colette to finish filming and then exhaled deeply. 'How was that? Do you think it went okay?'

'You were brilliant, Bruno. A natural.' Mademoiselle Cantagnac beamed at him, and Bruno heaved a sigh of relief. Years spent giving speeches at various student sports clubs had given him a crash course in public speaking; holding the attention of a room full of excitable youths had been exactly the preparation he'd never known he would need for this moment.

He mounted the steps, and moments later the automatic doors opened to reveal Claudette peering around the corner of the doorframe. 'All done? Can I stop standing guard at the bottom of the stairs?'

'All done, Claudette, *merci*.' Bruno smiled at the receptionist. 'I hope you let everyone know that the blockade was in aid of a good cause?'

Mademoiselle Cantagnac gave Bruno his phone back. She told him that she'd already saved the video to his GoogleDrive and sent herself a copy for safe-keeping. His attention was then drawn to a text that had just arrived from Fabien: 'New round of interviews at the old folks' home, do you want to come?'

Tapping out a quick affirmative, Bruno bade a hasty farewell to the women of the Mairie and set a fast pace towards the care home.

The first interview began a little awkwardly, with neither Bruno nor Fabien wanting to take the lead and upset the other. Luckily, it was with the junior gardener, who came across as a particularly oblivious individual – he wasn't sure if he and Mlle Quirit had ever worked the same shift, despite the rota Bruno was holding showing they were scheduled for the same hours three days per week and had been for as long as the older woman had worked at the home. As the young man left the room, Fabien turned to Bruno with an exasperated expression.

'That should have gone a lot better.'

Bruno nodded. 'Before we call the next person in, how do you want to play this?'

'Not good cop, bad cop, I take it?'

Bruno laughed. 'Not at this stage of proceedings. You've been running the case so far, why don't you take the lead?'

'If you're sure? You know these people much better than I do.'

'And me sitting back and observing them while you conduct the interviews will tell us as much as the words coming out of their mouths. Who do you want to bring in next?'

Fabien looked at his notebook. 'We've got the head gardener, two nurses, and the night-duty receptionist still to interview. The number of interviews the team has managed to conduct in the last few days has been really impressive. You trained them well.'

'I can't take much of the credit – it's Yveline who's been in charge of the new recruits, and she's taken to the role like a duck to water.'

'Everyone at the gendarmerie both admires and fears her, as far as I've been able to work out. Which is pretty much exactly as it should be in that role, if you ask me!'

'I agree. We're lucky to have her. Should we bring in the receptionist next?'

The night shift receptionist was another young man, just past adolescence. His cheeks still bore the pitting of a particularly unfortunate bout of acne, but he had warm eyes and a disarming smile. Unlike the previous young interviewee, Michel Daubain offered his hand to both Bruno and Fabien before sitting down. 'A pleasure to meet you, gentlemen. Despite the circumstances, of course. How can I help?'

'As you know, we're investigating the murder of Josette Quirit,' Fabien began. 'While our colleagues at the gendarmerie go through the CCTV footage your manager supplied of the care home in the days leading up to the incident, we're interviewing anyone who might have come into contact with her. You never know what small detail, seemingly unimportant to you, might prove to be the turning point for us.'

Bruno watched the young man carefully as the exchange went on, a keen eye on the alert for the smallest signs of physical discomfort or changes in atmosphere that could indicate a lie or obfuscation. He didn't have much of a basis to start from, as the man sitting in front of him was effectively a stranger, a half-remembered face from the streets of St Denis and a fairly recent incomer. There was no rugby pitch intel for Bruno to draw on.

'She wasn't unfriendly, but she certainly kept her cards close to her chest,' Daubain said. 'It was as if she'd landed in St Denis out of nowhere – there was never any indication of her personal life, or people she knew.'

Fabien cocked his head to the side. 'That's interesting. Could you expand?'

Daubain shrugged. 'You know what it's like – you're talking in the break room about your new coffee machine, or where you're going on holiday, and someone will say "Oh, my mother has that one," or "My friend went there last year, you'll love it". But never with Mlle Quirit. She could talk all day long and tell you absolutely nothing about herself.'

'If she never revealed much of herself, I suppose it's too much to hope you noticed anything different in her behaviour in the days leading up to the murder?'

'Not that I noticed.' He paused, eyes staring at nothing in the corner of the room. 'Except for the last week or so. She asked me to walk her to her car at the end of her shift on the nights we crossed over. It wasn't a problem for me; it took two minutes while Marine from the day shift was prepping her handover notes, but it was something she only started last week, maybe ten days ago.'

'Did she say why?'

'Only that as an older woman she wasn't feeling quite as steady on her feet as she used to be, particularly at the end of a long day's work.' He shrugged again. 'Made sense to me, and I'm more than used to being a steady arm for my *grandmère* when she needs one.'

The two nurses had very little to offer in their interviews. Mlle Quirit was a hard worker, never late to start a shift, and offered an excellent standard of patient care. By all accounts she was an exemplary nurse, if a rather private colleague, and both women had been far too occupied with their own workloads to notice any changes in the victim's behaviour.

When the head gardener, Jean-Charles Gommet, walked into the room Bruno felt an instinct that this interview would yield something. He had known Gommet for as long as he'd been living in St Denis, for in addition to tending the grounds at the care home the gardener volunteered his time to keep the flowerbeds at the tennis and rugby clubs in tip-top condition. Gommet's normally relaxed demeanour had given way to a nervous energy, and Bruno knew it wasn't because he feared the police. Unless he was sorely mistaken, the groundskeeper had something to reveal.

Under the table, Bruno gave Fabien's ankle a light tap with his foot. When the young man turned to look at him, Bruno raised his eyebrow. Fabien nodded and leaned back in his chair as Bruno took over.

'Jean-Charles, welcome. Thank you for finding the time to speak with us. As I'm sure you know, we're here to interview you about your former colleague, Josette Quirit.' The gardener nodded. 'What sort of relationship did you have?'

Jean-Charles cleared his throat. 'Not much of one. She wasn't at the home very long, and my work keeps me outside while hers was largely inside. But we'd exchange the occasional word about the weather, or the gardens. She always complimented my flowerbeds, said they reminded her of a place she used to work when she was younger.' A pause. 'Has anyone else mentioned the motorbike?'

And there it was. 'The motorbike?' Bruno asked.

'A Honda, I don't know the make. It started showing up not long after she started working here, at the beginning and end of each shift.' He settled and resettled himself in the chair. 'Parked up just along the road from the home, not far from the *pompiers*, and stayed for at least half an hour each time, the rider never dismounting.'

Bruno turned to look at Fabien, who gave a small shake of his head.

'Do you have any idea who it might have been?' Bruno asked.

'None whatsoever. The rider was wearing a helmet and leathers.'

'Were they tall, short?'

'Hard to tell. Average, I would say. Not tall.'

'And did you mention this to Mlle Quirit?'

The gardener nodded. 'I'd assumed it was someone she knew making sure she'd got to work and home again safely, a son or daughter perhaps. But it spooked her, and she started getting Michel on the front desk to walk her to her car each night.'

After they'd thanked the gardener for his time and were walking back to the station, Bruno asked Fabien, 'What do you think about the idea of a female killer now?'

'Now?'

'Now that we've had two witnesses describe our murder victim as having been followed, perhaps even stalked, by someone bold enough to be observed yet maintain their presence. According to the gardener, the rider's helmet and leathers covered up every inch of skin, but there's got to be something on camera that will help us.'

Fabien nodded. 'Hopefully the CCTV will be of use when we finally get through it all.'

10

Bruno was so happy to be back in the swing of things, conducting interviews and tossing around theories with the rest of the team, that it came as something of a shock when four o'clock rolled around, nearly the hour for him and Fabien to go to Fauquet for their meeting-slash-video chat with Claudine Jaboullier and Fabien's techy friend in Paris. It had been no trouble at all to get the Jaboulliers to agree to Claudine's participation in the revitalization scheme; Père Jaboullier had been one of Bruno's most fearsome opponents on the tennis court for the past ten years, and both he and his wife trusted their village policeman implicitly.

At sixteen years old, Claudine had no need for parental supervision during the meeting itself, but Bruno was a man who liked to do things properly, and it was his opinion that the proper way to do business with a teenager was to go through their parents. Alicia, Claudine's mother, had been enthusiastic about getting her daughter involved in a project that would do no harm at all to her eventual curriculum vitae, but a born negotiator at heart she had extracted a promise of a dinner cooked by Bruno in exchange for her family's cooperation. It had been no hardship for him to agree to the concession; there was little in life that gave Bruno more satisfaction than cooking for his friends and neighbours.

Getting from his office to Fauquet's was a matter of moments; Bruno only had to cross the market square. He made a point to arrive early; the extra window of time should be sufficient to choose Easter treats for Laura, Pamela, Florence and the twins, and to meet the new chocolatier he had heard so much about.

Bruno inhaled deeply as he crossed the shop, the warm embrace of chocolate mingling with the sweet air of caramelizing sugar and baked goods. The display case full of *viennoiseries* attracted his eye as he walked past, tight curls of *escargots* – the pastries, not the molluscs – calling to him from beyond the glass. A few paces past the baked goods stood another display cabinet, this one filled with handmade chocolates of every hue: dark, milk, white and ruby. The latter, recently discovered, made little sense to Bruno, although he had to acknowledge it had a good flavour, chocolate with a back note of berry, not unlike some of his favourite wines.

There were more varieties of chocolates than Bruno had ever dreamt possible. He peered down to read the labels – *bergamot*, read one; *passion fruit*, another. There was a whole shelf dedicated to pralines, and two just for truffles. Since he'd last been in this corner of the shop Fauquet's had transformed itself from a simple patisserie into a Willy Wonka wonderland. It was no wonder he'd heard such good things about the new arrival.

Behind the counter was a friendly face, that of Delphine Mausans. As a young girl Delphine had declared herself allergic to sport in all its forms, but that didn't stop her from coming along to the town rugby games, cheering on her older brothers as they scored tries and conversions for St Denis. If he remembered correctly, she and Claudine Jaboullier had become great friends on the sidelines, neither girl having much interest in sports beyond their shared desire to cheer on their siblings and school friends.

'Bruno, *bonjour!* How are you today?'

'I am very well, Delphine, very well indeed. I didn't know you were working at Fauquet's. How long have you been here?'

'Not long at all – I actually started last week. They were advertising for part-time help during the school holidays, and my parents said I could apply as long as it didn't interfere with my studies.'

'Very wise. And are you enjoying the work?'

She nodded. 'I'm still training, but I'm looking forward to getting my first pay cheque at the end of the month. It feels so grown up!'

Bruno smiled. 'I bet it does. Congratulations, I'm sure you'll be excellent.'

Delphine blushed slightly, both proud of and embarrassed by the compliment. 'Thank you, I hope so. How can I help you today?'

Bruno turned and gestured to the shelves behind him, which were stacked with all manner of Easter chocolates, bunnies and chickens and eggs, and even a lamb or two. 'I'm in the market for some Easter chocolates for some friends of mine. Do you have any recommendations?'

'Do I ever! You know we have a new chocolatier, a master from Brussels?'

'So I'd heard, but I didn't know he was from Belgium.'

'He's wonderful,' Delphine sighed, and Bruno could almost see cartoon hearts and flowers dancing around the teenager's head, so apparent was her crush. He couldn't help smiling to himself, remembering the strength of his own adolescent fancies. 'I'd offer to introduce you,' Delphine continued, 'but he's downstairs working in the cool room and mustn't be disturbed.'

'Another time then. Come, tell me – what would you suggest I buy for Florence's twins?'

Delphine made her way around the counter and joined Bruno in front of the shelving display. 'Now with twins it's tricky. Do you give them the same so they don't fight, or do you give them different ones to celebrate their individuality?'

Bruno was impressed by the young woman's thoughtfulness. 'I'm not really sure. I think as long as they're the same size, perhaps I should give them each something different?'

'Everything on the second shelf weighs five hundred grams; I know because I displayed them myself. The twins will probably prefer milk chocolate rather than the dark stuff.'

'And Florence would want me to stay away from the white, she's always telling me it doesn't qualify as chocolate.'

'I agree with her. So milk or ruby it is, then. Why don't you get a ruby egg for Dora, and a milk one for Daniel?'

Bruno cast his eyes over the display. 'I like the way you're thinking, but perhaps one of the animals would please them more. And I'll get three of your largest eggs – dark chocolate – for Laura, Florence and Pamela. The ones on the top shelf with the bronze finish would be perfect.' As Delphine reached for the eggs Bruno wondered how long after Easter it would be before he saw Laura to give her the chocolate, whether he was wasting time and money in the purchase.

'A very good choice indeed. And for the twins? Would you prefer the bunnies or the chickens?'

'I think the chickens, a tribute to my own birds. One ruby and one milk, please.'

Delphine retrieved the chocolates and began parcelling them up for him. 'Are you going home immediately, or do you have more shopping to do in town? Because I can always keep them in the fridge here for you to collect on your way home, reduce the risk of any melting.'

'Thanks, Delphine, but I'm actually about to have a meeting right here, so perhaps I could pay you for the chocolates now and come back for them when I'm ready to leave?'

Delphine clicked her heels together and issued Bruno with a mock salute. 'Of course, *monsieur le chef*. Here at Fauquet our number one goal is to keep our clientele happy.'

'So professional, and still in training. You're a credit to your family, Delphine.' At this, the young girl's blush extended to her hairline. He settled the bill, returned her salute, and made his way to the tables on the front terrace, where Claudine was sitting under an umbrella, tapping away at her phone.

'Claudine, thanks so much for agreeing to come along today.' Bruno bent down to kiss the young woman hello. 'I hope you haven't been waiting long?'

'Barely five minutes, Monsieur Courrèges. I ordered a drink, though. I hope that was all right.'

'Of course. And you must call me Bruno, Claudine, if we are to be colleagues.'

She made an apologetic face. 'Maman told me that I had to be professional, courteous.'

'And your mother is not wrong. But have I not always been Bruno to you?'

'To my brothers, yes. But you're their coach, you have a bond.'

Bruno was rather taken aback by this statement; he hadn't thought his connection with the youth of St Denis was restricted to those with an aptitude for sport. But before he could respond Fabien bounded across the terrace and pulled up a chair.

'Sorry I'm late, I got held up at the station,' he said, slightly out of breath, before turning to the other occupant of the table and thrusting out his hand for a shake. 'You must be Claudine, thank you so much for coming. I'm Fabien.' The younger officer turned a hundred-watt smile on the teenager, who visibly melted from the attention. 'Has Bruno explained why we wanted to meet with you today?'

'Not yet, he only just arrived. But Maman said it was something to do with social media and the market?'

Somehow Fabien's beam only grew bigger. 'Exactly. I have a friend who's going to help us use social media to promote St Denis, but we need help creating content for him to use. Does that sound like something you could do?'

Claudine's response to Fabien's question was interrupted by the waitress arriving with the young girl's drink, an ice cold bottle of Gini bitter lemon soda, condensation dripping down the sides and making Bruno's mouth water. Setting the small bottle down in front of Claudine with a glass full of ice, the waitress took drink orders from the two police officers and headed back inside.

'So does that sound like something you could do?' Fabien repeated his question after the brief interruption.

'That depends on what you need. I'm pretty good at filming and editing video, and my photos aren't bad, but I'm not great at Photoshop; I've never had the money for a licence, so can only use the free tools with any real competence.' She twisted her hands together on her lap, unwittingly betraying her nervousness.

Fabien nodded. 'I don't think that'll be a problem, my friend Vincent is a wizard when it comes to photo-editing. What we would need from you is content for him to work with. But it's not a one and done deal – we'd want you to be giving us new material throughout the summer. Are you okay with that level of commitment?'

Claudine nodded. 'I'd only be able to give you a couple of hours each week until my exams are over, but after mid-June I'll have more time, and by the beginning of July I'd be completely free till the end of the summer holidays.' She looked at the floor, clearly uncomfortable with what she was about to say, and her next sentence came out as one long incoherent word. '*Maman*sayswillyoubeabletowritemealetterofreference?'

Bruno and Fabien looked at each other for a moment in confusion before the words split apart in their brains. 'A letter of reference? Of course, that will be no trouble at all,' Fabien said, smiling at the teenager, who beamed back at him, clearly more comfortable than she had been moments earlier. 'If you're happy to come on board, shall we give Vincent a ring? He'll be able to brief you fully; I barely have half a clue when it comes to social media.'

Claudine reached into the rucksack at her feet and pulled out a notepad and pen. 'Yes please, that would be great.' She sat herself up straight in her chair and tucked a lock of hair behind her ear.

Bruno thought to himself that the gesture made her look more like the schoolgirl she was than her earlier awkwardness had done, and he was touched by her efforts to appear adult and professional. Claudine might not think that the two of them had a bond, but over the years Bruno had watched the young woman grow up and he felt the same paternal pull towards her as he did all the young folk of St Denis and its environs.

Fabien moved around to Claudine's side of the table and leaned his mobile phone against the umbrella pole that stood in the centre. Bruno couldn't see the screen, but he could hear the ringing from the speaker, and then an 'allô' as the call was answered.

'Vincent, *salut.* This is Claudine, the budding videographer I told you about?'

Claudine grinned at the introduction and waved at the screen. '*Bonjour,* Vincent.'

'*Enchanté,* Claudine. Happy to have you join our little team.'

'Can you give Claudine a rundown of the sort of material you need?' Fabien asked. 'I've told her you'll want photos and video, but I didn't know anything more than that to brief her.'

Vincent started to talk while Claudine took notes, and it was only a sentence or two before Bruno tuned out of the conversation, so unfamiliar was the vocabulary. He noted that the teenager was giving the video call her full attention, her pen scratching away at the paper as she took copious notes, occasionally pausing to ask what sounded to his untrained ear like pertinent questions.

After a few minutes, with Vincent and Claudine chattering away like lifelong friends, Fabien came back around to Bruno's side of the table. 'It seems to be going well,' he said *sotto voce*. 'I think you chose the right woman for the job.'

'I think so,' agreed Bruno. 'Don't let me forget to send Claudine and Vincent the video Mademoiselle Cantagnac filmed today; we did our first draw for the stalls.'

Fabien turned his grin on Bruno. 'So it's all coming together?'

'It seems to be. Mademoiselle Cantagnac is contacting the May winners this afternoon, and first thing tomorrow morning I'm going to meet with Fat Jeanne to finalize the details.'

'Fat Jeanne? That doesn't sound like the kindest of nicknames.'

Bruno shrugged. 'I thought the same when I first arrived in St Denis but trust me – she won't answer to anything else. Says that calling herself fat is no different to calling me brunet or Pamela red-headed, a factual description, nothing more and nothing less.'

'If you say so. But it doesn't sound right to me.' Fabien pulled a face. 'So who's this so-called Fat Jeanne anyway? What's her role in all this?'

Bruno laughed as he leaned back in his chair. 'Fat Jeanne is the queen of the market, for lack of a better description. For as long as anyone can remember, she's been the woman in charge of organizing which stallholder gets which pitch, of collecting their fees.'

'And does she control the list of applicants?'

Bruno shook his head. 'No, no. That's all done by the Mayor's office – there's a lot of paperwork and admin involved, and all of that has to go through proper procedure, making sure licences are in place and whatnot. But Fat Jeanne is like the market's mediator, its archivist, its UN peacekeeper. Without her, at its busiest the market would have descended into open warfare, vendors battling for prime position. No one dares cross Fat Jeanne – in St Denis, her word is law. We policemen are merely her enforcers.'

'She sounds like a fearsome woman.'

'Definitely not one to be crossed,' Bruno agreed.

'Excuse me, Fabien?' Claudine interrupted their gossip, holding out Fabien's phone. 'Vincent wants a quick word.'

Fabien took the phone and stood up, crossing the square to continue his conversation. Bruno smiled widely at Claudine. 'That seemed to go well. Are you happy?'

'Very much so, yes. It will be good for me to have a purpose to all my filming, a real project to work on. Thank you very much for thinking of me.'

'You were the first and only person who came to mind. I couldn't think of a better candidate, and I'm very happy that we've got you on board.'

Claudine busied herself collecting her notebook and pen, packing her things away into her rucksack. 'Please tell Monsieur Fabien how grateful I am for this opportunity. I hate to run off without saying goodbye, but Maman will want my help preparing dinner.'

Bruno took a card from his wallet, his phone number and email address on the front. Taking a pen from his breast pocket, he copied Fabien's number from his phone and handed the card to Claudine. 'Here are our numbers; if you have any further questions before we next meet please don't hesitate to get in touch. Oh, and before I forget – this morning Mademoiselle Cantagnac and I filmed the first of the draws for a slot in the market. Should I send it to you, or straight to Vincent?'

'Send it to me, please. I'll do any editing it might need and then pass it on to Vincent for posting. Do you have my email address?' Bruno shook his head, and she recited her details twice while he tapped them into his phone.

'I'm sending the file now. If you haven't received it by the time you get home, drop me a text and I'll send it again.'

Claudine nodded. 'Thanks again, Bruno. I'm very excited to be a part of this, and I promise you I'll give you my very best.'

Bruno smiled genially. 'I would expect nothing less from a Jaboullier, on or off the pitch.'

He watched as Claudine made her way across the market square, waving a farewell to Fabien, who was leaning against the low wall as he continued his phone call. After a few minutes the young man returned to the table.

'Well I'd say that went well. Very well indeed.' He sat down and took a long drink of the soda water that had arrived earlier. 'Vincent was most impressed with Claudine, said she asked him all the right questions. Did you send her the video you took this morning?'

'I did. And I've given her both of our contact information, so she might be in touch if she has any questions.' Bruno passed his own phone across the table. 'That's her info there, if you want to copy it.'

Fabien tapped away at the screen and seconds later his phone chimed an alert. 'No need to copy it, I just shared the contact with myself.' He handed Bruno's phone back. 'Thanks. So now that's all done and dusted, what's the plan of action for tomorrow? Will you be working from the gendarmerie, or are you sticking with your office at the Hôtel de Ville?'

'A bit of both, I think. I'm aware that this is your investigation, not mine. Anything I can do to assist you, I will, but I don't want you to think I'm breathing down your neck, second-guessing your every move.'

'And if I want you to do a bit of second-guessing? What then?'

'Then that falls under the umbrella of anything I can do to assist you, does it not?'

A shrug from Fabien. 'I suppose so. But wouldn't it be easier if we were working under the same roof?'

'It would. Now that it's clear solving this murder won't be a matter of moments, it strikes me that having you stay at the Hôtel St Denis is something of a waste of departmental funds. There's plenty of space at the new residences attached to the gendarmerie, if you don't mind living in the office, as it were.'

Fabien smiled, but Bruno could tell it was forced. 'Alternatively, there are plenty of *gîtes* in the area – Mademoiselle Cantagnac at the Mairie could organize one in minutes, if you'd prefer something a little more private?'

This time Fabien beamed. 'I think that's a great idea, Bruno – a place of my own would be brilliant. You're sure it wouldn't be too much trouble?'

'Not in the slightest. A short let will be cheaper for the police than the hotel, and whichever cottage owner gets you will be grateful for the income. I'll set Colette on the search straight away; we'll have you in your own place by tomorrow night.'

'In that case, Bruno, you have yourself a deal.' He extended a hand and the two men shook on it. 'I'll speak to Christophe tonight, let him know I'll be checking out in the morning.'

'Excellent news. Don't forget to let J-J know too.'

'I won't, don't you worry.' Fabien downed the rest of his glass. 'Can I buy you dinner, thank you for your help?'

'Don't even think about it. I was about to invite you to dinner, give you a chance to have a home-cooked meal. Tell me, do you have any allergies I should know about?'

'None whatsoever. My mother always said there was nothing on this earth I wouldn't eat. Even mud as a small child, apparently.'

'Well, I certainly won't be serving you any of that, unless I fail to wash the vegetables properly.' They both laughed, and Bruno continued. 'If you're going to be around for the foreseeable, why don't I organize a big dinner this weekend, introduce you to some people in St Denis?'

'That sounds like a lovely idea, if you're sure it's not too much effort?'

'Not at all. I'd been toying with the idea of having friends over to celebrate Easter, now we have two things to toast.' Bruno gestured to the waitress for the bill and fished a handful of coins from his pocket. 'Now if you'll excuse me, I must be off.'

11

It might not have been quite like the old days, Bruno thought to himself as he surveyed the vendors packing up their stalls at the end of the morning, but the first edition of No Traffic Tuesdays looked to have been a success – there was certainly a lot more footfall than he'd seen in recent months. Across the way he saw Fat Jeanne sharing a glass of wine and a gossip with Stéphane the cheesemaker and decided to join them.

'Bruno, *bonjour!*' Stéphane, a former rugby man and still the size of a Samoan prop forward, drew the policeman into a warm embrace. 'We missed you last week. I understand we have you to thank for the renewed interest in our little market.'

Bruno's attempt at a reply was muffled by the other man's barrel chest, and Stéphane freed him from the hug and bade him repeat himself. 'I did very little, *mon ami*. You'll have to thank Colette Cantagnac: she sacrificed a lot of shoe leather to the putting up of posters and the handing out of leaflets, not to mention the petrol spent driving to almost every hamlet in the Périgord.'

Fat Jeanne rolled her eyes. 'We'll have none of your false modesty here, Bruno – we all know you put in every bit as much effort as she did, and came up with the concept in the first place.' She took a long draw from her tumbler of wine, and it stained her teeth with a purple wash. 'But I'll thank the young lady nonetheless.' Bruno smiled, Colette was in her late forties if she was a day.

'So the morning has been a success, I take it?' Bruno knew that more people walking around the market didn't necessarily translate to more money being spent, although it did significantly increase the odds.

Fat Jeanne beamed. 'A resounding success. How much did you say you'd taken today, Stéphane? Over a thousand euros, wasn't it?'

'Just shy of twelve hundred. Which is incredible, given we don't even have the tourists yet.'

Bruno let out a long slow whistle – he was impressed. 'Twelve hundred euros in a morning, *mon Dieu*. That's peak summertime takings, am I right?'

Stéphane nodded. 'That's not profit, mind you – that's turnover. But given that last week I barely scraped three hundred . . .' The cheesemaker finished his sentence with raised eyebrows that said as much as words.

Bruno clapped his friend on the arm. 'I'm really happy for you, Stéphane. Now all we need to do is make sure this initial burst of enthusiasm can be sustained throughout the year. Curiosity will have driven a lot of people here today; our job now is to keep them coming back.'

Their little gathering was interrupted by Gérard Mangin, who approached the group with a smile, wrinkles gathering in the corners of his eyes. 'Bruno, Fat Jeanne! Just the people I wanted to see.'

'*Bonjour*, Monsieur le Maire.' Fat Jeanne proffered her face for a welcome kiss. 'It's good to see St Denis so busy, is it not?'

The Mayor clasped the old woman by the shoulders and smacked a loud *bisou* on each cheek. 'It most certainly is! Do you know who I just ran into?' She shook her head. 'None other than my counterpart at Le Croiseau, Dominique Renoir, and she pretended not to see me. Dove into the nearest stall and had to fake a deep interest in their plus-sized lingerie.'

Bruno chuckled. 'So we managed to lure the mayor of our rivals to our little market? That's no small victory.'

The Mayor laughed in response. 'We can't start thinking of our fellow villages as rivals, my dear Bruno. All us small towns are in this together; we need to support each other if we're to have any chance at all of beating the lure of online shopping and out-of-town megastores.'

'Tell that to the mayor of the town who deliberately moved her market in competition with our own,' Bruno replied. 'That wasn't remotely supportive. We've had this slot for seven hundred years, maintained it through plague and famine and war.'

'And faced off nearly every horseman of the apocalypse in the process,' the Mayor agreed. 'You neglected to mention Death. I hear that you're back on the murder investigation – what's the latest news on the case?'

Bruno gave the Mayor a stern look. 'Do you think I would be so indiscreet as to discuss such matters in the middle of the market?' The Mayor looked suitably abashed. 'Tell you what, Fabien is moving into the Durrands' old place on the river this evening; it seemed foolish having the Police Nationale pay for him to live in the Hôtel de Ville when so many holiday lets are sitting empty. I'd planned on having him to dinner tonight, save him doing a shop. Why don't you join us, we can update you then?'

'With pleasure, thank you,' said the Mayor. 'I'll bring along a loaf or two of that olive bread you like from the Moroccans, and some of Stéphane's cheese.' He nodded at the cheesemaker, who turned to his van and set about putting together an assortment of the Mayor's favourites. 'Eight o'clock okay?'

'Make it a little earlier, we can have a *petit apéro* before the main event. Let's say seven? Perhaps quarter past? And will Jacqueline be joining us?'

'She will not. It's bingo tonight, and she has her heart set on winning one of the mixed selection baskets from the butcher.' He rolled his eyes. 'To think that such a towering intellect can find fun in something as pedestrian as village bingo boggles my mind. Women. What can we do but worship them?'

Bruno and Stéphane laughed as the Mayor bade farewell to the group and continued his rounds of the market traders, seeking out their feedback on the first stage of his town's resuscitation attempt. Bruno reached into his pocket for his mobile phone and let Fabien know that they would be enjoying the Mayor's company at supper that evening.

Bruno was about to carry on his rounds of the closing market, taking the mood of the stallholders, when he felt a warm hand grasp his elbow and hot breath in his ear. 'Bruno! A word, if you please. *Privately*.' The fingers digging into his biceps squeezed a little tighter as she steered him into the shadows between Stéphane's refrigerated unit and the hotter-than-hell walls of the rotisserie chicken stall. Bruno felt sweat start to pool at the base of his spine.

'*T'as un problème,* Bruno,' Fat Jeanne said, close to his ear.

Bruno cocked his head to the side. 'A problem? I thought the market was happy with the increased footfall.'

Fat Jeanne shrugged. 'They are. But that doesn't mean I'm not hearing mutterings about your plan to find a "new market star".' Her air quotes in fingerless gloves gave the gesture a degree of menace. 'Did you not think to go stall to stall and tell the old guard how important they are to the success of your little scheme?' She spat on the ground to show her displeasure. 'How there would not even *be* a St Denis market to celebrate without their decades of loyalty?'

Bruno, surprised but not usually lost for words, was formulating his reply when she went on.

'Of course you didn't, because you are Bruno, Chef de Police, King Midas of the Périgord Noir. No one begrudges your enthusiasm for St Denis, don't misunderstand me. But maybe you should think of the bigger picture. People can be sensitive, have egos, you know. There's life outside the Mairie, you should remember. What's good for Gerard Mangin isn't always good for Bruno Courrèges.'

Before Bruno had a second to properly take in her critique, let alone respond to it, she had spun on her heel and disappeared with the speed of a woman many decades younger. Bruno, stunned, walked slowly away, pondering her words and wondering whether they were going to prove a rather uncomfortable truth.

It was not long past five when Bruno's mobile phone beeped with an incoming text message, Fabien saying he was finishing up at the station and would be at the Mairie within the quarter hour. To his horror, Bruno realized he'd yet to give a moment's thought to that evening's meal. A quick mental inventory of his fridge and cupboards and he was able to compose a meal both casual and celebratory.

He'd bought greens for a salad during his tour of the market, and having no fridge in his office had taken the precaution of wrapping the leaves in a damp tea towel and leaving them in the coolest corner to keep them fresh during the working day. His well-stocked larder always contained the makings of a vinaigrette for the salad; some of Stéphane's rich golden butter and tinned anchovies he could lay out on thin slices of toast to serve with pre-dinner drinks. The Mayor had promised to bring bread and cheese, which left only the main course to consider. His chickens had been particularly fruitful of late, and he'd not had the time for more than one proper breakfast all week, so omelette it would be. If he remembered correctly, there was still a small ball of black truffle sitting in the carton he used to store his eggs, infusing the whites and yolks with its earthy perfume.

No sooner had Bruno decided on the menu than he heard Fabien greeting Colette Cantagnac in the anteroom, his manner both respectful and warm as he thanked her for arranging his temporary home. As Bruno got up and readied himself to greet his new colleague, he was amused to witness his executive assistant being clearly charmed by the visiting officer.

With Fabien taking Balzac's usual place in the front passenger seat of the Land Rover, the basset was relegated to the back, from where he couldn't stick his head out of the window and watch the world go by. Bruno made a fuss of the dog as he installed him on the back seat, and once he'd buckled himself in Fabien stuck his left arm through the gap between the two front seats and started stroking the basset's soft ears, an action he continued for the whole drive home.

Fabian let out an admiring whistle as Bruno pulled into the courtyard. 'Bruno, your place is beautiful. It reminds me of home.' Fabien stepped out of the car and slowly turned in a circle, taking in the plane tree, the potager, and the chicken run Bruno and the Baron had built over the course of one very long and sweaty summer weekend many years back. 'Even your shutters are the same colour as my parents'.'

Bruno laughed. 'Aren't all the shutters in the Périgord the same shade of blue?'

'Not quite all! You see some rebels with grey ones, and once or twice I've even seen green.' He pulled a face of horror, but it was in jest.

'Shocking. I hope you reported them to the style police.'

'It was but my duty as a man of the law,' Fabien replied with a grin. He bent his head down to pass under the heavy boughs of wisteria that framed the low doorway, and when he was inside and upright Bruno was amused to note that his Sonic the Hedgehog shock had picked up a few small purple petals in his passage. He showed his guest the bathroom, and while Fabien was out of the room Bruno set to work preparing dinner.

Having put the salad greens straight into the fridge, still wrapped in their just damp cloths, Bruno began clearing off the dining table, which tended to become a repository for paperwork and half-read copies of *Sud Ouest* when he wasn't entertaining friends – or lovers, he thought wistfully.

This was not a formal dinner but a casual supper for friends, so he wouldn't use a tablecloth, he decided. Instead, he reached into the top drawer of the chest in the dining room and pulled out a pile of cork circles to use as placemats. From the dresser he took out three side plates, none matching, and three of the handsome red wine glasses with the generous bowls and short fat stems that he'd found at the same *brocante* where he and Pamela had bought the bed linens currently in use in the guest room. Salt, pepper, and a bottle of the sparkling water Gérard liked, and the table was almost ready for supper. He would be balancing out his wine with tap water, while Fabien's preferences had yet to be established.

As he went into the kitchen carrying the three dinner plates he planned to warm in the oven while he prepared the omelette, he heard Fabien's feet on the tiles. 'Help yourself to water – it's on the side,' he called over his shoulder as he bent down to turn on the grill for toasting, after which he would use the residual heat to warm the plates for the main course.

'Is there anything I can do to help?'

'How's your vinaigrette?'

'That depends. Do you have any walnut vinegar to hand?'

Bruno stood up, beaming. 'I think you and I are going to get along rather well.' He reached across the stove to grab the bottle, noting he was going to need to replenish it this week, and passed it to Fabien. 'There's a jam jar in the drainer by the sink, and everything else you might need you'll find on the shelf to your right.' He paused. 'Except salt and pepper, I already put those on the table.'

While Fabien got to work making the vinaigrette, Bruno took the remains of yesterday's baguette from the clay pot he used as a bread bin and began slicing it thinly in readiness for toasting when the Mayor arrived. He dusted the crumbs off the bread board and into the sink, and went into the pantry, where he fetched two tins of anchovies and was pleased to spy a bottle of *vinaigre aux noix* sitting on the shelf above, one small task struck off the week's domestic to-do list.

There was little left to do before the Mayor turned up, as both the omelette and the accompanying salad were the work of moments, and far better made in the minutes immediately before serving. 'What wine do you think with *omelette aux truffes*?' he asked Fabien, wanting to include the young man despite already having decided on the appropriate bottle.

Fabien turned to face him, shaking the jam jar as he spoke. 'I'm afraid I don't know much about wine – we were always more beer drinkers in my family.'

Bruno mimed a look of shock. 'Never mind, while you're in St Denis I shall teach you.'

'From what I've learned since I got here, you're on first-name terms with half the winemakers in the *département*.'

'I thought you were supposed to be investigating the Quirit murder, not me!' Bruno laughed. 'Speaking of which, before the Mayor arrives I wanted to reassure you that you can speak freely about the case in front of him. He's going to need to be briefed anyway, and you can trust in his discretion.'

A crunch of gravel in the courtyard heralded the Mayor's arrival, and Balzac ran towards the door, baying his song of welcome. Bruno put down the bottle of wine he was holding, and opened the kitchen door to his guest, who was immediately set upon by thirty-plus kilos of basset hound. A short honk of farewell from Jacqueline as she turned the car around and drove on to her bingo date, and the three men plus dog exchanged greetings.

'Bruno, take these off me before Balzac has a go at them?' The Mayor handed Bruno a canvas bag reeking of ripe cheese, two olive loaves emerging from the top. From the floor Gérard then gave the dog his full attention, pressing his face into the loose folds of fur by the basset's neck. 'Who's the very best basset in all the land?' Balzac preened at the attention and gave each of the Mayor's forearms an affectionate lick.

With the cheeses safely out of Balzac's reach in the furthest depths of the counter, Bruno reached for the bottle of Ter'Raz he had selected for the occasion, and opened it so that it might breathe before dinner. The Ter'Raz was a new addition to Bruno's roster of local favourites, a Malbec–Merlot blend from Château Le Raz in the Montravel, to the west of Bergerac. The producer, Patrick Barde, had elected to give up the *appellation contrôlée* award so that he could blend wines from different years and ensure a consistent product, something that was becoming ever more of a challenge for winemakers as a result of climate change. 'What can I offer you to drink, Gérard? We're having Ter'Raz with our dinner, but what would you like for an *apéro*?'

'Ter'Raz? I don't know it, but if you've chosen it I'm sure it will be delightful. As for that *apéro*, do you have any Crémant? A kir royale would go down nicely.'

'Of course.' Bruno opened the fridge, where no fewer than three bottles of Crémant sat chilling on the bottom shelf. 'Fabien, the cassis is on that tray to your left, could you please pass it to me?' He grabbed three champagne flutes from the shelf above the wine rack and busied himself making the drinks before realizing he hadn't asked Fabien what he wanted. 'I assume you're happy with a kir, Fabien? If not, don't worry – the extra glass certainly won't go to waste.'

'I'd love one, thank you. But is there anything else I can do to help you with dinner?'

'You could put the toast on to grill if you don't mind?' Bruno gestured with his head to where the slices were laid out in readiness, and Fabien popped them under the grill, crouching down to keep an eye on the thin wafers to ensure they didn't burn. When the bread was out from under the grill Fabien turned off the heat, put the dinner plates inside, and closed the door, all without being asked. His mother had clearly taught him well, Bruno thought, despite his years lost to boarding school.

Fabien's phone rang, and the younger officer ducked into the hallway to take the call. Meanwhile, Bruno put a slick of fridge-cold butter on each slice of toast and topped them with a pair of anchovies straight from the tin, the extra drizzle of oil providing another pop of flavour. He arranged the canapés on the breadboard and brought them out to the courtyard, where the Mayor sat at a table, the evening remarkably warm for April.

'These toasts are wonderful, Bruno,' said the Mayor as he reached for another. 'And so simple. Your own recipe?'

'I wish I could claim that they were, but actually Fabiola introduced me to them, apparently she and Gilles stumbled on them when they were on holiday in Firenze last month. The Italians call them *burro e acciughe*.'

Fabien was off the phone and walking across the courtyard, trying to tell Bruno something with his eyes. Bruno gave a subtle nod; he wasn't sure what the message was but he understood an update would be forthcoming.

'I didn't think the Italians knew what butter was,' Gérard said with a smile. 'Aren't they all olive oil all the time?'

'Evidently not. The Florentines are famous for their beef steaks, I suppose they have to get some use from the dairy cows.'

'But not milk,' joked the Mayor. 'Certainly not after ten a.m.!'

Bruno and Fabien joined in the laughter; the rivalry between France and Italy was almost as long-standing as that between the French and their cousins over La Manche, and it was almost a ritual to poke fun at their near neighbours, especially when their national team had been given a kicking on the rugby pitch by *gli Azzurri*, as had happened all too often in recent years.

'I used to have an Italian girlfriend,' Fabien offered, 'from Le Marche. Have you ever heard what they like to say about us?'

'I've heard them say many things about us over the years,' replied the Mayor. 'Not all of them kind.'

'Well this one I kind of like – according to them, we French are simply sad Italians.' The laughter that erupted following Fabien's comment rather disproved the notion.

'Looks like our glasses need refreshing. Excuse me a moment.' Bruno went into the kitchen and Fabien followed.

'That was Jules on the phone,' Fabien said. 'Not only have they found the bike Gommet described on the CCTV, but there's a second vehicle of interest. A black van, spotted at both the nursing home and the riding school.'

'*Putain.*'

'Jules is sending a car up there to keep watch overnight, but I'm not sure we've got the manpower to sustain a twenty-four-hour presence.'

Bruno nodded. 'We'd best get back to the Mayor. He's here

for an update on the case anyway.' Back at the table with the second half of the bottle of Crémant in one hand and the crème de cassis in the other, Bruno was amused to see that Gérard had polished off the anchovy toasts in their brief absence. 'I thought that we could finish this bottle and then you two can move into the dining room while I make dinner. It won't take me long.'

'I'm enjoying being out here, between the candlelight and the stars. Why don't Fabien and I move the plates and things outside while you cook, so we can take advantage of this lovely spring evening?'

Fabien nodded. 'Sounds good to me, I haven't had dinner outside yet this year. And your garden is glorious, Bruno. What are the flowers I can smell?'

'Probably the roses, which seem to be coming earlier each year, although the wisteria has started flowering earlier than usual too.'

'Don't I know it! Some of the petals fell out of my hair when I was in the bathroom earlier,' Fabien laughed.

'If I may be so bold,' Gérard asked, leaning across the table. 'What exactly is the motivation behind that haircut? It's rather . . .' He paused. 'Unusual. Striking, one might say.'

Fabien grinned ruefully. 'One of my cousins is training as a hairdresser, and I told her she could practise on me. She was so pleased with the result that I didn't have the heart to tell her I hated it.'

Bruno and Gérard laughed heartily, helped along by the bottle of Crémant they'd put away. 'That's good of you, son. And at least it's only hair, it'll grow back.'

'Which is all very well, Monsieur le Maire, except cousinly duty now obliges me to use her services.' Fabien pulled a face. 'I think you'll be stuck with Officer Sonic for quite some time to come.'

Seeing that his guests had finished their drinks Bruno swallowed the last of his own and got to his feet. 'Time for me to start preparing our dinner. I'll leave you two to set the table out here.'

'What are we having, dear Bruno?' Without waiting for a response, Gérard turned to face Fabien. 'If you've not had Bruno's cooking before let me tell you that you are in for a treat, whatever it is.'

'Just a simple supper tonight: *omelette aux truffes* made with eggs from my chickens and flavoured with the first truffle that Balzac found when we taught him to hunt them. With a plain salad to follow, and the bread and cheese you were so kind to bring along.' Bruno was gratified to hear the Mayor groan in pleasure at the sound of the menu, while Fabien surreptitiously licked his lips at the mention of truffle, the only acceptable reaction from a son of the Périgord.

Before getting to work on their main course, Bruno rang Pamela. But it was dinnertime, and he was unsurprised when the phone rang out. The omelette took but a few minutes to make, Bruno preferring to leave the eggs just underdone in the pan, secure in the knowledge that the residual heat in the cast iron would finish the job on the way to the table. He called for Fabien to come and bring out the plates, which had warmed nicely, and carried the large frying pan directly from stovetop to table, enjoying the fragrance of truffle carried by the steam.

He had originally planned to keep the omelette truffle-scented, but in the spirit of generosity decided to treat his guests to some fresh shavings on top of their portions. It was clearly the right decision, as both Gérard and Fabien exclaimed with pleasure when they spied the black diamond cupped in the hand not busy with the pan.

'What a treat this is, Bruno. I can't remember the last time I had your *omelette aux truffes*, it must be last year at least.'

'And I can't wait to try your cooking, it was all J-J could talk about on our drive down from Périgueux.' Fabien took his phone from his pocket and snapped a photo of the omelette in its pan. 'I'm going to send him this so he knows what he's missing.'

'You young people, always taking photos of your food.' Gérard shook his head as he passed the bottle of Ter'Raz for each man to fill his own glass. 'I don't understand the fascination with what other people have had for breakfast.'

'I might be a millennial, sir, but this is a rarity for me. I'm mainly doing it to wind up the boss.' Fabien grinned, then bent forward over his plate with his eyes closed, using his hands to waft the aroma to his nose.

Bruno served himself and sat down. '*Bon appétit!*' The next few minutes passed in near silence, the only noises small murmurs of appreciation from his two guests. In no time at all the plates were clean but for the faintest traces of the butter in which the omelette had been cooked. 'I'm going to get the salad, perhaps one of you could help me with the cheese?' He got to his feet, and Fabien followed him to the kitchen, where he showed the younger man the stack of wooden boards next to the toaster and set about dressing the greens he had bought from the market.

Back outside, the three men piled their used plates high with salad, Fabien's vinaigrette mixing with the truffle butter residue left over from the main course. Once each of them had made their selection of cheese and pulled off hunks of Bruno's favourite olive loaves, Gérard turned the conversation to the actual purpose of their dinner.

'So, Fabien,' he began. 'While it's been a delight getting to know you, as lead officer, I think it's time that you give me an update on the Quirit investigation. Where are you in the case? Have you any reason to believe that the killer will strike again? If there's one thing St Denis can't afford, it's to lose more of our tourist custom. I'm not sure how many of our businesses can survive another bad summer.'

Fabien wiped at his plate with a hunk of bread, soaking it in salad dressing before topping it with a small sliver of Stéphane's Tomme d'Audrix. 'Time and cause of death have been signed off by both the coroner and the medical examiner – would you like me to email you a summary?'

The Mayor shook his head. 'No, no, that wouldn't be appropriate. A verbal sketch will suffice.'

Fabien described the victim and what they knew of her past before pausing to draw breath. 'Mademoiselle Quirit appears to have been living under an assumed name, and we're still trying to work our way backwards through what looks to be a chain of aliases. As things stand, everything about her life before Menton is a mystery.'

'So let me get this straight,' said Gérard. 'We have a strange woman who arrives in St Denis with a false identity, and within a few weeks she's dead. Have you established any sort of motive for the killing, anything to make you think that she was a target rather than a random victim?'

'We have, actually. Not a motive, not yet, but we have evidence to suggest that Mademoiselle Quirit was being stalked in the weeks leading up to her death.'

'Stalked?' Gérard sounded shocked. 'By whom?'

'We don't know yet. We have a witness at the nursing home who says that the same *moto* followed Mademoiselle Quirit to work each day. The rider – always in full leathers and a helmet – waited outside the building for half an hour each morning and arrived at a similar time before the end of her shift. We've requested all the footage from CCTV cameras both public and private that cover the nursing home and the fire station, but it's a long process reviewing it all.'

'Whoever followed her seems to have had access to her shift rota,' Bruno added.

'What about licence plates?' the Mayor asked. 'Surely you've looked up the bike?'

'Based on the footage reviewed so far it was obscured by mud, a different smear every day, which suggests that her stalker was smart enough to clean off the plates when out of the camera's reach so they didn't risk getting stopped by one of your gendarmes. The bike itself is a Honda Forza 125, the best-selling model in the country, so that was no use.'

'And what of the riding school? I assume you've checked the CCTV there to see if our stalker made any appearances up where the victim was living?' Bruno, unused to taking a back seat when briefing the Mayor, was privately amused by the Mayor's questions. He hadn't realized his friend would have made such a good cop, but the Mayor was asking the same questions he'd asked when being brought up to speed on the case.

Fabien nodded. 'We have. No suspicious mopeds or bikes, but for the past two weeks a large black van – plates also obscured – has driven past the gates slowly each evening, usually between six and seven o'clock. At the weekends it's been harder to predict. Once very early in the morning; twice in the early afternoon and five times after seven p.m.'

Gérard whistled. 'Exactly the window in which the murder took place. I assume you've taken precautions to ensure the safety of those living up at the riding school?'

'Excuse me one minute, I think this discussion calls for something a little stronger.' Bruno got up from the table and went inside, where he fetched three tumblers, a bottle of his beloved Lagavulin, and another of the Malvern water Jack Crimson had insisted was the only acceptable accompaniment to the top tier malt. Back outside he poured each of them a glass, too busy thinking to instruct young Fabien in the sipping and rolling and breathing that the whisky normally demanded. Gérard, he was pleased to see, completed the routine automatically. He was less pleased to see that the Mayor downed the rest of his glass in one; it was disrespectful to such a fine spirit.

Bruno took a small sip of his whisky and enjoyed the peat in his nose and on his tongue before the sensation of smoky liquid fire filled his gullet. 'To summarize, then. Our murder victim turns out to be a mystery woman of no known origin beyond ten years ago, with a stalker who knew where she was working and where she was living.'

Their conversation was brought to an end by the appearance of headlights sweeping along the trees that lined the road to Bruno's property, followed by Jacqueline's car. The woman herself bounced out of the driver's seat, oblivious to the heavy mood at the table. 'I did it! I won!'

'To think this woman teaches at the Sorbonne, and is a visiting fellow at the Wilson Center.' Gérard got to his feet shaking his head, but the grin on his face betrayed his pride in his partner. 'Gentleman, I must take my leave. Bruno, thank you for a delicious dinner. Fabien, it was a pleasure to meet you and thank you for the briefing. Can we drop you off in town? We'll pass by the Mairie on our way home.'

'That's very kind of you, sir.'

Gérard gave Bruno a resounding smack on the cheek, thanked him for dinner, and followed Jacqueline to the car, Fabien along for the ride. Bruno set about clearing the table, Balzac weaving between his feet in the hopes of a dropped morsel or two. Once everything had been brought into the kitchen, Bruno took Balzac out into the garden before turning in.

While the basset sniffed around before doing his business, Bruno turned his gaze to the night sky, cloudless and star-filled thanks to the lack of street lighting this far above St Denis. Fabien's summary of the case had given him a lot to think about: Mademoiselle Quirit's stalker, her mystery past – the two had to be related somehow – and Pamela's safety. He checked his watch, it was far too late to call a second time. He whistled for Balzac, and as the pair of them made their way to bed he decided that first thing tomorrow he would give Jack Crimson a ring. The old spy had to have seen something.

12

When Bruno awoke the next morning dawn was only just beginning to break behind the hills. After a quick shower, he changed into his work clothes before padding along the hall to the kitchen in his socks, where he put the water on to boil for his morning coffee. While he waited, he checked his phone, which had been left charging in the kitchen overnight. There was already a message from Fabien, sent twenty minutes earlier, and nothing from Laura, as was becoming all too familiar. He missed the traces of her scent on his pillow, waking up to her legs curled around his. He couldn't remember the date of their last sleepover – it was far too many weeks ago. Was he even in a relationship with this woman? He tapped out a text asking when she might be free for dinner before calling his colleague.

'*Bonjour,* Fabien. You're up early.'

'Always. Especially in a new place. Please thank Mademoiselle Cantagnac for arranging it, the place is great, very comfortable.'

'I'm glad to hear it. So what are your plans for the morning? If you don't need to head straight to the station, I thought I could pick you up and we could go over to the riding school, have a word with Pamela about this potential stalker?'

'That sounds like a very good idea to me. I know you two are close – you must be worried about her?'

'Pamela would hate to think it, but yes, I am. A woman more capable of looking after herself I've never met, she's fiercely independent. But the grounds are so big, and we know that there's a murderer at large. If there's any chance at all that she might be at risk, we have to warn her.'

'At least she's not alone up there, what with the Englishman and his daughter, plus the young boy who helps with the horses.'

'There is at least that, although I'm not sure how much use Félix would be if things got dangerous. We should have a word with Jack. If there's been any suspicious activity on site I'm sure he would've told me, but we should talk to him all the same.'

Before setting off for the riding school Bruno had rung Pamela and asked her to gather Jack and Miranda so that he and Fabien could speak with all three of them together. As he parked the Land Rover in front of her house the door opened and her sheepdogs burst through it to greet them, tails wagging as one, the sight of which had Balzac jumping up and down on the back seat in excitement.

Pamela stood in the open doorway, waiting for the men and dog to finish greeting the pack before waving them through the house and onto the rear patio, which no longer bore any traces of the previous week's gruesome attack. Jack and Miranda were sitting next to each other at the big wooden table, a tray in front of them bearing a large cafetière, a small bowl of sugar cubes, and a stack of delicate painted espresso cups, plus two dog biscuits for Balzac.

On seeing them approach Jack got to his feet to greet the new arrivals, while Miranda set about pouring coffees and putting one in front of each chair, after which she embraced Balzac and Bruno in turn, offering her cheek to Fabien for the traditional *bise*.

'Bruno, my dear chap,' said Jack. 'I can't tell you how happy I am that you're back on the case.' He turned to Fabien. 'No offence intended, young man.'

'And none taken. Of course you'd find comfort in the presence of a detective with whom you've worked so closely in the past, it's only natural.'

'Wise beyond your years, I see. Please do take a seat.' He sat back down himself and reached for the tray. 'Do you take sugar with your coffee?' Seated, Fabien declined, and Jack passed the bowl to Pamela. 'I told you these lumps were only fit for the horses.'

Pamela rolled her eyes, but there was a smile on her face. 'That you did, Jack.' She turned to face Bruno, who was seated to her left. 'Don't think I'm not happy to see you, but something tells me there's an ulterior motive to your visit, and it's not introducing Fabien here to Hector.'

Bruno noted his colleague counting the number of chairs with a puzzled expression and gave him a nudge. 'Hector is my horse. If you'd like to meet him I can take you to the stables after we're done.' He angled himself back towards Pamela. 'I'm afraid we come bearing some troubling news, and it has the potential to affect all three of you. Fabien, it's your case. Why don't you bring everyone up to date?'

'Of course, chief.' Fabien sat up straight and pushed his coffee to one side. 'During the course of our investigation it has become clear to us that Mademoiselle Quirit was being watched, stalked even. By whom, we have not yet been able to establish, but it seems highly probable that the person was also her killer. From the CCTV footage you provided us, and corroborated by other cameras in town, we have determined that this individual spent much of the past fortnight recceing the victim's place of work and the riding school, using both a moped and a large black van, although we have not yet been able to determine ownership of either vehicle.'

Across the table Bruno saw Miranda blanch, while Jack's face took on a stern impression. To his left, Pamela took a deep breath and held it for a long few moments before exhaling.

'Gosh. Well that does put the cat among the pigeons rather.' Pamela stood up. 'I'm just going to fetch a drop of brandy for these coffees. Please excuse me for a moment.'

'I know that very little escapes your notice, Jack,' said Bruno. 'Have you spotted anything unusual over the past few weeks? Any suspicious movements around the property?'

Jack shook his head. 'Well there is one thing, I suppose. I'd noticed a few cigarette butts dotted around under some of the trees, but I'd assumed Félix had started smoking again and didn't want us to know since he's supposed to have given up.'

'We must ask him. I don't suppose you were able to identify the brand?'

'Afraid not. The butts were brown, not white, but that doesn't narrow it down much. I binned all the ones I found, but we've had two rubbish collections since the murder, so unless there are new ones out there I fear I can't be much help.'

'Could you take me and Fabien to the trees where you found them? It's a long shot but some more might have turned up.'

'Certainly. But what do you propose we do to protect ourselves?' asked Jack.

'Keep your eyes open, and make sure your doors and windows are locked at all times. Do you still have the permit for that gun of yours?'

'I do.' He looked grim at the prospect of having to use it, a sentiment Bruno shared wholeheartedly.

'A little target practice might not hurt.'

Pamela returned just in time to hear Bruno's suggestion and plonked the brandy bottle down in the middle of the table with a loud thump. 'I'm afraid it's more for cooking than for drinking, but it'll have to do.' Jack reached for it and poured a half measure into each of their cups before topping them up with the remains of the coffee.

'I might have some small words of comfort,' said Fabien. 'We haven't seen either of the vehicles on the CCTV footage from here in the days immediately following the murder, although I'd like to have a look at the most recent recordings while I'm here if you don't mind?'

'Why don't you and Pamela go and take a look at the latest footage while I give Bruno a tour around the trees?' said Jack. 'I'd like whatever reassurances I can get that we're safe here; it's where my grandchildren live.'

Miranda, who had been uncharacteristically silent as she absorbed the news, gave her father an affectionate slap on the arm. 'I live here too, you know.'

Fabien took out his phone. 'I'm fairly sure that having had

Yveline and the crime scene investigators on site for a few days will have kept the stalker at bay, but I'm just issuing instructions to the gendarmerie now to increase their patrols of this area. We can't spare officers up here full-time, but the regular appearance of police vans should act as a significant deterrent in the event that Mademoiselle Quirit was not deliberately targeted.'

'Could you download the past week's video onto a USB stick for us to review at the station while you're at it?' asked Bruno. 'I've yet to review any of it, that's the next job on my list once we leave here.'

Jack got to his feet, and the others followed his lead. 'In that case, don't let us keep you. Miranda, will you join us on our tour of the grounds?'

'No, I'll go and help Félix with the horses. I don't like the idea of him being in the stables on his own right now, and there's a lot to be getting on with as it is.'

The five of them parted ways, Balzac and the sheepdogs following Miranda in the direction of the stables. Bruno knew that when he and Jack finished their patrol he was almost certain to find the basset in Hector's stall and was of a mind to leave him there for the day, an added layer of security for his friends at the riding school.

'How was Biarritz?' Bruno asked. 'A pity you had to cut your holiday short – I hope the children weren't too upset?'

'They soon got over it when we bribed them with the promise of a McDo on the way home.' Jack rolled his eyes. 'The extent to which that company has managed to get its claws into the children of France never ceases to amaze me. But you'll never guess who we ran into down there.'

'Who?'

'Do you remember Bobo, the young bloke with the mobile pizza van?'

'Do I? I still dream of his white pizzas with goats' cheese, walnuts, and the thinnest drizzle of honey. No matter how I try, I just can't replicate his crusts.'

'Well you'll have to make your way down to the coast for your next holiday because he's only gone and opened up a pizzeria! And he's made quite a success of it too – queues out the door and local awards in the window.'

As a moody teen, Bobo had resisted all Bruno's attempts to get him to join the local rugby team, and had only shaken his adolescent angst when he discovered an aptitude in the kitchen after getting a job washing dishes at Ivan's bistro.

Jack's sharp mind had travelled the distance from Biarritz while Bruno's was still lost in memory. 'So tell me, Bruno. What's your gut feeling on all this? Are we at risk of being attacked by a crazed intruder, or do you think Josette was the victim of a deliberate assault?'

'My gut says the latter but that's not enough. I want to be sure.'

Jack led Bruno towards a cluster of walnut trees a few hundred metres from the main house and ducked under a low-hanging branch, gesturing for Bruno to follow. 'Under here was the first place I spotted them, the kids lost one of their balls and there were four or five butts by this tree when I retrieved it.'

Bruno turned back to face the house; from their concealed spot in the small thicket he had a clear sightline to the patio where they'd just finished their coffees, and to the unshuttered kitchen window. At night, with the lights on inside, any hidden observer would be more than capable of monitoring the household's dinner preparations.

Jack stood next to Bruno, his service-trained eye making the same assessment. 'Not great, is it? I'll talk to Pamela about putting up a curtain or blind.' He crouched down, examining the ground around the roots of the trees that shielded them. 'No sign of any cigarette ends here. Shall we move on?'

As the pair of them made their way around the grounds, a clear pattern emerged. While there were no errant butts to be found in any of the places Jack had previously found litter, each of the spots gave them a clear view of a different angle of Pamela's house while providing full concealment for the watcher. Perhaps there was something to his Scottish friend's dislike of the local tendency for thickets of trees, Bruno mused.

'Well that was rather less productive than I'd hoped. Sorry, Bruno.' The two men started walking back towards the house.

'Not at all. I've been able to draw two conclusions from our little excursion, and it would surprise me if you weren't thinking along similar lines.'

'That our stalker hasn't been back, and that they were only interested in Josette Quirit?'

'Exactly.'

'I must confess it was a relief when I worked out you couldn't see mine or Miranda's windows from any of the hiding places. But I suppose we can't discount the risk, no matter how small, that Pamela might still be in their sights?'

'Unlikely, but yes. Until we have the killer behind bars I'm going to ensure that the patrol vans Fabien has organized keep you on their beat.'

'Shall we take a quick look around the stables? There's no tree coverage, but there are some decent lines of sight up to the house.'

Together they walked the perimeter of the stable building, looking in the longer grass that abutted the walls, but found nothing of interest. The stables were always busy from sunrise to sunset, riders coming and going for classes or private tuition, horse-mad teens polishing tack in exchange for the occasional hour or two on horseback. It was an unlikely place for someone to hide away, but not impossible, especially not at night or early morning.

In one of the vacant stalls a flash of pink caught Bruno's eye, mostly concealed in the hay. He crouched down, and used his pen to poke around, uncovering what was unmistakably the end of a Sobranie cigarette, pink filter with gold branding.

'Jack! Come here!'

His friend joined him at ground level. 'It's a butt all right, but it's definitely not like the other ones I found.' He stood up. 'I thought only Russians smoked Sobranies.'

'The sign of an accomplice, or a simple aberration?' Bruno carefully folded the cigarette end into his handkerchief; he would file it as possible evidence when he got back to the station. 'I think I need to go and have a chat with Marcel. There can't be many people smoking these; he's the only one around here who stocks them.'

The two men headed back towards the main house, where Pamela and Fabien were waiting for them, an ice-cold bottle of sparkling water dribbling condensation on the table.

'Here, I thought you'd be thirsty.' Pamela handed a glass to each of the men before refreshing her own. 'Fabien? A top-up?'

'*Merci.*' He held out his glass before reporting to Bruno what he'd seen on the footage, that they'd seen no sign of any van or moped.

'Well we think we didn't,' Pamela interjected. 'Several bikes of the model Fabien was looking out for went by over the three evenings we scanned through. But,' she looked at Fabien, 'you didn't think any of them looked suspicious, did you?'

Fabien shrugged. 'One was clearly a pair of teenagers who need writing up for helmet violations, and the others went by too quickly, didn't even look in the gates.'

'That sounds a little reassuring,' said Jack. 'We found one new butt in the stables, but it wasn't of the sort I'd been seeing—'

'In the stables?' Miranda was furious. 'Someone has been smoking in the stables?'

Pamela shook her head. 'All that dry hay. What the hell were they thinking?'

Bruno patted his shirt pocket, where he could smell the cigarette end despite its age and handkerchief wrapping. 'The butt we found might not have any bearing on the case – Jack said it wasn't the sort he'd found before. Perhaps you should have a safety chat with your volunteers as a precautionary measure, remind them of the fire risk?'

Miranda nodded. 'I'll take care of that.' She turned to her father. 'Sorry, Dad. Do go on.'

He reached across and squeezed her hand. 'Based on the spots where I found the butts previously, I'd guess that the intruder was only interested in the goings-on at the main house, not the cottages or the riding school.'

'That's hardly reassuring to me!' Pamela looked to Bruno and read encouragement in his eyes. 'What I don't understand is how someone managed to get onto the grounds without the dogs barking up a storm.'

Bruno laughed. 'That's easy enough to answer. You have so many clients coming and going for the riding school that your pack of shepherds only greets known friends. They've become immune to strangers.'

'I suppose you're right. Perhaps I should think about getting a guard dog of sorts, adding to the pack.'

'My dear,' said Jack, 'you'd domesticate Cerberus with kindness given half a day. I'm not sure a guard dog is the answer. Besides, I'm your guard dog.' He puffed out his chest and barked, breaking the tension at the table.

'Fabien and I must be off, get back to the station to give this new footage a more thorough review. But before we go, what are your plans for Easter Sunday? I was thinking of hosting a feast, both to celebrate the holiday and to introduce Fabien to more friendly faces from St Denis.'

'That's a marvellous idea,' Pamela said. 'Do count me in.'

'And me,' said Jack, 'and Miranda, plus the kids.'

'Great stuff. I was going to invite Alain and Rosalie, and Florence and the twins. Perhaps Cassandra and Kirk from Château Rouffillac, with their daughter Patsy. And of course not forgetting J-J, the Baron, Horst and Clothilde, the Mayor and Jacqueline. Mademoiselle Cantagnac. Fabiola, if she's not on duty at the surgery that day, and Gilles if he's back from Ukraine. And Laura, of course.'

'A veritable horde! But there's one small problem with your plan, dear Bruno – you're looking at around twenty people, and you don't have that sort of space around your table. Why don't you have it here? The kids can splash around in the pool, assuming this weather holds, and we grown-ups can pull a few more tables up onto the terrace.'

Bruno beamed. 'That would be great, Pamela. Thank you.'

'And what were you thinking of cooking?'

'It has to be lamb, don't you think? Perhaps even a *méchoui*?'

'I don't think you can have a *méchoui* and not invite Momu and his family,' Pamela pointed out. 'Perhaps those patio tables will have to be a series of picnic blankets on the lawn?'

'I think you're right.' Bruno looked at his watch. 'We really must be off now. I'll be in touch tomorrow to make arrangements for the feast, once I know who's coming.' The group bade each other farewell, and asking Pamela to say goodbye to Miranda on his behalf reminded Bruno that he'd not had time to retrieve Balzac from Hector's stall.

'Actually, do you mind if I leave Balzac here for the day? He would love it and it would help me.'

Of course, Pamela didn't mind one bit.

'The wonders of modern technology!' Bruno tapped away at his phone as he and Fabien walked towards the Land Rover. 'Thanks to the magic of WhatsApp I've been able to issue nearly two dozen invitations via a single text message.'

'And you'll spend the rest of the day buzzing with notifications as the group chat takes on new life without you,' Fabien joked.

'Any time I'm added to one I automatically set it to mute or I'd go insane.'

Fabien was proved right again and again over the course of the drive to the gendarmerie, Bruno's phone lighting up like the Eiffel Tower with incoming messages as all and sundry voiced their enthusiasm – and their availability – for the proposed Easter feast. 'I suppose I should call the butcher, order a thirty kilo lamb for the occasion before he's all sold out. Perhaps even thirty-five kilos. Remind me when we're parked up, would you?'

His passenger nodded, busy with his own phone. 'By the way, thanks for putting me in touch with Gabrielle Teyssier, she's already busy trying to track down our victim's real identity.'

'I knew she'd be an asset. Has she dug up anything so far?'

'Not yet, but she's writing a bot to trawl through digital archives, addresses, utility bills, that sort of thing, see if she can find any crossover between what we know about Josette Quirit and anyone else who has occupied the same premises over the years. She's bet me a lunch that she'll have found out our victim's real name before the end of play tomorrow, suggested a place called Le Bistro d'en Face. Do you know it?'

Bruno nodded. 'I knew that young woman had impeccable taste. Count yourself lucky she's not gone for Le Vieux Logis.'

Fabien gulped. 'I don't think my salary would stretch that far. Not if I want to pay rent on my apartment this month.'

'Why don't you invite her to the Easter feast instead? J-J can bring her down in his car when he comes.'

'That sounds like a much more affordable idea, if you're sure you don't mind another mouth to feed?'

'From what I remember she subsists largely on coffee; it won't be a problem. Besides, the more the merrier!' Bruno indicated to turn into the gendarmerie car park, where all the shady spots had already been taken by conscientious officers who had arrived far earlier than they.

'Have you got a large-screen monitor in your office, or shall we use the viewing room?' asked Bruno. 'I hope you don't mind if I review that footage.'

'Not at all,' said Fabien. 'The more eyes on it, the better. My office will be fine. I'm reasonably confident I could land a space shuttle with the set-up they've given me.'

Three hours of viewing and reviewing jerky CCTV footage had done a number on Bruno's eyeballs. They'd started with the most recent clips from the riding school, and had established that there had been no sign of either van or moped since the previous Saturday afternoon, roughly twenty-four hours before the murder.

Then they'd moved back in time, checking through the feeds from the fortnight leading up to the attack, both at the riding school and from the cameras stationed outside the fire station and nursing home. They saw the moped in town and the van at Pamela's, and the two vehicles never appeared on either feed with less than a ninety-minute gap between them, which suggested to Bruno that they shared a driver, someone who appeared to only have limited access to the van. There was something else about the bigger vehicle that teased at the edges of his brain, but it was like a butterfly, fluttering in and out of the edges of his thought patterns. It would come to him in the middle of the night or not at all, he knew from experience.

He tapped out a quick message to Pamela, letting her know that they'd not identified the stalker near her property – or in St Denis – since the night before the murder, half a week ago.

'I don't know about you, but I'm more than ready for a break. Shall we go and have a chat with Marcel at the *tabac*?'

Fabien stood up, moving his shoulders to uncrunch his spine. 'Are all the chairs in the gendarmerie this uncomfortable, or do I have an enemy I'm not aware of?'

'If you do I can assure you that they loathe all policemen equally. I have exactly the same torture device in my office in the Mairie.'

'Why is your office in the Mairie and not here in the station? I've been meaning to ask.'

Bruno raised an eyebrow. 'Politics. Now that I'm responsible for the entire Vézère Valley it was decided that an office in the Mairie would prevent the other gendarmeries from feeling neglected by my absence there and my presence here.' He shrugged. 'I've been there for years anyway – if you ask me it's because there simply isn't enough room for us all.'

Fabien snorted back a laugh. 'Because what every worker wants more than anything is to share an office with his boss. Have these politicians ever met real live people, or is their human contact limited to focus groups?'

Bruno shook his head. 'Your guess is as good as mine.'

They made their way up the rue de Paris towards the *tabac*, Bruno pausing occasionally to bestow a kiss or a greeting on the passers-by. He was pleased to note a small increase in the amount of foot traffic on the street and counted half a dozen posters advertising the St Denis loyalty card in the shop windows they passed. Little by little, his plan was beginning to come together.

'Sobranies?' Marcel coughed. 'Used to be only Russians smoked them, but they've become a lot more popular among young people recently. The ones who don't vape think the colours look cool on Instagram.' He rolled his eyes.

'So you've got multiple customers?' Marcel nodded. 'Was one of them Félix?'

'Félix?'

'The kid who helps with the horses up at the riding school?'

Marcel shook his head. 'No, he quit. Asked me to promise never to sell him another pack.'

'You do know he's still seventeen? You shouldn't have been selling him any cigarettes at all.'

Bruno turned to Fabien. 'So either Félix is buying his cigarettes elsewhere or that butt belonged to someone else.' He turned back to Marcel. 'Thanks for your help. Looks like I need to have a chat with Félix.'

As they left the shop, Bruno got out his phone and called him. He answered instantly.

'*Salut,* Félix, a quick question. Have you started smoking again? Yes, I know it's a personal question, but I'm afraid it's to do with a case. Well I'm sorry to hear that. And what brand are you smoking?' He looked at Fabien and shook his head. 'Thank you, Félix, see you soon.' Hanging up the phone he went back into Marcel's and bought a few packets of nicotine gum. With Bruno's support perhaps Félix could kick the habit for good.

Back on the street, Fabien was looking at a still of the motorbike they'd extracted from the CCTV footage, which gave Bruno the opening to float an idea he'd had. 'I'd like to make a suggestion about the case, if that's okay?'

'Of course.'

'Given that we have all this footage of the two vehicles, why not make an appeal to the press, see if publicizing their existence turns up a few leads? We're sure to get the usual cranks phoning in, claiming that the van is owned by Elvis and the moped by Princess Diana, but maybe we'll find something useful, that is if you feel ready to reveal their existence to the public.'

'I'm willing to give it a try. I assume you have contacts in the local media?'

'Certainly do. In my office I have the contact information for France3, FranceInfo, TF1, as well as all the local radio stations. Still photographs would be no use on their broadcasts, of course, but we can supply them with images for their websites. I think the most useful man in this instance would be Philippe Delaron, of *Sud-Ouest*. He's always after a scoop.'

'Then by all means, go ahead. I'll message Yveline now, see if she can get someone to extract clear images from the footage and get them to you for sending on.'

'Tell her to email them directly to Colette Cantagnac in my office, she has her details.' As they walked on, Bruno quickly called the assistant and advised her that an email would be incoming from the gendarmerie and gave her the necessary instructions.

Before he and Fabien had finished their walk up the rue de Paris Bruno's phone rang. It was Colette, informing him that she had already passed on the images of the vehicles to all the media on his list, and that he should expect a call from Philippe Delaron within the hour, the newshound seeking an exclusive quote for his article. Bruno decided that when the moment came he would pass on that particular responsibility to Fabien, who was lead in the investigation and so more appropriate for the task.

'And now on to important matters,' said Bruno. 'What are you doing for dinner tonight? The Pergola does an acceptable pizza, and you have to eat at Ivan's bistro while you're in town.'

'Why don't you let me cook for you? I owe you, and you've found me a base with a well-equipped kitchen. I make a mean mushroom risotto, thanks to my Italian ex, and I can get everything I need in town.'

'That would be a real pleasure, thank you. Can I bring anything?'

Fabien wrinkled his nose in thought. 'Some dry white wine? Something both we and the risotto can drink. Come over around seven thirty.'

Bruno and Fabien were sitting at the younger man's patio table, empty plates pushed aside and wine still in their glasses. The risotto had been excellent, the liquid used to rehydrate the mushrooms serving a second, flavourful duty as stock. Fabien had the makings of a very good cook indeed. The relaxed atmosphere, helped by the wine, persuaded Bruno that this would be a good moment to try to get some answers to the questions that had been on his mind for the duration of the meal.

'These Catholic boarding schools, what are they like?' Bruno asked the question matter-of-factly, although his interest was anything but casual.

Fabien grimaced. 'I wouldn't like to tar them all with the

same brush, but the one I attended was . . .' Bruno watched as Fabien searched around for the appropriate word, a kaleidoscope of unexpressed emotions crossing his unlined face. 'Barbaric.'

Bruno nodded slowly. 'And your faith?'

'My faith? What do you mean?'

'Are you still a practising Catholic? Do you attend Mass?'

Fabien shook his head vigorously, his hair flopping violently with the movement. 'I wasn't a practising Catholic when I arrived, and I was a confirmed atheist by the time I left.'

Bruno was puzzled. 'But if you weren't a practising Catholic, why send you to a Catholic school?'

Fabien shrugged. 'You'd have to ask my parents, I didn't have any say in the matter. I think they thought it would give me the best possible start in life – a good education, a sense of discipline, strong moral fibre, that sort of thing.'

'But you're young. If you were my age, I'd have understood, but haven't things changed? The Church's influence has been dwindling for decades, hasn't it?'

'You have to remember who my parents are, Bruno. Two kind and industrious people from a very small village. They're small-c conservative, traditional, country people.' He looked directly into Bruno's eyes with an intensity that made the older man feel slightly uncomfortable. 'Good people.'

'I don't suggest they're not and forgive me if you thought otherwise. Barbaric, you said. That's a pretty strong word. Barbaric how?'

'I'm not sure what discipline was like in your schooldays, I don't want to make presumptions about your age. But I started in Bandol long after they formally banned corporal punishment in schools. No flogging, no canes, no priests whacking us on the palm of the hand with sticks whenever we got an answer wrong.'

Bruno nodded, memories of his own schooldays flitting through his brain, all those power-crazed teachers who had been all too ready with the rod or worse to punish the most minor of infractions, 'saving the child', as the old adage went. 'Based on my own experience at both school and the army, I can tell you that physical deterrents were never particularly effective; they just tended to lead to more defiance and rebellion.'

'Only to be expected. People don't respond well to violence, as a rule.' While they had been speaking Fabien had picked up his knife and was tapping its blunt edge on the side of the wooden table. Tap, tap, tap-tap. Tap, tap, tap-tap. Bruno didn't think he'd noticed what he was doing. 'So instead of punishing us physically, they punished us emotionally, psychologically.'

'Punished you how?' Bruno was well aware of the many methods mankind used to inflict psychological cruelty on his fellow human beings, the ease with which one could break another man's spirit. His years in the army, the war crimes to which he'd borne witness, had taught him just how much more permanently devastating emotional pain could be than the physical variety.

Fabien shook his head and looked away. Bruno saw his colleague close his eyes and breathe in deeply through his nose, expelling the air from his pursed lips as though he were blowing out the candles on a birthday cake. It was a technique Bruno recognized as mindful breathing, a way of staving off a panic attack or otherwise trying to get a handle on tumultuous emotions. It was a minute or so before Fabien turned back to face Bruno.

'Where to start?' He reached for his wine glass and drained it, then reached for the bottle and poured himself another. Bruno placed a hand over his own when the bottle was offered, he wanted to keep a clear head for any revelations to come.

'Minor misdemeanours qualified for endless laps of the rugby pitch in place of dinner; we had to recite Hail Marys as we ran. More serious offences meant up to a week of isolation in the infirmary, nothing but bread and water to eat once a day, the matron coming by to drop off a new tray each morning. At least, we assumed it was morning.'

'Just like the army,' Bruno muttered, but Fabien evidently hadn't heard the aside.

'But the real *coup de grâce* was what they called the assessment of our loyalties, which they determined by having us stand on the stage in the auditorium, in front of the whole school – pupils, teachers, ground staff, you name it. You had to stretch your arms out to the side, like Jesus on the cross, palms facing skyward. On one hand the teacher who had determined you were in need of discipline would put a copy of the Holy Bible, and on the other a bound hardback of the school's history and rules, books of similar physical and moral weight. Whichever you let fall to the floor first was the power you respected the least. All the time, your classmates were baying for your blood like the crowds at a gladiator death match. It was horrible.'

Bruno shook his head. 'Brutal.'

'It was. There were even rumours that a boy died doing it, but if it ever actually happened it was certainly before my time. I'm sure you know what playground gossip can be like.'

'I do. Did you ever tell your parents what it was like?'

'After everything they sacrificed to put me there? The hours they worked to cover my fees?' He shook his head. 'They thought they were giving their only child the best possible start in life, how could I disabuse them of that notion?' Fabien pushed his glass of wine to the side, untouched since he'd refilled it. 'I've rather lost my taste for this, I'm afraid. If you don't mind, can we call it a night?'

'Of course.' Bruno cleared the table, piling the plates and risotto pan in the sink before Fabien steered him in the direction of the front door. Once in the car he took out his phone to call Pamela, who answered on the third ring.

'Sorry, sorry. I meant to call you, but Jack insisted that he give me and Miranda a few lessons in marksmanship, and we carried on for so long that it completely slipped my mind. Would you mind terribly if I kept Balzac here tonight? He's been fed and is currently curled up indoors with my pack. You can come and collect him in the morning; we'll go for a ride, make arrangements for your feast.'

'At least I know he'll be well looked after. Enjoy the rest of your evening. I'll be over bright and early.'

13

Despite the heavy pall cast over last night's dinner, a phone call from Laura raised Bruno's spirits on Thursday morning. She apologized for the radio silence and invited him to dinner the following week: she would be carving out space in her schedule to spoil him. He turned on the radio and filled the old whistling kettle – much more pleasurable to use than its electric cousin – and left it to heat on the stovetop while he went out to service the needs of his poultry. While he missed Balzac's presence this morning, his birds seemed not to. The flock flapped around his feet unbothered by barks while he scattered yesterday's scraps for them to eat, mixed in with a few generous scoops of the chicken feed he'd bought to ensure they were getting enough calcium to produce strong shells. When the bucket was empty he set about retrieving that morning's eggs.

He hadn't quite decided how to deal with last night's emotional conversation, but in the end thought that the best thing would be to take his cues from Fabien. Back in the kitchen the radio played a familiar pop song whose name Bruno didn't know and didn't care to find out, and when it ended the local news bulletin included the request for information on the moped and van that he and Fabien had set in motion the night before.

'Anyone with information relating to either of the vehicles should contact the St Denis gendarmerie *at info-stdenis@mairies-dordogne.fr or by phone at—'* Bruno turned off the radio and called his colleague, who answered on the first ring.

'*Bonjour,* Bruno. I assume you heard the bulletin that was on the radio just now?'

'I did. And with any luck, half the *département* will have heard the same. Did you happen to have the radio on last night? Do you know if it ran yesterday?'

'I'm not sure about the radio, but I was checking the local news websites on my phone first thing, and *Sud-Ouest* published their piece last night – there were already more than three hundred comments when I looked, but I haven't had time to read them.'

'I wouldn't bother. The media team at the station will already be on that, and I'd bet you anything that at least half of them will be from people decrying the various ways in which the world is going to hell.'

Fabien laughed. 'Changing the subject entirely, I forgot yesterday to remind you to order the lamb for the weekend.'

'Don't worry, I took care of it. And Momu has agreed to come and give us the benefit of his expertise. I don't think you've met him yet. He's the local maths teacher, works at the school with Florence, Alain and Rosalie, my cousins. You haven't met them yet either, have you?'

'No, but I remember you mentioning their names at Pamela's when you were putting Sunday's guest list together.'

'Well Momu is a dear old friend, and every year he's in charge of doing a *méchoui* for the annual tennis club dinner, turns up with a box of herbs and spices – his secret blend, he calls it, although we've all worked out that he uses cinnamon, cumin and allspice, along with some garlic and chilli. They smell so strong you couldn't mistake them, and the taste . . .' Bruno rolled his eyes with rapture.

'What can I do to help?'

'Well the lamb will be Momu's baby, but you and I can certainly be of use building and maintaining the fire. We'll want to have a selection of salads, some couscous, the usual trimmings.'

'Given the fattiness of the lamb, what do you think of a red onion and citrus salad?'

'Perfect. When I get to the station I'll give Momu a ring, see if he's got any other ideas. With a crowd of more than twenty we're going to want a range of options for people to choose from, including a few the children won't turn their noses up at. And we'll have to pick up all the ingredients by Saturday. Nothing will be open on Easter Sunday.'

'Sounds good to me,' said Fabien. 'I'll start making a list.'

Before driving to the station Bruno took out his mobile and gave Pamela a ring. When she answered, he could hear Balzac baying joyfully in the background.

'*Bonjour*, and how's my beautiful boy this morning?'

Pamela laughed. 'I'm sure you can hear for yourself. He's having a wonderful time in the garden with the sheepdogs. They're trying to round him up and he's being as stubborn as ever. Are you on your way round?'

'I'm not, I'm afraid. Duty calls, and I have to go into the office earlier than expected. Sorry about this.'

'Is it anything to do with the news bulletin about the van and the moped? I must have heard it half a dozen times since I woke up.'

'You're right, as usual.'

'As always, I think you'll find!' Pamela's laugh was joyful.

'As always, then! I'm going to leave Balzac with you for the day, if that's okay? I think he'll have a much better time with Hector and your mob than he will sitting in my office.'

'You'll get no arguments from me on that front.'

Inside the police station, Sergeant Jules found Bruno in Fabien's office. 'Yveline wanted me to come and find you as soon as you got here. The phones have been blowing up since six a.m. – we must have had two hundred tips come in already.'

'Anything we might actually be able to use?' asked Bruno.

The sergeant shrugged. 'You know what it's like. Nothing useful has come in yet.'

'And have you found anything?' Bruno turned to Fabien. 'I mean beyond people reporting their neighbours for boundary infringements, for having affairs, to try and convince us that UFOs have been seen flying above Beynac.'

'We have exactly the same up at Périgueux HQ,' Fabien said with a smile. 'Although our UFOs tend to be spotted over the hospital and are identical in shape and size to the medical helicopter.' The three policemen laughed; people were people wherever they happened to be from.

'Anything come in from the retirement home itself?' Bruno asked Sergeant Jules. 'Given we've had the moped there twice a day for several days on CCTV, I was hoping one or two of the sharper residents might have noticed something.'

The sergeant shrugged again. 'You'd have to ask Yveline that, chief. She's been running the show. I'm just the messenger.'

'Right. When you see her, can you tell her that Fabien and I will be in his office? If she could swing by when she has a minute, I'd like to take a look at what's come in so far.'

'Of course, chief.' Sergeant Jules turned on his heel and made for the large open-plan office at the rear of the building, where, ever since her promotion, Yveline had ruled the roost with an iron fist in a velvet glove.

Yveline leaned against the open door. 'Knock, knock. Jules said you wanted to see me?'

'Please, come in. Take a seat.' Bruno pulled up an empty chair.

Yveline sat down and took out her notebook. 'Where do you want to start?'

Fabien looked at Bruno, which he took as his cue. 'Has anything of interest come in from the media appeal?'

'Not yet. We've had the usual.'

'Madame Cartier accusing her neighbours of being *collabos* again?' Bruno asked.

Yvette nodded.

'Old Besson blaming immigrants?' Another nod. 'Then I'm inclined to agree. Fabien? What do you think?'

The younger officer leaned back in his chair. 'But that can't be all, surely? We must have a few concerned members of the public with leads worth looking into?'

Yveline looked down at her notebook. 'We've had twenty credible sightings of the Peugeot van, and I've got a team of gendarmes following up those leads, but given what a popular vehicle it is I can't say I've got a high degree of confidence that any of them will go anywhere.'

Bruno nodded. 'On the off-chance one does, though.'

'Don't worry, chief. I've got my newest recruits answering the phones and monitoring the inbox, taking all the salient details. Others are going through the reports and pulling out anything worthy of investigation, and Sergeant Jules is in charge of the teams doing the follow-up. By the end of the day, if there's any good info to come from the appeal, you'll have it.'

'And what about the retirement home? Anything there?' asked Fabien.

Yveline flicked a few pages back in her notebook. 'I interviewed the head nurse, the home's manager, and the head of HR.' She laughed. 'She called herself the head of HR, anyway, but she was the only one on the team. The majority of the staff interviews were conducted by junior officers, with Jules and Celestine supervising, and the short version is that there was nothing unusual reported.' She paused. 'Aside from the not infrequent sighting of a certain police officer asking questions off duty.' She raised an eyebrow and Bruno coloured slightly.

'Is that in the general staff interviews, or across all the interviews?' Bruno asked, deciding not to respond to her comment. 'Because we're all aware of the irregularities in Mademoiselle Quirit's recruitment, her lack of the proper paperwork – what did the HR woman have to say for herself?'

Yveline couldn't quite disguise her amusement at Bruno's neat avoidance of his off-duty overstepping. 'She tried to fall back on the reference from Menton, saying that Quirit had come with excellent references and it wasn't her problem that the last place hadn't done the proper paperwork checks, which went down as well as you can imagine. She then moved on to the "challenging recruitment environment", with all the young people fleeing to big cities and no one wanting to do an honest day's work any more.' Yveline rolled her eyes. 'You know the routine.'

'I do. You've talked about interviewing the staff. Who interviewed the residents?' asked Bruno.

'The residents?' Yveline looked blank. 'No one.'

'Why not? Is it a facility exclusively for those suffering from dementia?'

'No.'

'Then some of them may well have something useful to add to the investigation, don't you think? Don't forget the stereotype of the curtain-twitching elderly neighbour. Given half the old boys in wheelchairs spend their days on the sundeck out front, I'll bet you they know more about the comings and goings around there than anyone on staff.'

'I'll get onto this immediately and report back. Apologies for the oversight.' She left the room, clearly flustered.

Bruno turned to look at Fabien whose face betrayed his dismay.

'I can't believe I didn't pick up on that,' he said.

'Look, I know this is your first time leading an investigation, but you should have thought of it yourself, don't you think?'

Bruno felt a twinge of sympathy for the younger man but he pressed on; this was important. 'We all make mistakes, and investigations are full of them. But the reason we run investigations as a team is because we know it takes different pairs of eyes, different brains, to get a result. Tell me – have you been leading briefings, or have you been listening at briefings?'

'I thought I was doing both.'

They were interrupted by Bruno's phone; he showed Fabien that the display read Gabrielle Teyssier. '*Salut*, Mademoiselle Teyssier, I'm with officer Panton.' He put the phone on speaker, so Fabien could hear the whole exchange. 'You're on speaker. It's just us in here, so speak freely.'

'Hello, Bruno, I hope you're well. Do you want the good news, or the bad news?'

'Let's start with the good news. What have you got for me?'

'It's less for you, really. The good news is that Fabien doesn't need to buy me lunch.'

'You mean the bad news is that you haven't tracked down our victim's original identity.'

'Correct. But to be fair, it's only been a little more than twenty-four hours since you set me the task – I didn't give myself much time when I issued my little wager. My bots are trawling, and I'll get you your answers sooner or later, you can be sure of that.'

As they listened, Fabien's body language underwent a transformation from the earlier tense moment. Bruno got the impression that his colleague liked the smart young woman quite a lot. Which was no surprise – she had impressed Bruno no end with her work during the crypto case the previous autumn, and much of the Périgueux brass besides, her efforts to prevent hacking of the police systems earning her both a promotion and a pay rise. 'I have every confidence in you, Gabrielle. And bet or no bet, I'll make sure that Fabien buys you that lunch whenever you do track her down.'

'I shall look forward to it.' Bruno was sure that the young woman was smiling down the phone. 'Anyway, I suppose I should get off the phone and back to work – Josette Quirit's past won't stay hidden for long, I promise you.'

Fabien was grinning when Bruno got off the phone, confirming his first impression although he was too professional to tease his colleague about it. In the office, at any rate – he might test the waters with some gentle ribbing over a coffee.

'Nothing we can do now but wait,' said Bruno. 'If Gabrielle can't track this woman down then I'm the queen of Sheba.' The comment got the laugh out of Fabien that Bruno was hoping for – the officer's oversight was a lesson learned and they could move on. There was a knock at the door.

'Come in!' The door opened to reveal Jules, who was escorting a young woman. Bruno knew he'd seen her somewhere before, and recently, but his brain wasn't telling him when or where.

'Mademoiselle Marchant here came in response to the radio appeal, chief. I thought I'd bring her straight to you.'

'Thank you, Jules.' Bruno asked the woman to take a seat across the desk from him and Fabien.

'I came as soon as I heard the appeal on the radio,' Mademoiselle Marchant said nervously, twisting her hands around each other as bright spots of colour appeared on her prominent cheekbones. 'I heard the announcement, and then I checked out the photos on the website, and I knew I had to come in and see you. I'm afraid this was the first moment I could spare from work.'

'You're here now, *mademoiselle*.' Bruno leaned forward with what he hoped was a reassuring smile on his face. 'So, what is it that you think you have for us?'

Still twisting her hands together on her lap, her fingers long and rather bony, the young woman's eyes flicked between Bruno and Fabien as though they were watching a match at the Stade Roland-Garros. It was beginning to make Bruno feel almost dizzy, but he knew that he should wait it out. Any attempt to hurry the issue was likely to send her running back to wherever she'd come from.

A quick glance at Fabien in his peripheral vision and Bruno was relieved to see he was waiting just as patiently.

'Why don't you begin by telling us your full name.'

She took a deep breath to compose herself. 'My name is Odelie. Odelie Marchant.'

Then Bruno placed her, the young woman he'd seen a week or so ago on the terrace at Fauquet's, being chewed out by her colleague for spilling water near his laptop. He decided not to reveal that he'd noticed her there, among the Netflix crew, and nodded for her to continue in her own time.

'I'm a contractor with Netflix, you know the series set in St Christophe de la Domaine?' Bruno and Fabien nodded as one. 'I'm sure everyone in the *département* knows it, sorry. Anyway, I'm the production coordinator. I keep the budgets on track, sign off on the shooting schedules, all the boring back-end stuff that keeps the show on the road. One of my jobs is to make sure our vehicle records are kept up to date, to track that our mileage matches our petrol spend.'

Bruno glanced at Fabien, who had one eyebrow raised. 'Go on,' he said.

'Well, for a period of several weeks, my records weren't matching up. The mileage on one of our vehicles was considerably higher than the petrol spend, although there was never any budgetary shortage, so I couldn't get anyone to care about it.' She took another deep breath and smoothed imaginary creases from her lap. 'But I don't like mysteries. My job is to know where every centime is supposed to be, and where they've all gone, and I noticed that one of our vans was doing around three hundred kilometres more per week than we were paying for in petrol.'

'One of your vans, you say? Could you describe the vehicle in question?'

Odelie shrugged. 'It's a black Peugeot people carrier, Expert model, from I think 2016, although I'd have to check the paperwork to be sure.'

Fabien stood up. 'Would you excuse me one minute, Mademoiselle Marchant? I'll only be a second.'

'Of course. But please, call me Odelie,' she said to his back as he walked to the door.

'Odelie,' said Bruno. 'Does your van have tinted windows?'

She nodded. 'It does. Is that important?'

'Perhaps. Would you mind staying here a few minutes longer? My colleague will be back any second, and I think you may just have been very helpful indeed.'

She smiled then, for the first time since entering the room. 'I'm not used to praise. In my job we get shouted at a lot.'

'If you don't mind me saying, that doesn't sound like a healthy working environment.'

'It's not, but what can you do? I've got a relatively secure gig for the entertainment industry, and I'm working on one of France's biggest TV exports. Whatever I have to suffer now will be worth it to look good on my CV.'

Bruno smiled at her. 'Before I joined the police, I served in the military. Believe you me, when it comes to suffering in order to progress, I can fully sympathize.'

Fabien came back into the room, holding a sheaf of papers. 'Odelie, would you mind taking a look at these stills, see if you can identify the vehicle?' He spread out half a dozen hi-res printouts from the CCTV footage on the desk between them. 'Take your time.'

With the young woman's head bent over the pictures, Bruno and Fabien had a silent conversation comprised entirely of eye contact and facial expressions, both men aware this could be of real significance to the inquiry. Odelie took her time, going back and forth between two photos in particular before raising her head to speak.

'I'm pretty certain this vehicle is ours. Or the one we rented, anyway. Do you see here, the rear panel on the passenger side?' She pointed at the spot on the printouts she'd isolated from the pack. 'If you can get a better image of this panel from your footage I'd be able to confirm for sure, but I'm almost sure that this is our van. We dinged it on a bollard the first week of the current shoot, and it looks like there's a mark in the same place, do you see?'

Bruno didn't realize he'd been holding his breath until he let it out in one long exhale. He picked up his phone. 'Gabrielle? If I send you over some CCTV footage, is there any way you or one of your colleagues can clean up the images for us? You can? Great. As soon as possible please. I'll send you the link to the intranet folder as soon as we're off the phone. You're a star.'

Fabien leaned on the desk facing Odelie, his back to Bruno. 'Odelie, you've been incredibly helpful. Are you able to stay with us a while longer or come in again, perhaps within the hour?'

'I'm afraid I really can't – I'm already risking my job being here. If they start shooting before I'm back from lunch I'll be out on my ear. I could come back this evening, though, after about eight o'clock, once they've signed off the rushes from today's filming.'

'Okay,' said Fabien. 'I suppose that'll have to do. At least it gives the techs more time to clean up the footage. Please, not a word of this to any of your colleagues. I assume we can trust in your discretion?'

Odelie smiled. 'You most certainly can. I'll see you both this evening.' She made to leave, but before she had reached the door, Bruno had a thought.

'Why don't we meet at my office in the Mairie? If you're worried about being spotted, that way you won't be seen coming to the police station again. It's in the Hôtel de Ville, on the market square over the road from the *tabac*.'

'That would be great, thank you.'

Bruno handed her his card. 'Call me on this number when you arrive. The front door will be locked at that hour; I'll come down and let you in.' Odelie tucked the card into a small nylon backpack and hurried out of the office, almost as skittish as she'd been on arrival. When the door had closed behind her, he raised both his eyebrows at Fabien. 'Well, what do you think? Is this the breakthrough we've been waiting for?'

'Let's hope so, Bruno. Let's hope so.'

14

Thursday afternoon saw Bruno and Fabien at the care home to conduct second interviews with two of the residents the gendarmes had considered worthy of further questioning. Several residents were in the home for advanced dementia care, and there was little that they could contribute, but of those who used the place like an assisted living facility, Yveline's notes had identified two with observations useful to the case.

The front desk was unmanned when they arrived, a small sign reading 'Back in five minutes'. It was less than two before a young woman emerged from a door marked private, rubbing her hands together. Bruno could smell the sharp tang of alcohol-based sanitizer. 'Good morning, officers. I hope you haven't been waiting long. How may I help you?'

Bruno stepped forward, smiled and introduced them both before explaining that they were there to interview two of the residents. He rifled through his notebook, but before he found the page with the names on it the receptionist provided them.

'Madame Reynaud and Monsieur Poillier, I have a note of it here. You'll find Madame Reynaud in room 211 on the second floor, while Monsieur Poillier is one floor up, in room 303. Wait here a moment, I'll let them know you're coming.'

They waited while the two residents were informed by phone of their presence. 'Would you like me to show you the way?'

Bruno shook his head. 'I'm familiar with the building but thank you.' He led Fabien up the stairs and along the third floor hallway. 'Let's start at the top and work down.'

After Bruno knocked on the door of room 303 he heard a strong voice call out '*Entrez*'. Opening the door he saw a man in his late eighties or early nineties sitting in a wingchair facing the window, a wheeled walker to his right. On the small table to his left sat several jars of prescription medicine, a couple of balled-up tissues and a pair of reading glasses.

'You'll have to excuse me if I don't get up, my knees aren't what they were.'

'Monsieur Poillier, I am Bruno Courrèges, chief of police here in St Denis, and this is my colleague Fabien Panton. We're here to follow up on the interview you gave regarding the murder of your carer here, Mademoiselle Quirit.'

Poillier coughed and spat into a tissue. 'Of course, please take a seat.' Bruno took one of two chairs from a small dining table and made space for himself next to the old man, while Fabien remained standing. 'How can I help?'

'In your first statement you said that Mademoiselle Quirit seemed to be on edge in the weeks leading up to her death. Could you elaborate on that?'

'Well, she wasn't her usual self, always had half an eye on the window as if she was waiting for someone to come down the road. And she was very jumpy – I knocked over my walking stick one day and she jumped two metres in the air at the noise.' Another cough, another tissue. 'You might not think much of it, but it was certainly out of character. Anyone could tell she'd seen things.'

'Seen things?'

'I'm not about to start speculating. But you know how it is – life knocks some people about a bit, and others have a smoother ride. Mademoiselle Quirit had definitely experienced a few bumps, you could see it in how she carried herself, how carefully she guarded her expressions.' He shook his head. 'Beyond that, I know nothing.'

'In your first interview you said that you spent a lot of time together during her tenure here. Did you ever ask her about her life?'

'Her business was her business. The woman was here to do a job. She didn't need some interfering old oaf like me sticking his nose into her private life.'

Bruno nodded. The attitude was one he respected on a personal level, however unhelpful it might be on a professional one. 'And this jumpiness. Could you pinpoint roughly when it started?'

'Whenever it last rained, whatever day that was.' Bruno made a note to check. 'I remember running into her one morning on my way into breakfast; her hair was wet and she looked like she'd had some kind of shock. I asked her if she was on her way to get a towel, but she was lost in her head and didn't hear me.' He laughed. 'Or maybe it was an idiot question and she chose to ignore it. But I don't think so.'

A little more probing of Monsieur Poillier didn't turn up anything else of interest, so Bruno and Fabien made their way down to the second floor, Bruno using the time to tap out a message to Jules asking him to find out the date of the last rainy morning.

The door to room 211 was already open when they approached, but Bruno rapped on the frame to announce their arrival. 'Madame Reynaud? I think you're expecting us. May we come in?'

'Please do!' called a voice from a corner of the room. Its owner was busy at a small table, her back to them. 'Take a seat on the chaise while I finish making coffee. Which one is Bruno?'

'That's me, *madame*, and this is Fabien.'

She turned around, a wizened walnut of a woman with a deeply tanned face criss-crossed with lines, and startlingly black eyes that sparkled with intelligence and humour. 'Would you both like a cup?'

When it became clear that the elderly woman was loading up a tea tray with cups, saucers, a cafetière, milk jug, sugar bowl, and a small vase of flowers besides, Fabien sprang forward. 'Here, let me. Would you like me to put it over on that table?'

Once the business of serving coffee had been dealt with, Bruno turned to the task at hand. 'The statement you gave our colleague says that you spent a lot of time with the carer, Mademoiselle Quirit. But based on what I've seen so far you seem fairly independent and not to need much in the way of care.'

Madame Reynaud laughed. 'That's very sweet of you to say. I do what I can, but I need rather more support than I let people see. But yes, Josette and I got on well.'

'Another resident mentioned she'd been out of sorts of late, jumpy. Had you noticed anything out of character?'

'I wouldn't say out of character, no. There was a moped she was convinced was following her to work, and whenever she saw it she was on edge all day. If you ask me, it's the main reason she spent so much time in my room.' The old woman waved a hand at the window. 'Because of the trees, and the layout of the street, this room probably has the best views of the road, despite not being on a higher floor.'

'This moped, did you ever see it? Did she point it out to you?'

The old woman pursed her lips. 'Pfft! Maybe I saw it, maybe not. Every time one went along the road, she said it was the one following her. Maybe it was – they all look alike to me.'

Madame Reynaud seemed to disappear somewhere for a moment, her eyes blank, and when she came back to herself they sparkled once more. 'There was one morning, only last week, when she was in a real panic. She'd been crossing the road from the car park, and there'd been a van parked up right outside the care home. She came into my room still in her street clothes, dripping wet and shaking like she'd seen a ghost.' The old lady cleared her throat and took a sip of water.

'It took me some time to get it out of her, but apparently while she'd been waiting to cross the road, the driver of the van had held her eyes and made a slashing gesture across his or her throat, like something out of a movie. Josette was incredibly flustered by it.'

'If they made eye contact, she must have seen the driver. Did she describe them to you?' Bruno asked.

The old lady shook her head. 'Anything she might have said I'm afraid I can't remember. I was more concerned with making sure she was okay than with taking notes.'

Fabien leaned forward. 'If I may, *madame*. Is there any particular reason why Mademoiselle Quirit chose you to confide in? It seems odd that she would entrust a resident with her fears when her job was to provide you with support.'

'I assume it's because we're related.'

Bruno was glad to have finished his mouthful of coffee before that particular revelation. 'Related how?'

'Distantly. Cousins-in-law by marriage, and several cousins removed.'

'And you knew each other before she started working here?'

'Lord no. But Quirit is my maiden name, and so it was only natural when she introduced herself that I asked her if we might share a family connection. It turns out that she was married to Yves, my second- or third-cousin, from the Marseille branch of the family.'

'You say *was* married?'

'Yves died years ago, in the late eighties or early nineties I think it was, but I don't remember much about it. I'm afraid we only saw that side of the family at the occasional wedding or funeral, we were never particularly close. There was some family feud that pre-dated even my parents, and the ties frayed with time.' She smiled. 'Sorry I can't be more helpful.'

Bruno stood up. 'On the contrary, *madame*. You've been very helpful indeed. Thank you, for both the coffee and the information.' After ushering Fabien out of the door Bruno turned to the old woman and bowed. It felt somehow appropriate.

Once outside, Bruno rang Gabrielle. 'We've got a lead for you on one of our victim's aliases. She was married to an Yves Quirit, who lived in or near Marseille and died at some point in the late eighties or early nineties. No, we don't know when they got married. Nor where. I know it's frustrating, but at least it's something. Either way, I'll let you know if we get any more information.'

He ended the call and Fabien asked, 'What's the plan now? Back to the gendarmerie?'

Bruno shook his head. 'Not yet. How hungry are you?'

'Not starving. Why?'

'We need to pick up supplies for Easter, and we may as well do that while we wait for a response from Gabrielle and our meeting with Mademoiselle Marchant this evening. I thought the supermarket first, get that out of the way, and then Fauquet after, if that's all right with you?'

'Fine by me.'

'Great. I've got more chocolates to buy for Sunday, and I don't want to leave them in a hot car while we eat.'

'What are we getting from the supermarket? I thought everything you ate was homegrown, or from one of your local friends.'

'Unless you have a particular urge to spend the next two days rolling semolina into couscous by hand?'

Fabien raised an eyebrow. 'I most certainly do not. So couscous for thirty, and what else?';

'All the citrus, so lemons and limes for the cooking, and was it oranges you wanted for your salad?'

'It was. Can we get enough red onions at the market?'

Bruno thought for a second. 'Maybe not in the numbers we'll need. We'll be taking a gamble if we try and buy kilos of them at the small market tomorrow morning.'

'Will there even be a market? Isn't it a *jour férié*?'

'In most towns, no. But Fat Jeanne wouldn't let anything as

trivial as a holiday stop the stallholders from earning a sou.'

Fabien shook his head as he tapped away at his phone. 'I don't think I'll ever get used to that nickname. Couscous, oranges, lemons, limes, red onions. Do you want me to add Greek yoghurt to the list?'

'Well remembered. Garlic I have heaps of at home, the herbs we'll take from my garden. Add some carrots too.'

'Done and done.' Fabien looked up from his phone just as Bruno was indicating to turn into the supermarket car park.

The pair of them made short work of the supermarket, the hardest part of the job being pushing the trolley with its kilos of ingredients back to where Bruno had parked the Land Rover in a shady corner with the windows down. Fabien was an efficient shopping partner, and the two men were in and out in under fifteen minutes, including the time spent gossiping with Minette, who was manning the register.

'We may as well leave the car here,' said Bruno. 'It's only a short walk over the bridge to Fauquet, and it will take us as long to find a new parking spot as it will to walk over.'

They strolled to the café on the market square, pausing at the far side of the bridge to give a wave to Marcel, who was hiding in his usual fug of blue smoke in the doorway of the *tabac*.

Fauquet's was bustling, almost all of the terrace tables occupied. 'Here, you go and stake a claim to that table, and I'll head inside to get those chocolates organized. If they come to take our order, a *pain au chocolat* and a double espresso for me. I won't be long.'

Delphine Mausans was behind the chocolate counter at the back of the shop, talking to a tall thin man in a chef's toque.

'Bruno! How nice to see you again. May I introduce you to Léon, our chocolatier?'

Bruno offered a hand across the glass cabinet displaying the man's wares and introduced himself. 'Very pleased to meet you, Léon.'

'And I you, Bruno. I assume you've come looking for chocolates?'

'You assume correctly. Delphine helped me choose some of your Easter animals the other day, and I realized I've actually got two more, older kids to buy for. And I was thinking of getting a couple of your selection boxes, perhaps a small one of pralines as a thank-you gift, and an exceptionally large one that I can offer in lieu of dessert at a lunch I'm throwing. What would you recommend?'

'A cool box to store it all in,' joked Léon. 'Delphine, can you make sure there's space in the fridge for Bruno's purchases?'

'*Oui, chef!*' She scampered into the back room and Bruno could hear the sounds of a door opening, objects being moved before her head popped around the partition. 'Plenty of space now, *chef*.'

Bruno picked up two milk chocolate eggs from the shelves along the back wall for Miranda's two and put them on the counter. 'That's the easy bit done. Could I ask you to help me put together the two boxes I mentioned? You're the expert, after all.'

Léon beamed. 'I'd be more than happy to. Why don't you go and have your coffee; by the time you come back everything will be ready and waiting in the fridge.'

'Perfect, that would be great. Thank you so much, Léon, and welcome to St Denis.'

*

As the bell tower struck eight, Bruno's phone rang, an unknown number on the display. '*Allô bonjour?*'

'Chef Courrèges? It's Odelie Marchant. I'm outside the Mairie.'

'Come to the side door, it's around the corner to your right if you're facing the building. I'll be right down.'

Bruno left Fabien in his office on the second floor while he fetched Odelie. By the time the pair of them were back upstairs, Fabien had dragged Colette Cantagnac's comfortable chair into the back room for their visitor, leaving two less comfortable seats for the officers.

'Thank you for coming in again. I hope it wasn't too much trouble to get away?'

Odelie was markedly less nervous than she had been that morning. 'None whatsoever. Thank you for meeting me so late.'

'We've managed to enhance the photos of the side panel, and you're right – there is obvious damage. The question is, does it match the damage on the Peugeot you have in mind?'

Odelie took her time examining the photos, and Bruno was left in no doubt that she was a very methodical person. More than a minute had passed before she put the printouts back on the desk with a grim nod. 'It's ours all right, no doubt about it.'

'In that case, we have a few more questions for you. First, how many people on your staff have access to the vehicle?'

Odelie shrugged. 'All of them, to be honest with you. It's a crew vehicle – when it's not being used the keys are kept in the production office, which everyone on the team can access.'

Bruno nodded. 'And can you furnish me with a list of everyone on your team? Names, ID card numbers, home addresses?'

'I can give you the names now, but the rest of it is on the computers at work. I can send you over a full list in the morning?'

'That would be very helpful, thank you. And one more question – do you happen to know if any of your colleagues rides a moped?'

She made a face. 'We're French. I assume that all of us know how, but let me try to remember who's been using one to get to work.'

'Could you highlight their names in the list you send over?'

'I'll do my best.'

'Okay. Then I think that'll be all for now, unless you have any questions?' Bruno turned to look at Fabien, who shook his head. 'Thank you for giving us your time this evening, Odelie. You've been incredibly helpful.'

'Can I ask you a question?'

'Of course.'

'Is this going to have any impact on our production? I don't mean to sound flippant, I know you're investigating a murder, but it's my livelihood we're talking about here. I just bought an apartment, I need to know if I can keep paying my mortgage.'

Bruno smiled. 'Not flippant at all. That depends on the outcome of our investigation, so I'm afraid I can't give you any reassurances.'

Odelie winced and got to her feet. 'No good deed goes unpunished, does it?'

'I fear not, *mademoiselle*. Let me take you back downstairs, you won't be able to get out without my key.'

15

On Good Friday morning Bruno had several reasons to be optimistic. Not only had Odelie Marchant come up with some potentially very useful information, but she would be following through with staffing data this morning – something relevant had to be lurking in there somewhere, it was simply a matter of finding it. And there was good news on the personal front, too – Laura had rung to confirm their dinner invitation, her workload on pause for the long weekend. She'd made him promise not to cook a thing, nor to select any wine. Tonight was to be Laura's night, and Bruno her valued guest.

While it was officially a day off, Bruno knew that for police officers working on an active murder case there was rarely such luxury, not even in the depths of rural France. It was still early enough for a decent jog before heading to the station, so he put on his trainers and made for the ridgeline, Balzac trotting along at his heels.

Bruno had long considered running one of the most effective forms of meditation; he couldn't count the number of breakthroughs he'd had while his conscious mind focused on putting one foot in front of the other, on spotting obstacles, on maintaining his breathing, leaving his subconscious to make connections and draw hypotheses in the background. There were no such breakthroughs this morning, not so far as the case went.

Instead, and in lieu of his usual single-minded focus, all he could think about was Laura, about the way he had fallen head over heels – yet again – with a woman in a matter of moments. Was it his years in an orphanage that had him chasing connection with strong and loving female figures? Was he seeing relationships where his partners saw affairs? Or was he falling for the same woman again and again but expecting a different result?

He stopped, nowhere near the top of the hill, and only a little out of breath. Balzac, who was slightly ahead at this point, stopped to see what was going on. Bruno threw himself down on the ground and leaned on his elbows to look up at the sky, ignoring the stabbing of a thousand small twigs in the flesh of his lower arms. Balzac snuffled over to investigate, certain his friend was in need of some form of comfort. A few snuffles and a lick and Bruno pulled the dog tightly to his side, basking in the sensation of love in its purest form.

As he and Balzac were returning from their run, Bruno felt his phone buzz with an incoming message. He checked the screen, Fabien was summoning him to the station. 'There in 20', he tapped back.

Fabien, his jacket slung over his forearm and his sleeves rolled up to his elbows, was waiting on the steps of the gendarmerie when Bruno arrived with Balzac in tow. 'I can't believe it's still only April and it's this hot. It can't be normal.'

'It's not. But you must be used to far warmer, what with your years in the Var?'

'Yes, but in the Var we have the sea breeze to take the edge off. Here the heat just seems to sit in the valley, unmoving.'

'You must remember our summer storms? The way the lightning rolls around the edges of the hills like water circling a drain?'

'I used to love watching them every August,' said Fabien. 'I'd sit on the covered terrace behind my parents' house, protected from the rains but with a perfect view of the forks as they appeared. God, nature can be majestic when she wants to be.'

Bruno nodded, he too loved to watch the late summer storms, delighting in the newborn fresh air that followed. 'Your summons. I assume you've heard from Gabrielle bearing news of Josette Quirit?'

'I have. To be precise, I come bearing news of Joséphine Taun. Gabrielle's bots have finally worked their way to the bottom of her layers of aliases. Josette Quirit's real name is Joséphine Taun.'

'Taun? You can't be serious, no wonder she changed it.' Her name was a homophone for ugly person.

'I know, poor woman. But there's more. When Gabrielle ran a search for Joséphine Taun, a criminal record appeared.'

Bruno whistled. '*Merde*. What does it say?'

'Gabrielle is sending the file as an attachment as soon as the archivist in Bandol finishes scanning it. Whatever Mademoiselle Taun was up to, it pre-dates our digitized records.'

'Sounds as though you owe Gabrielle Teyssier that lunch after all. So what does Google have to say about Joséphine Taun?'

'The news only just came through and I thought we could look together.' Fabien got out his phone and tapped away. He went very still and his eyes widened as he stared at the screen.

'What is it?'

'It can't be. Impossible.'

'What can't be?' Fabien stayed mute, and Bruno reached for the phone. Google was still parsing the results, but there were thousands of hits, the first page of results dominated by archived news articles from *Le Monde*, *Libération*, *Le Figaro*, *Les Echos* – all the nationals, as well as local papers from *Var-Matin* all the way to *L'Alsace-Le Pays*. His eyes boggled as he scrolled.

'If this is the same woman, we have a dead murderer on our hands,' said Bruno, handing the phone back to his colleague. But Fabien, staring straight ahead, dropped it. 'Fabien? Are you okay?' Bruno bent down to pick up the phone; the screen was undamaged.

'That's my school, in Bandol,' Fabien said.

Bruno scrolled back up to the top of the page and clicked on the first article. '*Putain*, no wonder she changed her name. I'm amazed she didn't leave the country.'

12 DECEMBER, 1994 – BANDOL, FRANCE

Following a three-month trial, the Tribunal de Grande Instance in Bandol, Var, found Joséphine Taun guilty of the homicide of Matthieu Ventou, aged 12. A pupil at Union Chrétienne de St Ambroise, near Bandol, Ventou died during the Michaelmas term of 1993, the result of a punishment meted out under the authority of Mademoiselle Taun, then the school's matron.

Over the course of the trial, lawyers for the defence argued that Mlle Taun could not be found guilty of murder, as the prosecution had established neither l'élément matériel *nor* l'élément moral. *The prosecution in turn argued that so great was the violation of*

Mlle Taun's duty of care over her young charge that it could not be morally defended by the French courts, and that her decision to discipline her pupil was in itself a statement of intent.

According to Article 121-3 of the Criminal Code, 'There is no serious crime or major crime in the absence of an intention to commit it.' It's hard though, many observers feel, to countenance the death of a young child going unpunished – Mlle Taun's intention was to discipline Matthieu Ventou, who was reportedly caught in possession of cannabis, and the circumstances of that punishment were entirely within her control.

Pupils at the Union Chrétienne de St Ambroise have described the punishment Ventou faced as 'the test of loyalties', during which the guilty party was required to balance a bound history of the school and the Holy Bible on outstretched arms. Allowing either volume to fall to the floor was an indication of disrespect and led to further punishment. Multiple pupils, past and present, have come forward to say that the test of loyalties was traditionally performed during school-wide assemblies, making Mlle Taun's decision to punish Ventou in her own quarters most unusual.

According to the coroner's report, Ventou's death was caused by severe trauma to the skull. On the stand, Taun conceded that the boy had fainted during the course of the punishment, hitting his head on the flagstones. She immediately called for an ambulance, but Ventou suffered an intercranial haemorrhage and died from his injuries.

Joséphine Taun has been sentenced to fifteen years without the possibility of parole at the Centre Pénitentiaire de Rennes, the only high security women's prison in France. Matthieu Ventou is survived by his parents, Marc and Julie, and by four siblings, all unnamed minors.

'Let's go back to the gendarmerie. We must break this news to the team.' Bruno looped Balzac's leash over his left arm, and with his right took hold of Fabien, steering his shocked colleague away from the stairs and in the direction of the Rue de Paris.

Once they were back in the gendarmerie, Bruno asked Fabien, 'Do you think you could handle a few questions? I just want to get my timeline in order.'

Fabien nodded. 'Of course.' They retired to a quiet corner of the room.

'When did you attend the school?'

'I graduated in 2009.'

'And when did you start?'

'I think 2002? Maybe 2003.'

'It doesn't matter. Around ten years after the death, at any rate.'

Fabien nodded.

'And you said the other night there had been playground rumours about a boy dying.'

'Not rumours at all, it seems.'

Bruno raised an eyebrow. 'Definitely not. Either way, Mademoiselle Taun would have been long gone before your arrival.'

'I never heard the name.'

'And yet these punishments persisted? You saw them carried out yourself?'

'I suffered them myself. More than once.'

'What I don't understand is how the school stayed open. And why any parent would choose to send their child there afterwards. It was a national scandal – based on the archived news results, it dominated the headlines of the day.'

Fabien laughed, but it was bitter. 'Why does any parent send their child to a Catholic school, allow them to attend sleep-away camps with Catholic priests? We've had years of headlines detailing sexual abuses in the Church, no country is immune. And yet the faith lives on. No one thinks it's their priest, their child. God is good, remember?'

'These are not the actions of God, but the actions of man. But you're right. Globally, the Catholic Church operates in a sphere of quasi-immunity, crimes on Earth punishable only in the afterlife.' Bruno paused. 'Your school friends – would any of them have had siblings old enough to be at the school when it happened?'

'I don't know, offhand, but I imagine not. They'd have been able to confirm the playground rumours if that had been the case.'

Bruno nodded. 'Good point. I suppose we have our motive. Or a strong candidate for a motive, at least.'

Fabien's eyebrows rose in an unasked question Bruno was nonetheless able to read.

'Do you remember when we spoke of Agatha Christie, of Miss Marple? People kill for money, for sex, for power and for revenge. Given the ferocity of the attack on Joséphine Taun, we'd already come to the conclusion that there was a personal reason behind her killing, and given her history I don't think it would be much of a stretch to assume that we're looking at revenge for the death of Matthieu Ventou.'

Fabien nodded. 'A surviving family member?'

'Perhaps. The article mentioned his parents and four siblings, although as minors none of them were named. I think our first step is to track them down and eliminate them as possible suspects, don't you?'

'Can I stay on the case, knowing my connection with the school?'

'I'll check with J-J, but my instinct is that it won't be an issue, given you enrolled a decade or more after it happened. Mademoiselle Taun was long gone by then, serving her sentence. While I give him a call, could you get in touch with Gabrielle, ask her to set her bots on tracking down the surviving members of the Ventou family?'

Back at the gendarmerie Fabien held it together long enough to call Gabrielle without revealing his state of shock, but Bruno offered to take the reins when it came to briefing the team, assigning a different member of the Ventou family to each of his investigating officers.

'I want everything you can find on every last member, anyone who might remember the boy. We're talking everything from long forgotten social media accounts to unpaid parking tickets, book club memberships, any trace at all. We need to know who in the family is still alive, and if any of them have been within a hundred and fifty kilometres of St Denis in the last two months.'

He turned to address Yveline.

'Gabrielle Teyssier is going to be sending us a scan of Joséphine Taun's complete criminal record as soon as it's been uploaded. Could you please let me or Fabien know the minute it arrives?'

'*Oui, chef.* I'll call the station down in Bandol, see if anyone down there remembers working on the case.'

'Good idea, let me know what they say. And that goes for all of you – we need to make sharing any information a top priority; there are a lot of threads to follow right now.'

After such an exhausting day Bruno found it hard to drum up his usual level of enthusiasm about dinner with a beautiful woman and had he and Laura not found it so difficult to make plans of late he would have cried off, citing the pressures of work. He'd been tempted to do so just to prove a point. But it wasn't in his character to be petty, so despite the lure of an early night he spruced himself up in a nice shirt and jacket and added a quick spritz of aftershave.

Laura hadn't said where they were meeting, only that it was a surprise, and she sent him a map link on WhatsApp. When it opened, he recognized the location but couldn't remember any restaurants in the vicinity, and he set off full of curiosity about the evening to come, the Taun investigation temporarily relegated to the back of his mind. With the map telling him he was less than two minutes from his destination Bruno was beyond confused – he knew there was nowhere to eat for miles around – and then he spotted Laura's gleaming Range Rover parked up at a nearby rest area.

Parking his own vehicle behind hers, Bruno looked to the picnic tables a few hundred metres uphill, where Laura sat in the setting sun, her shoes kicked off and the legs of her trousers rolled up her calves as she sunned them. Beside her on the bench was an old-fashioned picnic basket made of rattan, and next to that a garish modern plastic cooler. She stood up as he opened the door and called out, 'Bruno! I'm up here!'

Moments later he was up the incline and in her arms, inhaling the scent of her hair, her perfume, relishing the very fact of physical contact with a woman who had proven so elusive for so long. 'Laura.' He kissed her. 'Laura, Laura, Laura.' Every word a kiss. 'It's wonderful to see you.'

'I hope you like picnics,' she said, breaking away from their embrace and turning to open the cooler. 'And oysters.'

Much as Bruno wanted to lose himself in the delights of Laura and her perfectly chosen picnic, there was no denying that the Quirit investigation – Taun investigation, he should say – was weighing heavily upon his mood that evening. Fabien had clearly been deeply shocked by the connection with his old school, but he was resilient and would recover. Bruno was confident that knowing the victim's real identity would lead them swiftly to her killer, and for all that he wanted to swim in Laura's eyes, drown in her scent and more, he knew he wasn't giving her the attention she deserved.

'A lot on your mind tonight?' Laura passed him a plate of thinly sliced cured trout and wedges of lemon. 'You've been awfully quiet.'

'It's the murder case. We've had a breakthrough, and I know we're getting somewhere. I just don't know where yet.'

'All confidential, I assume?' Bruno nodded. 'What about on the team? Is there anyone there you can hash things out with, try and look at things from different angles?'

Bruno laughed and took Laura's hand in his. 'Laura, are you delegating?'

A squeeze, then she broke their hold to pass him the oyster knife. 'I suppose I am. Twice, in fact. I assume you know how to shuck an oyster?'

As they worked their way through a tower of seafood, Laura gossiped about her work, and Bruno sensed a lightness about her that he'd not seen in months. Rather than moaning about office politics and power plays she was enthusing about a new chateau they were bringing onto the books, and its owner, a Canadian emigrant who'd made his money exporting North American lobster to European restaurants. He was now connecting fishermen and restaurants around Europe via an app he'd designed to make it easier to ensure ethical supply chains without any middlemen. Bruno was happy to see Laura's enthusiasm and to know that she was back on form.

'So what's a man of the sea doing living in the Périgord? You can't get much more landlocked than here.'

Laura laughed. 'I asked him the very same question. Apparently the chateau is roughly equidistant from his favourite restaurants in the country, so he never has to travel more than four hours in any one direction.' She rolled her eyes. 'You know what North Americans are like, they don't think twice about that sort of a drive.'

Bruno shook his head. 'And have you taken him to Le Vieux Logis? One meal there could save the man a lot of fuel.'

'If he likes it, it could save the planet!' She laughed. 'That's a very good idea, Bruno. I should have thought of it myself.'

The rest of the evening passed as perfectly as Bruno could have hoped, the two of them driving back to his house in convoy once the sun disappeared below the hills and the temperature fell with it. After a rapturous welcome from Balzac, Laura and Bruno disappeared for a little rapture of their own.

*

Waking up on Saturday morning Bruno couldn't have been happier. He wrapped himself around the still sleeping Laura, burying his nose between her neck and shoulder before peppering the spot with kisses. 'Wake up, my love.' She stirred, rolled away, and pulled the sheet up over her head. With a quiet laugh, Bruno went to tend to Balzac, who'd been left to his own devices for hours, with water and a choice of bedding in the kitchen and hall.

The basset sped across to the furthest corner of the garden as soon as Bruno opened the kitchen door, baying a crescendo. The quick flash of a ginger tail as it disappeared over the wall showed that Balzac had bravely fought off an intruder, and Bruno made a fuss of the dog when he strolled back into the kitchen, scratching his belly in just the right spot. He was so involved in the interaction that it took a few moments before he felt the weight of Laura's gaze in the doorway. She'd wrapped a sheet around her like a Grecian statue.

'Sorry about the noise, there was a cat in the garden.'

'Say no more,' she laughed. 'What time is it?'

'A little before eight. Would you like to go back to bed, I can bring you a coffee?'

'That sounds glorious. But actually, seeing as I'm up, why not go into town? I'm sure you've got things you need from the market.'

Bruno nodded. 'And we can have our coffees at Fauquet. How long will you need to get ready?'

She opened the sheet wide and beckoned him in. 'I think that's rather up to you.'

The Saturday market would have to wait a bit today.

*

It was just gone ten when Bruno's Land Rover pulled up in the lot behind the bank, and sheer luck that they turned in just as another car was leaving. Even the Saturday market was seeing increased signs of life, although Bruno had to acknowledge that some of the people present would be Easter visitors, that it was the start of the natural upswing that came with the tourist season. It would be unwise to rest on his laurels just yet.

They'd left Balzac sunning himself in the garden, doing his best to demolish one of the dried pig ears Bruno bought for him as the most special of treats. Bruno knew that the 'disappearing' ears would all be revealed the next time he did a bit of heavy work in the garden – Balzac was a master of burying his treasures, digging them up and burying them again.

Hand in hand, Bruno and Laura strolled across the bridge to the market square, stopping every so often in order that Bruno could introduce Laura to the curious citizenry. When they reached Fauquet's, Bruno took her inside to meet the owner.

'*Enchanté*, my dear, *enchanté*,' said Fauquet, lifting Laura's hand. 'It's so nice to meet you.'

'Actually, we've met before, although it was a few months ago.'

'Don't tell me.' He thought aloud, muttering through scenarios. 'I've got it! Before Christmas, you were here with the confederation of bassets. And yours was the most beautiful lady . . . what was her name?'

'George Sand.'

Fauquet tipped his head back and roared with laughter, flashing traces of ancient fillings. 'Perfect. And what can I get you to drink?'

'A double espresso, please.'

He nodded. 'Bruno, your usual? And a basket of croissants? I'll bring them. There's a table free on the terrace if you're quick.'

After breakfast, interrupted by a couple of curious well-wishers hoping to get an eyeful of Bruno's date, they began their rounds of the Saturday market, which was much smaller than Tuesday's edition. Rather than running the length of the Rue de Paris and beyond, it was restricted to the two small squares by the river which were used as public parking the rest of the week. A nursery had set up shop a few years earlier, selling potted plants and trees, but otherwise the stallholders were all local farmers and producers, the men and women whose forefathers had sold their wares in St Denis for hundreds of years, the ones they called the old guard. He must ask Fat Jeanne who the longest-running family was. He knew of several whose forebears pre-dated the Napoleonic Wars, but he bet that some could trace their roots even further back.

'I need to get a load of onions for the feast tomorrow, but we've got everything else we need.'

Laura laughed. 'I love that you call it a feast. Makes me think of the closing scene in an Astérix, all the villagers eating boar and drinking Getafix's magic potion after vanquishing the Romans once again. *Vive la France!*'

'Is there anything more patriotic than a good meal and good wine, enjoyed in the company of one's compatriots?'

'Especially when the food and wine are French?'

'Of course, goes without saying. To add French after "good" would be a tautology.'

Laura laughed again, and Bruno felt a warm glow at having caused it. The glow evaporated seconds later, when they reached the front of the small queue for Lorraine's vegetable stall. Instead of the warm greeting to which he was accustomed, the old lady made eye contact and then deliberately turned her back on him.

'*Bonjour*, Lorraine—'

'I'm out.' Her voice was like ice.

'I'm sorry?'

'I'm out. Whatever you want, I don't have it. Next!'

Bruno didn't know what to say or do but felt Laura gently steering him away from the trestle tables and curious eyes.

'What was all that about?'

Bruno shook his head. 'I have no idea. I buy greens from Lorraine most weeks, have done for years.'

'I assume she's not the only person with onions in St Denis?'

'She's not.' He turned to look back at the stall, where Lorraine was happily chatting away with a customer, her unusual exchange with Bruno seemingly of no concern.

At the next stall, he was frozen out entirely by the youngest son of a farmer whose root vegetables he'd bought for as long as he'd been living in St Denis. The boy discovered a sudden and debilitating bout of Bruno blindness, and Laura once again pulled him away from the scene.

'Once is an aberration, Bruno. Two looks very much like the beginning of a pattern. Are you sure you haven't done something to upset these people?'

There was a cough. 'If I may interrupt for a second?' It was Stéphane, the cheesemaker. After Bruno had introduced him to Laura as a good friend, Stéphane asked him for a quick word in private.

'You two take as long as you need,' said Laura. 'I'm just going to check out the competition in the window over the road.' She strolled off in the direction of a high-end holiday rental company displaying pictures of chateaux and farmhouses.

Stéphane cleared his throat. 'I'm sorry, Bruno. I want to say you know how it is with the old guard, that they're stuck in their ways and resist change.' He looked uncomfortable. 'The fact of the matter is that, however good your intentions, you stormed in here with a plan for the market, all guns blazing, and at no point did you consult the people most likely to be affected.'

Bruno was shocked but had to concede that a fair point was being made. He also had to concede that Jeanne had made a very similar point to him not all that long ago and he hadn't given her comments the consideration they deserved.

'Do you really think that we stallholders haven't been brainstorming ways of boosting our profile, increasing foot traffic? Of course we have. This is our livelihoods we're talking about. While we're setting up, we talk about the successful markets we've done this week. While we're closing down, we bemoan our collapsing takings in St Denis. And in between, while we're serving our customers and pausing for our coffees, we come up with ideas to make things better.'

'You're right. I should've taken soundings, talked to you before.'

'You should. Instead of asking what Bruno could do for St Denis, you just assumed you knew what needed to be done and that you were the man to do it. It's not a mortal sin, Bruno, but a little more self-awareness might not hurt.'

Bruno reached across and squeezed Stéphane's forearm.

'Thank you. Thank you for making sense of it and thank you for making sure Laura didn't have to hear that.'

Stéphane chuckled. 'Don't worry, Bruno. If she's half as smart as the other women you've dated, she'll have clocked your saviour complex by now.'

16

There would be at least another hour of darkness before daybreak, Bruno thought when his alarm sounded on Easter Sunday, his room far colder than he was used to. He reached for the thick dressing gown he'd had the foresight to drop on the floor the night before and wrapped it tightly around him before padding over to the dresser for a pair of thick woollen socks. Seeing that there was no light coming from underneath the guest room door, he gave it a quick rap on his way to the kitchen to get the coffee going – Balzac had sensibly decided to stay asleep a little longer, the basset having opened one eye, clocked the darkness, and closed it again.

It had been decided that Fabien would sleep over in view of the early start. Satisfied his colleague was awake after his knock was answered by a groan, Bruno flicked on the set of low wattage downlights, and set about boiling the kettle in the cosy gloom. Waiting for the whistle, he tapped out a message to Momu. 'We're up, eta 1h'. Receiving nothing but a thumbs up in reply, he smiled – even Momu, whom he knew to be the original early bird, had little to say at this hour.

A series of gentle burbles from the kettle returned his mind to the task at hand, and he'd only just finished spooning coffee grounds into the cafetière when Fabien stumbled in, his hair in full electric shock mode.

'I'm not sure whether to wish you a good morning or a good night, but either way I'm glad you convinced me it would be easier to stay here last night,' he said. 'Are you sure we have to be up and out quite this early?'

'If you want to eat before night falls, then yes. A *méchoui* takes between six and eight hours to cook, and with the size of our lamb it's likely to be eight.' The kettle whistled, and Bruno waited a minute or two to take the edge off the boiling water before decanting it over the grounds. Despite his apparent lack of enthusiasm for the early hour, Fabien had managed to assemble cups and a pot of chestnut honey, and pour them each a glass of water.

The younger man was rubbing his face with the heels of both hands, dragging his skin around like a cement mixer, his eyes bleary. 'I won't be much use until I've had at least one coffee inside me, I'm afraid. It took me forever to get to sleep, I can't have had more than three or four hours.'

Bruno pressed the plunger down and poured them each a coffee, adding a generous spoon of honey to each cup. Fabien reached both hands out, evidently not trusting one to hold the cup steady.

'I'm going to get dressed,' said Bruno. 'Then I must feed the birds. I'll be back in a minute.'

True to his word, Bruno was soon back in the kitchen, having tossed the bucket of scraps over the fence but deciding to leave the hunting of eggs for another day. There would be egg hunting on Easter Sunday, of course, but aimed at an age group considerably lower than his. Which reminded him – he mustn't forget the chocolates that Delphine Mausans had kindly helped him with; it wouldn't do to leave Daniel and Dora disappointed. Nor Pamela and Florence, for that matter. Would Laura manage to turn up?

Laura had promised to put her work on hold for the weekend. Bruno opened up their message thread and began to type before checking himself. If she had taken the time off as promised, she wouldn't appreciate the sound of a message arriving at this hour. He deleted his words and offered up a quick prayer to whoever might be listening that she'd be on his arm come lunchtime.

He was relieved she'd not borne witness to Stéphane's taking him to task, and she had been discreet enough not to say anything when he turned into the supermarket car park to get the remaining shopping. But Laura not raising the topic of his market shunning hadn't stopped him from brooding once she'd left for the office. He knew the importance of community, it was the foundation of his personal philosophy. How could he have been so blind?

While Bruno busied himself getting things ready, taking a wicker basket and a handful of cool bags from the back of the pantry door, Fabien stared into his coffee, a glazed look in his eyes. Bruno snapped his fingers in front of his face. 'Wakey-wakey! Time to get going!'

Fabien shook his head and downed his cup. 'Sorry. One more coffee and I'll be up and at 'em, as they say.' He poured them each a refill and stood up to drink. Having downed the second coffee and after a sharp slap to each cheek, he was looking decidedly more alert. 'Right. What should I be doing?'

Bruno pointed at the baskets on the counter. 'First things first, take the chocolates from the fridge and put them in the wicker basket. That can go straight to the car, front passenger seat. The sun's not up yet, they'll be fine and I won't be forgiven if I forget them.'

While Fabien followed his orders, Bruno set about packing up the spoils they'd collected. The multiple boxes of couscous could go in one bag, while the kilos of citrus, the onions and olives could go in another. Pamela had plenty of olive oil, and Momu would have his usual box of secret ingredients.

'What next?' Bruno started; he hadn't heard Fabien come back inside.

'Could you go to the potager and cut an armful of parsley, and another of coriander?' Bruno held out the kitchen scissors. 'When you've done that, wrap them in damp kitchen towels and put them in the bags with the couscous and the lemons and limes?' Fabien nodded, using the torch on his phone to illuminate the vegetable garden.

From the fridge, Bruno pulled out several tubs of Greek yoghurt – *labneh* was still a rarity in their part of the world, and more's the pity, he often said – and emptied the vegetable drawer of the three kilos of carrots they'd picked up on their shopping trip. That left the oranges, the fennel and the red onions to retrieve from the giant wicker basket on the counter. Momu was in charge of bringing home-made flatbreads, the special Persian cucumbers he grew in his own potager, and who knew what else besides. The maths teacher was one of the most generous hosts in St Denis, Bruno knew; he was certain to have more than a few tricks up his sleeve.

Fabien's eyes boggled at the load. 'Seems like we're going to be feeding an army, not just thirty.'

'Eating in the fresh air always seems to make people hungrier. Especially if they've spent half the day salivating over the smell of lamb roasting on an open fire.'

'I'll get started, then. Is there any method to your loading, beyond putting the heavy stuff at the bottom?'

Bruno shook his head. 'However it fits. I'll help you with these and then go and get Balzac.'

It took them three trips before the kitchen was clear, and Bruno went to rouse the basset, several dog biscuits in his pocket to sweeten the deal. A quick lap of the garden and they were on their way.

They drove in darkness, both passengers quickly asleep, and it was only as they were rounding the final bend on the approach to the riding school that Bruno noticed the first fingers of dawn breaking through, pink tendrils just starting to colour the thin wisps of cloud to the east.

He pulled up alongside Momu's battered Renault hatchback, not at all surprised to find that the head chef had beaten him to Pamela's. There were lights on inside, and once he'd woken Fabien and Balzac, the three made their way to the front door, where Pamela was already waiting. After a half-hearted greeting, Balzac shuffled past her and headed straight for his favourite spot under the window.

'Come in, come in. There's coffee in the kitchen if you want it, and Momu's already outside building the fire.' She ushered them inside, where an eight-cup cafetière stood sentry next to a stack of espresso cups and a basket of mini *pains au chocolat.*

'They're only frozen ones from Picard, I'm afraid, but it was the best I could do before dawn on a holiday.'

'You're an angel.' Bruno reached for the basket and offered it to Fabien, before taking two for himself. 'I'll go see how Momu's doing before we start unloading the car. Could you clear some space in the fridge for me?'

'Already done. Everything bar the top shelf has either been cleared already or is my contribution.'

'What a woman!' With that, he headed out of the kitchen door and made his way across the patio, past the swimming pool and down the lawns, where Momu's outline was at work on this side of a small fire. 'Sous chef, at your service!'

Momu stood and turned to face Bruno, his arms held wide for an embrace. 'Happy Easter, my friend. I can't tell you how touched I am that you've invited me and my family to take part in your celebration.'

Bruno grinned. 'Easter means lamb, lamb means *méchoui*, and *méchoui* means Momu. I'm just happy you could join us. It's been far too long since we last did this.' Momu nodded. 'So what's the plan? I see you've got the fire started. Do you need me to start constructing the spit?'

'Not quite yet. It'll take another half hour or so before the flames have died down, so we can use the time to get everything from my car. Pamela told me you dropped the lamb off yesterday?'

'Packed in its box with plenty of ice and left on the table in the dining room overnight. And I've got enough couscous and salad ingredients to feed a cast of thousands.'

Momu nodded. 'Why don't we head up to the house so you

can introduce me to your new colleague? Pamela tells me he's not so bad in the kitchen.'

'Not bad at all. I thought he could take care of the salads, I'd do the couscous, and you could tend to the meat?'

'Do you remember how to make the green couscous I taught you?'

'Do I? Momu, we must have made it together at least a dozen times! I'm sure it won't be quite up to your wife's standards, but if the rest of your family can give me a hand when they arrive it will certainly pass muster.' Momu said nothing, but raised a heavy eyebrow, and Bruno knew when to concede. 'Would you like to be in charge of the couscous? I can baste the lamb according to your exact specifications.'

'Perhaps that would be wise.'

Back in the kitchen Fabien had not only perked up considerably, but had taken it upon himself to unload the Land Rover and organize the ingredients – by recipe, no less – in the fridge. Their hostess was sitting on one kitchen chair, her legs stretched out across a second, three sheepdogs and one basset looking mournfully at the pastry in her hand.

'Fabien was just giving me a rundown of the menu you three have planned – it sounds an utter treat. And even better not having to lift a finger myself,' she said with a grin. 'Will you want a hand bringing the lamb down to the spit?'

Momu smiled. 'I'm sure that we three can manage between us, thank you. Is there any more of that coffee going? We've just about got time for another round.'

*

The morning passed in a blur of activity. Momu taught Fabien how to build the spit for an above-ground *méchoui*, with Jack Crimson watching on, offering unsolicited and inexpert advice. The four men made light work of carting the lamb down from Pamela's dining room table in its insulated box, the task made easier when Bruno pointed out they could drain the melted ice onto the lawns and lighten their load.

Once the animal had been prepped, speared, and hung over the hot embers, Momu begged some large mixing bowls from Pamela, and fetched several litres of cooking oil and his magic box of herbs from his car. He banished the others indoors while he set about preparing his secret baste, keeping a watchful eye on their makeshift furnace.

While Pamela's kitchen was hardly short of prep space, Bruno and Fabien decided it would be more convivial to make the salads on the patio table, where they would be well positioned to smell the first hints of roasting lamb once their Easter beast started to come up to temperature. The sun was steadily climbing in the sky, and the worst of the predawn chill but a distant memory.

Splashes from the pool drew their attention: Jack had dived in and was beginning a series of laps, neatly avoiding his two young grandchildren, who were practising their diving in the deep end. Bruno and Fabien both smiled at the sight.

'Did you remember to bring your trunks with you? If not, I'm sure Jack will have a spare pair you can borrow.'

Fabien nodded, not looking up from the pile of onions he was slicing thinly and adding to the heap already sitting in a bowl of iced water. 'I'm wearing them under my trousers.'

'Excellent. Then once you've finished that onion, why don't we join them in the pool? I'll go and change.'

Bruno and Fabien stayed in their swimming shorts long after they'd finished splashing around in the pool with the kids, playing a game they'd invented. It was part water polo, part hide and seek, and seemed mostly to involve throwing an inflatable ball at Bruno. When they made it back up to the patio a little before noon, Pamela was clearing the table.

'I've moved your salad makings back inside; people will be turning up in the next half hour or so, and I want the snacks laid out before anyone arrives.'

'Snacks? We didn't make any snacks,' said Bruno.

'Not to worry, Miranda and I have done them. You can't invite people for lunch and then not feed them till mid-afternoon, especially not with children involved.'

'You're a life-saver. What have you made?'

'I wasn't sure where to go with the North African theme, as it's not really my thing, but I thought that a little bit of Mediterranean wouldn't go amiss, seeing as the eastern end of it seems to live on lamb.' Bruno nodded. 'So we've got piles of veg to dip in tzatziki that Miranda made, and I put together some of that green olive and walnut tapenade you showed me how to make last summer. Again to eat with the vegetables, and I'll put out a few bowls of crackers and breadsticks. Then there are radishes with butter and salt, and cherry tomatoes. Not because they're from the Med, but because they're from the garden and they needed eating.'

'Ah, Pamela, so talented!' He reached over to hug her, only to be pushed away.

'Time you put some clothes on. I could do with a hand bringing things out.'

'Yes, ma'am!' Bruno clicked his heels together and issued a salute. 'You heard the lady,' he said to Fabien. 'Let's make ourselves decent before the forced labour begins.'

Bruno was soon back on the patio, a cold glass of Bergerac sec in one hand and a carrot baton loaded with tzatziki in the other, surrounded by half of those he held nearest and dearest. The first car pulling up in Pamela's long drive unleashed a veritable deluge, and the patio was heaving with friendly faces, chatter and laughter ricocheting off the flagstones and down into the valley.

First to arrive had been Florence and her twins; they'd hitched a lift with her neighbour Alain and his wife Rosalie, Bruno's cousins and closest relatives. All three were teachers at the school in St Denis where Momu worked, and lived side by side in a row of apartments built to ensure that the faculty could afford to live in the town – St Denis's simple and effective solution to a global problem. The twins ripped off their outer layers and plunged straight into the pool with Miranda's children; it was the very place where Bruno had taught each of them to swim, and watching them play he was overcome with memories of giving them their first lessons, infant bravado quickly making way for real proficiency.

In Florence's wake had trailed Momu's wife, Dillah, his son Karim, and his daughter-in-law, Rashida. Dillah had immediately taken over the kitchen, pulling Fabien indoors to describe the selection of salads they had chosen to accompany the *méchoui*, while Rashida had followed to make sure her mother-in-law spared the poor boy the worst of her fierce but loving criticisms. Karim had accepted Bruno's offer of an alcohol-free beer, and made his way straight for the pit where Momu tended the lamb.

Jack and Miranda were busy flitting between groups of guests, taking the hosting weight off Pamela's shoulders as they ensured everyone had a drink, a towel, knew where to find the bathroom. Every time Bruno turned his head, it was to spot another familiar face, friends from St Denis and from much further afield. Last to arrive was J-J, who had come all the way from Périgueux, bringing Gabrielle Teyssier with him. As soon as he spotted them in the crowd, Bruno went to greet them. 'J-J, Gabrielle! I'm so pleased you two could make it. Fabien's in the kitchen, but I'll let him know you're here; I'm sure he'll be out as soon as he's able.'

'Anything for one of your feasts, Bruno,' boomed the *commissaire*. 'Where is the delightful Laura?'

'I hate to disappoint you on two fronts, but Momu is the one in charge of our food today, and it looks like Laura's stuck at the office.'

'On Easter Sunday!?' J-J shook his head. 'Momu,' he went on. 'Is he the one who does the *méchoui* at your tennis club dinners?'

'The very same.'

'Then there will be no disappointing me! I don't think I've ever had more succulent lamb.' Ever theatrical, J-J touched his fingers to his lips in a chef's kiss and nudged Gabrielle. 'That man's lamb could convert a vegetarian, you're in for a real treat.'

Many mouths made light work of the canapés, and Bruno went into the kitchen to fetch a new batch before being shooed out by Dillah, who was busy teaching Fabien to make the flatbreads they would be serving with the lamb.

'*Non, non!* Away with you! This kitchen is occupied.'

Bruno held up his hands in defeat. 'I just came looking for more crudités, some dip – we're running out fast, it's like a plague of locusts out there.'

'Pamela said there's more of everything on the bottom shelf,' said Fabien. 'Let Bruno take it out and we can get back to our lesson.'

Dillah beamed. 'I like this one. He's a much faster learner than you, Bruno.'

Suitably chastised, Bruno took refills from the fridge and retreated to the patio, where he replenished the tzatziki and tapenade, and the plates of vegetables and crackers, before heading across the lawn to Momu and Karim, two bottles of alcohol-free beer in one hand and a glass of wine in the other.

'How's the lamb? Can you trust me to look after it while you say hello to everyone? All the guests are here now.' Bruno offered them each one of the beers.

'What do you think, Dad? Can we trust *le flic*?'

Momu laughed. '*Les flics?* No. This *flic*? Yes. Come, let's go to where the party is.'

By the time the *méchoui* was ready the hordes were salivating. There wasn't a single crumb remaining of Pamela's snacks, and Fabien – finally released from his kitchen duties – was back in the pool with Karim, where they'd delighted the children with a game of chicken, each man hoisting a child onto his shoulders as they competed to push the opposing pair into the water.

Then Momu and Karim – now dried off and back in his street clothes – between them carried the lamb on its spit to where the guests had gathered. Fabien and Dillah brought an endless stream of home-made flatbreads out from the kitchen, and Pamela and Miranda set up the buffet on the patio table.

'We're not standing on ceremony here, everyone – grab a plate, load it up, and then head down to Momu, who will carve you off some lamb,' Pamela explained. 'Wine, water and juice are all on the side in the kitchen, so help yourselves.' The crowd surged as one towards the patio table. 'In an orderly fashion! We're not savages!'

Bruno found himself queueing next to Gabrielle Teyssier, and noticed she was only putting a few small portions of salad on her plate while he piled his high. 'Are you not hungry?'

She shrugged. 'I don't tend to eat much. I was born with a small appetite. And the appetite I do have I am very much saving for that lamb – it smells sensational!'

'Sensational it is. Come, I'll introduce you to Momu, make sure he gives you the best bit.'

They walked to where Momu and Karim were busy serving up plate after plate of lamb, and Bruno introduced Gabrielle to the chefs. 'That reminds me, have you met Fabien yet? In person, I mean.'

She laughed. 'Not yet. I understand he's been chained to the stove?'

'That would be my wife's doing.' Momu grinned. 'I think she's besotted with him, says he's a natural in the kitchen.'

'When he wasn't helping cook he was engaging me in battle with the kids, but I think he's been released at last,' said Karim. 'He took a plate over to the pool a couple of minutes ago.'

Having introduced Gabrielle to Fabien, Bruno made short

work of reading the room and retreated. He was no Cupid, but he could recognize chemistry. He bade them both a *bon appétit* and bid a hasty retreat, instead finding a hearty welcome from Florence, whom he'd barely seen all afternoon.

'Bruno, come sit! The twins are off playing spies in the bushes, and I have this blanket all to myself.' Bruno handed her his plate while he lowered himself to the ground, relieved to take the weight off his feet.

'You'll have to excuse me. I've been up for hours.'

'I can imagine, you must be exhausted. This is a wonderful feast you've helped put on, you should take a moment or two to enjoy it. No Laura today?' Bruno winced, and with sympathy in her eyes Florence deftly changed the subject to Dora and Daniel's latest exploits. Before his plate was empty, Bruno was laughing along at her description of an unsupervised five minutes that ended in several broken tree branches and a shredded pair of pyjamas but not a single scratch.

The sun was beginning its slow fall behind the hills, casting shadows on the lawn. He spied Fabien and Gabrielle sitting side by side on one of the loungers by the pool, clearly lost in conversation. 'Fabien! Sorry to interrupt, but I was hoping to steal you away? I want to introduce you to the rest of the guests.'

Fabien jumped up, and from the way Gabrielle smiled, Bruno was convinced that Cupid's arrow had indeed struck. 'I'd say I'll have him back to you in a minute, Gabrielle, but I can't promise the Baron won't talk for hours.'

'I should find Pamela to thank her for hosting.'

'Then come. If I know Pamela, she'll be holding court on the patio.' Bruno turned to face the house and there she was in the centre of a big group, laughing at something Horst had just said. 'If I may interrupt? I wanted to introduce you all to Fabien, who's been working with me at the station, and to Gabrielle, another colleague.' There was a chorus of hellos and questions, and Bruno held up his hands. 'Stop, stop, I want to do this properly!'

He started with Kirk and Cassandra. 'Gabrielle, these two own Château Rouffillac.' He looked at Gabrielle. 'This woman is the brains behind the safety of your American VIPs last year.' The *châtelains* were effusive in their greeting, with Cassandra pulling Gabrielle in for a hug.

'We owe you the continued health of our business, you're an absolute rock star,' she said. 'We can't thank you enough.'

Gabrielle smiled gratefully.

'And this,' Bruno went on, 'is Fabien Panton. His parents own the butchers' in Lalinde.'

Fabien leaned in for a kiss. 'Please don't mention the duck salami, it's all anyone in St Denis can talk about when they hear my name.'

Kirk laughed. 'And with good reason, it's superb. Pleased to meet you, young man. So are you a gendarme in St Denis?'

J-J cut in. 'Actually, he's one of my rising stars, on secondment to Bruno. But not for long, we need him in the *police judiciaire*.'

Horst stepped forward to shake Fabien's hand. 'I'm Horst, and this is my wife Clothilde. We both work at the Prehistory Museum in Les Eyzies, I'm sure you know it?'

Fabien nodded. 'Annual visits during the summer holidays. I'm very happy to meet you both.' He shook Horst's hand, and gave Clothilde a double *bise*.

Bruno looked around. 'Fabiola, Jack and Miranda you already

know, and the Mayor and Mademoiselle Cantagnac, of course. Gérard, where is Jacqueline?'

'Off with the Baron; he's taken it upon himself to give her a tour of the vegetable garden. He's promised to teach her all the tricks.'

'Let me guess. Herbicides and chemicals galore?' Bruno shook his head, and the Mayor laughed.

'So you've had the benefit of his folk wisdom?' he said. 'He's a big fan of chemical warfare.'

'You're far safer with his salads than you are with his *mique*.'

Fabien butted in. 'I don't think I've heard of a *mique*?'

'Count yourself lucky, dear boy,' J-J boomed, keen to be centre of attention. 'A boiled wodge of dough with uncooked lardons hiding inside. It's disgusting.'

'Fabien is actually very good in the kitchen,' said Bruno. 'Handles his knife like a trained chef.'

'I'd expect nothing less from a local,' said Gérard, 'and the son of a producer to boot. Tell me, why haven't I seen you around St Denis before this? Lalinde isn't a million miles away by moped, your boys are always coming across to hit on our girls.'

Fabien shrugged. 'I used to, in the summers.'

'I sense a "but" coming.'

Fabien winced. 'I don't want to be impolite . . .' He tailed off.

The Mayor looked stern. 'I insist. We're trying to breathe some life back into St Denis. Criticism might not be welcomed, but will at least be given its due consideration.'

'If you're sure?' Fabien looked uncomfortable. 'To be honest, your night market has got a little bit, well, rubbish.'

Gérard's eyes boggled for a second, but J-J's laugh cut the

tension. 'Don't mince your words, do you?' He patted Gérard on the arm. 'From the mouths of babes, eh? He said it, but I must admit I've been thinking it for some time now.'

'Rubbish? In what way rubbish?'

Fabien took a draught from his beer. 'Night markets are supposed to be about promoting the region, right?' The Mayor nodded. 'Then why does St Denis sell burgers, raclette and German sausages? If you go to Audrix on a Saturday night you'll find foie gras *poêlé* with a drizzle of honey from hives you can see from the market square. In Belvès and Cadouin you get duck, both Issigeac and Les Eyzies have grandmothers selling home-made *rillettes* and local *charcuterie* with bread baked in the village oven. Come to St Denis and it's second-rate versions of food from other countries, and a terrible DJ besides. Why bother?'

'Actually,' Pamela cut in, 'Fabien's right, although I hate to say it. These days I only go along if someone is organizing a gathering; it's definitely become more about the people than it is about the food. And if you're a tourist, you won't know the people.'

There were nods, and one by one the gang voiced their support for Fabien's thesis. In the hubbub, Colette Cantagnac nudged Bruno. 'I think we've found the next phase of our little project.'

17

The following morning in the gendarmerie, Fabien suggested they start interviewing the Netflix crew.

'Agreed,' said Bruno, 'but we have to work out how best to handle it. We want to maintain the element of surprise, make sure people haven't got time to get their stories straight.'

'Then let's go to see them on set rather than call them out to the station. How many people are we talking, anyway?'

Bruno shrugged. 'I'm not sure. Both times I've seen them out and about it's been a group of around seven or eight, but that's just the production team. We'll have to find out from Odelie whether any of the cast are in the area, and how many support staff such a big show requires.'

While Bruno went back through his notes, Fabien called Odelie Marchant, who over speakerphone informed them that there were more than eighty people from the show currently in the Périgord – actors, directors, the costume and make-up people, plus lighting teams, caterers, drivers, assistants, the list went on and on. Bruno's heart sank as he listened to the summary.

'Odelie? It's Bruno. When did you start filming this season's episodes?'

'Our first day shooting was last Tuesday, but we had the cast down for table readings on Monday. Why?'

'We're trying to establish just how many people from your show were in the area in the window we're interested in, how many interviews we'll need to conduct.'

'Oh, that's easy enough. Would you like me to send you over copies of the call sheets?'

'Call sheets? What are those?'

'They're a detailed timeline of who we need on set and when. Each member of cast and crew, details of the vehicle they've been assigned, the hotel they're staying in, the time we need them to be on set. I have one for every day of production, days done and those yet to come.'

Bruno beamed. 'Your organizational skills are a godsend, Odelie. Please do send them over. And have you prepared the list I asked for, the information of everyone who could have had access to the Peugeot?'

'I'm working on it now. Give me half an hour, and everything you need will be in your inbox. I'm sending you copies of the spreadsheets I've created so that you can sort the data as needed; I'm not giving you the masters because I can't risk you accidentally deleting something I need, but I can run a macro to extract any changes to my masters at the end of each day and send them over, if you'd like?'

Bruno's head was swimming. 'Maybe set up that changes thing, but don't send them over unless we request them – we don't want to get thrown off course by an excess of information.'

'Got it. Is there anything else I can do for you?'

'Nothing at all, thanks, you're being a great help. I'll confirm receipt once you've sent those documents through. *Merci beaucoup.*'

'Thanks so much, Odelie,' added Fabien, and cut the call. He looked at Bruno. 'Well?'

'Well, Odelie Marchant may well be the most efficient human being I've ever encountered. Even more so than Colette Cantagnac.'

Fabien mimed a faint. 'Don't let her hear you say that!'

'I'm not brave enough, never you fear. When we get those timesheets I suggest we start by interviewing those people we know were in the Périgord in the run-up to the murder. We might strike gold and save ourselves having to interview all of the eighty-plus people currently on site.'

'Let's hope so. Shall we head over to your office? By the time we get there, Odelie's sheets should be sitting in your inbox.'

Bruno tried to focus as he and Fabien scrolled through pages and pages of spreadsheet data. 'This is giving me a headache. Can you make any sense of it?'

'Sorry,' said Fabien. 'I've never been great with Excel.'

'Isn't your generation supposed to be digital natives? I thought you all grew up online.'

'Not in a Catholic boarding school I didn't. And besides – I grew up with phones, not computers. Apps that are designed to be instinctive to use. If you want someone who knows what they're doing with software, you'll need to find yourself an elder millennial. They grew up online at a time when nothing worked, so they actually know how to manipulate tools, get things working.'

'But I'm an elder millennial,' said Bruno. 'Well, just about.'

Colette Cantagnac rapped on the open door between the two offices. 'I don't mean to eavesdrop, gentlemen, but it sounds to me like you're fighting a losing battle with Excel?'

'That we are.'

She came into the room and looked expectantly at Bruno. 'If you want my help, you're going to have to give me your seat.' She rolled her eyes sky high. 'Why you didn't come to me immediately I simply don't know. Half the work I do for you is Excel-based. Now move over. Tell me – what am I looking at, and what are you hoping to get from it?'

Bruno explained. 'We need to know which of these people was scheduled for any and all days leading up to the Monday before Easter. If you can figure out who was around two weeks before that, even better.'

Colette beamed. 'Child's play.' Bruno tried to follow what she was doing as her fingers flew across the keyboard but gave up a few taps after she'd typed 'vlookup', pleased to note that Fabien appeared as confused as he was. It was a matter of minutes before Colette turned to face him with a smile. 'There you go.' She highlighted a column of text. 'That list there is all the names who were here before the Monday.' Another click. 'In bold is everyone who was here from the beginning of April. Do you want me to pull up March?'

'You never cease to amaze me.' Bruno shook his head. 'I think we've got enough to be getting started, but I may well call you back in later to work more of your magic. Thank you very much.'

The extracted list of names stretched to eleven people, eight of whom had been around since the beginning of the month. Bruno compared it with the list Odelie had sent across indicating the members of the production team who had access to the Peugeot van, and found it was the same eight who had been around all month, and very likely the same eight he'd spotted both in St Christophe and on Fauquet's terrace in recent weeks. He was pleased to note that the young woman had included herself on the list and hadn't presumed that her help made her any less of a suspect. He thought it showed good character.

'I think we start with these eleven, don't you?' said Bruno.

'But we can't discount the others – just because they didn't have cause to be down here for work doesn't mean they weren't here at all.'

'True, true. But how do you propose we interview all eighty-odd people on the list without giving them time to come up with a cover story, get alibis in order?'

'I think Gabrielle could help us here, don't you?' Without waiting for a response Fabien reached across the desk and forwarded Odelie's documents to the Périgueux tech wizard.

Bruno followed up with a call. 'We've just sent you a spreadsheet of names. Could you please cross-reference every name on this list with the records of visitors at every hotel, *gîte*, and campsite in the Périgord? Any and all matches from 1 April to this morning, please.'

'Of course. I should be able to get back to you within the hour.'

'Great, thank you.'

He turned to Fabien. 'Perhaps we should wait to begin our interviews until Gabrielle gets back to us. I'd rather we arrived on set with as much information as possible, not get interrupted mid-interview by a revelation from one of her bots. Let's go for a coffee while we wait; I have a feeling this might be our last chance of a relatively quiet morning for quite some time.'

Fabien nodded and stood up. 'Marcel's, or Fauquet?'

'I think Fauquet, don't you? Balzac loves the terrace there.'

Gabrielle Teyssier was true to her word. Less than an hour later Bruno's phone pinged with an incoming message. 'It's Gabrielle. She's sent me back the spreadsheet, do you want to take a look?'

Fabien shook his head. 'Not on that tiny screen I don't. Can you summarize it, or should we go back to the office and open it on the computer?'

'No need, Gabrielle has done a summary herself. Listen. All the names on the list match the hotels listed on the call sheets, and for the dates cited. Four names also appear to have booked private accommodation before being called onto the set: Alain Dennel, Sébastien Gosselin, Noémie Lavigne, and Marion Perrin. Perrin and Gosselin were booked into Le Moulin du Roc for three nights before their first days on set, sharing a room.' He looked up. 'That last one is almost certainly a lovers' getaway; it's one of the most romantic hotels in the Périgord.'

'Lucky them!' said Fabien.

'Netflix obviously pays rather well if they can spring for a five-star break. Of the other two, Dennel came down the night before he was first scheduled, stayed an extra night in the crew hotel, while Lavigne had two weeks in an Airbnb in Saint Cyprien before checking into the crew hotel with everyone else.'

'Interesting. How do you want to play this?'

'We could call Odelie, give her notice that we're coming and will need space to conduct our interviews, but I think we want the element of surprise.'

'As far as Odelie is concerned, we lost the element of surprise the minute we got her to send us all her data. But I think we just turn up, don't give anyone time to prepare.'

'Agreed.' Bruno stood up. 'Let's leave Balzac with Colette. Even with only eleven people to worry about, these interviews could take hours.'

According to Odelie's call sheets, the production would be filming at a farm just north of St Christophe all week, and nine of the people they hoped to speak to were scheduled on site that afternoon. Bruno wasn't familiar with the spot, so Fabien had plugged the address into Google Maps. Most of the journey was as familiar to Bruno as the roads around St Denis; it was only when he turned the Land Rover onto an increasingly inhospitable series of minor roads above St Christophe that he started to rely heavily on the automated voice for guidance.

'Did you know that they've done studies, and that we're more likely to ignore the instructions our GPS gives us if it's a woman's voice than a man's?'

Bruno chuckled. 'I didn't, but it doesn't surprise me. Far too many men feel emasculated by a woman knowing more than them.'

'You'd think that, but actually they found that the same applies to women. A female voice and we argue, we ignore it, we go our own way. But a male voice, and both sexes obey.' Fabien shifted in his seat. 'I'm not sure what that says about us as a species, but I don't think I like it.'

'Given that research has shown that to be the case, I wonder why all the tech companies persist in making the female voice the default. Do they want us to ignore it so we can gather more data for them while we're busy getting lost?'

'It wouldn't surprise me, we're all commodities now. This should be the turning here, don't you think? I'm not sure the satellite has quite caught up with us in all these trees.'

'Aha! Ignoring the woman, are we?' said Bruno. 'She doesn't want us to turn for another two hundred metres. But I think you're right, the turning was supposed to be just before the fork, and I can see the road splitting ahead.' He indicated left and slowly manoeuvred the Land Rover along a rutted farm track, the two of them having agreed that Bruno's private vehicle would be far better suited to the rustic terrain than the official police van. Also, they hoped, rather less of a trigger for those they were about to interview.

As they jiggled their way down the track it became clear that the Land Rover had been the right call – at certain points the ruts were almost thirty centimetres deep, and the standard issue police vehicle would never have made it.

'I wonder how they all manage to get to site,' Fabien mused. 'The ride height on that Peugeot they rented can't have had anything like enough ground clearance.'

'Odelie said it was only one of their vehicles, don't forget. It's a huge production. I'm sure they'll have covered all eventualities, especially if the rest of them are even half as organized as she is.'

Bruno navigated the Land Rover around a final bend, cresting a small hillock, and the true scale of the show was laid out in front of them down the slope and into a broad valley. They saw a mass of trailers, a huge marquee with flaps rolled up that looked to house the catering, and a network of lighting rigs and camera tracks that stretched across at least three fields. Scores of men and women dressed all in black were scurrying around the place, some with clipboards and others talking into headsets, while a group of a dozen or so people dressed like nineteenth-century farm workers were standing in a huddle, being shouted at by a tall man with gesturing hands. 'Looks like this is the spot. Where do you think we can park?'

Before Fabien could answer, a large, heavily tattooed man with a long grey beard and egg-sized holes in his earlobes came running over and gestured for Bruno to open the window. 'This is a closed set; I'm afraid you're going to have to turn around.'

Bruno smiled. 'We're here with the Police Nationale, could you please let me know where I can park?' Fabien shuffled around in his seat and produced his warrant card, offering it through the window for inspection. The giant nodded and pointed to his left.

'Park up in that field over there, anywhere you're not blocking another vehicle. When you've done that, come back here and I'll take you over to the production office.' Bruno followed his instructions, and in the rear-view mirror saw their guide whip out a walkie-talkie and start barking into it, presumably notifying his bosses of their arrival.

Outside the production office, a small portacabin in the corner of the field next to the one being used as a car park, Bruno and Fabien introduced themselves to Odelie, who managed to look suitably surprised by their presence before sending her assistant inside.

'We'll need a room, one where we won't be disturbed, and with three chairs. Can that be arranged?'

'How long would you need it for?'

'A few hours, maybe more. Not everyone we need to interview is on site today.'

Odelie nodded. 'Why don't you use the production office? You're already here, half the team are inside. I can stand guard in the unlikely event anyone wants to get in.'

Inside, Bruno and Fabien introduced themselves to the five members of the production crew sitting around a large oval table studded with laptops, tablets and phones, familiar faces all from sightings at Le Croiseau and Fauquet's. 'We're here investigating a murder. We'd like to speak with each of you in turn. You are witnesses, helping us with our inquiries, not suspects, which is why we've come to you, not called you into the station. Understood?' A series of nods. 'Our inquiry is confidential; you must not discuss your interviews, with each other or with anyone else. Any objections?' Shaking heads all around. 'You're under no obligation to speak to us but we hope you'll help us. The first person we would like to speak to is Sébastien Gosselin.'

The team packed up their tech and decamped elsewhere to continue work while each waited their turn, leaving one man. Bruno recognized him as the shaven-headed spectacle-wearer who had given Odelie a very public dressing-down on Fauquet's terrace.

Sébastien Gosselin stood up and approached them, his hand held out for a shake. 'Sébastien. *Bonjour.*' His outwardly calm countenance was betrayed by the slick of his palm.

Bruno indicated a chair opposite him before sitting himself, while Fabien remained standing, just out of Gosselin's eyeline. 'We're trying to establish a timeline of events relating to our investigation. How long have you been working on this production?'

'Since it was still a pilot. I've been on board since before the first season.'

'What about the current season? When did you come down to the Périgord to prepare?'

'That depends how you look at it. We were location-scouting last summer, while filming of season three was still under way. But in terms of the real balls-to-the-wall work, I've been down here full-time since the beginning of March, and also for some short trips in January and February, maybe two or three nights at a time.'

'Do you ride a moped?'

'In Paris, yes. Do you want the plate?'

'But not down here?'

He shook his head. 'I've probably borrowed a bike on site once or twice, getting from one side of the set to another, but not out on the roads, never.'

'And how often do you drive crew vehicles?'

At this Gosselin laughed. 'Absolutely never. I don't have a licence to drive a car.' He saw the puzzled look on Bruno's face and explained. 'A car in Paris is utter madness, and until I started working on this show, I'd only ever left the Périphérique to go to the airport.'

'So how do you get around here?'

'The crew vehicles. We're always out in pairs at a minimum, so it doesn't really matter that I can't drive.'

'And after hours? Does your girlfriend chauffeur you around?'

'My girlfriend? I don't have a girlfriend.'

'Not Marion Perrin?' Gosselin both shrugged and shook his head, a combination Bruno took to mean that whatever the pair had going between them it was probably pretty casual. 'The two of you shared a room at the Le Moulin du Roc for three nights just before your pre-season work began.'

'Oh. You know about that?' Bruno raised an eyebrow. The question didn't merit an answer. 'We try to be discreet, make sure our colleagues don't find out. Don't want it changing the way we all work together as a team.'

'And what did you do on this minibreak? Besides the obvious.'

'We hardly left the room, the hotel will confirm that if you ask. We ran up a hefty room-service bill, appeared in the bar once or twice, and were otherwise occupied in our room.'

'Thank you, Monsieur Gosselin, that will be all for now. Remember – you're not to discuss this, not even among the crew.' Bruno escorted Sébastien to the tent where the rest of his team was now assembled, all tapping away at keyboards, to collect their next subject. 'Marion Perrin? Kindly come with me.'

On their way to the portacabin, where it was Fabien's turn to sit and interview while Bruno stood and watched, Marion asked after Balzac. It was for this very reason that he and Fabien had decided to swap roles; Bruno had admitted to liking the young woman during their brief exchange on Fauquet's terrace and didn't want to prejudice the questioning in any way.

When questioned by Fabien, Marion's story about the lovers' getaway was identical to Gosselin's, and Bruno saw no reason to disbelieve either of them. She rode a moped; she regularly drove all manner of crew vehicles and had no specific recollection of any out-of-hours use of anything relating to the production. Alain Dennel said the same, as did the next five members of the production team. Everyone had access to the Peugeot, and no one would admit to any form of after-hours joyriding. Noémie Lavigne was the last to be interviewed.

'And your holiday in St Cyprien?' Fabien asked. 'Is there anyone who can account for your movements during the trip?'

Noemie was strikingly pale, a curtain of white-blonde hair almost matching her skin. She shook her head, her eyes strobing in and out of view behind her fringe. 'Not for the whole thing, no. I met up with friends a few times for dinner, but mostly I was on my own.'

'And what were you doing? You booked the accommodation privately, so it doesn't sound like work.'

She blushed, and against her pale skin her cheeks glowed a deeper pink. 'Is this confidential? From the rest of the crew, I mean.'

Fabien nodded. 'But we can't guarantee that what you say here wouldn't eventually come out in court, were it deemed relevant to the case.'

'I told them I was visiting friends and family. It's partly true, and I did grow up not too far from here. But I'm working on a book. My editor sent me a pile of changes, and I thought if I could hole up in the countryside for a few weeks before work got going, I'd be able to bash out the next draft without any distractions.'

'Understood,' said Fabien. 'But could you please give us contact details for your editor? Your draft could account for some of your movements, time stamps on your document history cross-referenced with the location data of your devices.'

'Not a problem.' Noemie took her phone from her pocket and started scrolling through her recent contacts.

'While you're doing that, could you also put together a list of your dinner reservations, and contact details for the people you met?' Fabien made a note on his phone. 'We might be able to eliminate you entirely.'

After finishing with Noémie Lavigne, Bruno and Fabien handed the portacabin back to the group.

'What do you reckon?' Fabien waited until he was buckled up in the passenger seat of the Land Rover before asking for Bruno's opinion. 'Should we get a warrant so we can ask France Telecom to start matching phones to cell towers?'

'Why don't you call J-J while I'm driving,' said Bruno. 'See if he can get one arranged. I would prioritize the four: Gosselin, Lavigne, Dennel and Perrin.'

Fabien took out his phone, but before calling J-J he read out Gabrielle's latest update, which had arrived while they were walking back to the car. 'Here's an interesting detail for you – Marion Perrin is married. Several times, in fact. And none of them to Sébastien Gosselin. Gabrielle is running searches on her previous names, including her maiden name.' He looked up. 'That puts rather a different spin on their lovers' getaway, don't you think?'

Bruno raised an eyebrow. 'We shouldn't jump to conclusions – she and her husband might be divorced, separated, even polyamorous. Marriage isn't the institution it once was.'

'I'm surprised you've heard of polyamory.'

'Why, because I'm in my forties? People did have sex before you were born, you know – your generation hardly invented it.'

Fabien rolled his eyes. 'By the way, did you know that virginity is hereditary? If your parents didn't have sex, you won't either.' It took a second, and then Bruno erupted in laughter.

'I'd not heard that one before, it's woefully bad.'

'And not wrong! No, I wasn't implying anything about your age, I just didn't think that polycules had made it this deep into France.'

'You'd be surprised at the different ways people find to amuse themselves during our long winters. Stick around and you might find out.' Bruno turned briefly to grin at him. 'I've made it sound like there's a hotbed of swingers in St Denis. If that's the case, I know nothing of it.'

18

Thursday was a particularly frustrating day in the office – or out of it, given that Bruno and Fabien had been back on set, where they once again commandeered the production portacabin as a temporary interview suite. First on the day's list had been the final two members of Odelie's team, neither of whom had been on the site rota during their previous visit. Their stories were very like their colleagues', and so the two policemen finished interviewing the eleven people they knew to have been in the Périgord during what Bruno was calling 'the stalking window' without any fresh leads. There was nothing for it but to cast a wider net – one that encompassed nearly eighty names.

'How do you propose we should break this list down? I'm not coming up with any bright ideas on who to prioritize.' Fabien's body language spoke his frustration as he hunched over the small table.

'Why don't we start with hair, make-up and wardrobe?' Bruno suggested. 'If what I've read about Hollywood is true they should be the people on set likely to know the most gossip.'

'It's as good a place as any to begin, I suppose.' Fabien ran his finger down the columns of the printed call sheets. 'Head of wardrobe is Dione Baudin, let's start with her.'

Baudin was not the gossip of silver screen cliché, but the wardrobe mistress turned out to be a useful interview nonetheless. While she had little to offer about unauthorized use of production vehicles, she was able to tell them that everyone from the make-up and wardrobe teams had travelled down together from Paris on the same coach, and were being ferried between set and the crew hotel in a series of minivans, none of the contractors meriting their own vehicle. According to Baudin, the hotel bar was full of carousing crew every night, there being nothing else to do in the vicinity, but it would be impossible for anyone to know who was where when.

'The hotel, it's in the middle of nowhere. One of those awful motorway places where the entire room and bathroom are made from one piece of moulded plastic and the only food comes out of a vending machine.' She grimaced. 'No one could get in or out without a taxi. Maybe reception could tell you if anyone's been ordering cabs.'

Fabien had left for Périgueux and the dinner date he'd arranged with Gabrielle Teyssier two hours previously, after securing J-J's blessing to request a warrant to obtain the four mobiles, and then what felt like hours on the phone to brief France Telecom. Bruno had dropped him off at the station in Le Buisson, from where he could get a fast train direct to Périgueux. While St Denis still boasted its own railway line, budget cuts over the past decade meant that there were only two trains a day that went to Périgueux, neither of which was at a time that was of much use to commuters. Privately, Bruno felt that this poor approach to scheduling was one of the reasons the train company was struggling to make a profit, but he was wise enough to know that one did not publicly question the decisions of the French railway unions, nor of the communists who had traditionally controlled them.

Bruno had his own date to get ready for, presuming that Laura kept her promise. He took extra care with his toilette, checking that his nails were tidy before dabbing on aftershave. Given the recent spell of warm weather he elected to forego a jacket, and instead rolled his shirtsleeves up to just below the elbow; more than one woman of his acquaintance had confessed to finding a man's forearms the sexiest part of the male body. If circumstances had been ideal Bruno would've collected Laura and driven her to the restaurant but, given that she would need her car in the morning and he had no intention of completing a round trip to Sarlat before dawn, the two of them had agreed to meet at the bistro Laura had chosen.

Le Bistrot du Marché was a new business, open for two or three months, the latest attempt to make a success of a small corner building in Limeuil that had yet to find the right occupant. It was Bruno's first visit, but the place was on his radar – Pamela had been for dinner shortly after the restaurant opened, and had said they must go, while Stéphane had mentioned supplying the cheese.

He parked his Land Rover in the car park by the bridge and looked for Laura's vehicle, but if she'd arrived before him she must have left her car elsewhere. As Bruno approached the *bistrot* he could see candlelight glowing through the windows of a room with high ceilings and stone walls that looked more inviting than imposing. Opening the door, he was hit with a wave of clinking cutlery, low conversation, laughter, and quiet jazz playing beneath the buzz. He smelled garlic, fat, and roasting meats, and his stomach rumbled in response.

Happily, he spied Laura at a corner table, her face soft in the candlelight. He raised a hand, and she stood to meet him, stunning in a simple shift dress and chunky necklace.

'Bruno, you have to excuse me. I've come straight from the office, I must look a fright.'

He took her into his arms and placed a kiss on each cheek. 'You look wonderful. I'm so happy we could do this.'

They took their seats and Laura asked, 'Do you know this place?'

Bruno shook his head. 'Some friends have eaten here, but this is my first visit.'

'And mine. Two of my colleagues came a couple of weeks ago; they've been raving about it ever since. But enough about that. How are you? How have you been?' She reached across the table and placed her hand on his. 'I've missed you. I'm sorry I've had to work so much. I can't imagine how let down you must have been feeling lately, and not just by me. That was nasty business at the market.'

'It was. But it needed to be said, so it's not all bad.' He smiled, but the memory of his shunning still felt like a bruise. On his phone sat a reminder to schedule a meeting with the stall-holders, both *mea culpa* and atonement. There was still a lot of ground to make up, he knew. 'Have you had a chance to look at the menu?'

'*Salade des gésiers* for me. I can't resist ordering it when I see it.'

'Which in this part of the world means you order it most days?'

Bruno teased. 'I don't blame you – when done well gizzards are so tasty, unbeatable in a warm salad.'

'And what are you having?'

'*Poisson du jour* for me, I'm in the mood for something light. But shall we share a cheese plate afterwards? The supplier is a good friend of mine.'

'Cheese is my favourite thing. You will get no complaints from me! Does your friend make cheeses, or just sell them?'

Bruno launched into a speech about the virtues of Stéphane's Tomme d'Audrix and the many uses of *aillou* that only ended when the waiter came to take their order. 'Sorry, I must have been boring you.'

'Not at all. Passion is attractive.'

'Even passion for cheese?' Bruno laughed.

'You jest, but to me a passion for food implies a passion for life and a generosity of spirit. Do you agree?'

'Absolutely. So how are things at the *conciergerie*? Taking tonight off isn't going to cause you any problems?'

She shrugged. 'Sisyphean? Never-ending? I thought I was an equal partner in the business before Monique died, but clearly she was carrying much more of the load than any of us appreciated.' She smiled. 'Which isn't to say it's not satisfying, but my god is it hard work.'

'You're telling me! I thought a murder investigation was about as time-consuming as it gets. But the challenge of managing the leisure time of the rich and famous beats it if your schedule is anything to go by.'

Bruno had aimed for a light-hearted tone, but the look on Laura's face told him he'd misfired.

'Are you disparaging my business?'

'Of course not—'

'The salaries I pay, the employment I provide, the money I bring to this community? Managing leisure time? Is that what you think I do?' Laura hissed, her volume low but her body language loud and clear. Despite her attempt at discretion, several pairs of eyes had turned to their table.

'Of course not,' he repeated, raising his hands in surrender. 'And I didn't mean to suggest otherwise. The *conciergerie* is serious business, I know that. I was trying to convey my sympathy and admiration for the twenty-four-hour service you provide. It just didn't land as intended.'

The beast soothed, work chat carried on as they waited for their food, Laura updating Bruno on changes she hoped to make to the business to increase growth and revenues. But as he listened Bruno felt his heart sink. Every word coming out of Laura's mouth sounded like another hour she wouldn't be able to spend with him, and the fish, a beautiful fillet of grilled river trout, failed to raise his spirits.

But before the fine cheese selection arrived the atmosphere changed. Under the table he felt what he certainly hoped was Laura's foot start to caress his calf, and he smiled encouragingly, grateful for whatever form of attention she was happy to bestow. Laura ate her cheese ostentatiously, licking her fingers and holding his eyes, and it wasn't long before they asked to settle the bill and raced back to St Denis as quickly as the law would allow.

When Bruno picked up Fabien at Le Buisson station on Friday morning he was in excellent spirits. His evening with Laura had turned into another sleepover, their second of the week. Before she left for work early that morning they had shared a rather drawn-out kiss and muttered promises of many more kisses to come, and another date the following evening. Bruno felt a renewed sense of optimism.

He pulled into the station car park a few minutes before Fabien's train was due and decided to take Balzac to meet him on the platform. Balzac took his time sniffing his way across the car park and through the station, and even though the train pulled in two minutes behind schedule they had only just reached the platform when the bell started ringing to announce the closing of the level crossing a hundred metres or so further along the track.

Fabien was one of the first off, jumping onto the platform and swinging a large backpack onto his shoulder, the smile on his face even bigger than Bruno's.

'Bruno! Balzac! I assumed you'd be waiting for me in the car.'

He dropped to a squat and received a hero's welcome from the dog, who was baying furiously and whipping up a storm with his tail. 'Yes I missed you too, I did, you're such a fine fellow.' Fabien buried his face into the folds of fur around Balzac's neck as he gave the dog a big hug. 'Your dog has got me wrapped around his little finger, Bruno. I'm not sure I can imagine life without him around me.'

Bruno grinned. 'Exactly what happened to me when I first met his predecessor, my beloved Gigi. I have bred Balzac before – perhaps you'd like to put your name down for one of his next litter?'

Fabien smiled. 'We'll see. I'm not sure anyone could live up to the high standard you set, could they, Balzac? Not even your own offspring.' He stood up and brushed himself down before picking up the backpack. 'Lucky that I brought clothes back from my flat, you've got me covered in hair and dusty pawprints.'

'How was your dinner? Did Gabrielle enjoy Le Bouteille Bleu?'

'She said so, but you've seen how little she eats. Just the soup, a small piece of fish.'

'You couldn't convince her to share a dessert? That's a shame, the *chef pâtissier* there has real talent.'

'Something better than dessert, though – she's got her own contacts at France Telecom, and they're going to send her the phone data so she can analyse it herself.'

'Isn't she rather busy?'

'Yes, but she wants to test a new programme she's working on, and this is the perfect data set. It looks at Bluetooth connectivity in league with tower data, and she thinks that when it's up and running she'll be able to cross reference it with existing databases to identify the owners of unregistered and burner phones, as well as any linked devices – smartwatches, wireless headphones, sport trackers, that kind of thing.'

'Interesting. Well, if France Telecom are okay with sharing the data,' said Bruno, 'I certainly have no objections. Let me know what she finds. Are you happy to lead on that going forward since you had an in-depth briefing over dinner?' He grinned.

'I'd be more than happy to. If she finds anything, that is.'

'Not if, when. She'll make it happen, I promise you.' Before putting the key in the ignition Bruno turned to look at Fabien. 'Did you have breakfast, or should I stop at the *boulangerie*?'

'I've eaten, thank you. Are we going to your office, or mine?'

'The gendarmerie, I think. Once the France Telecom data has come in and we've had a chance to analyse it, we might need to summon some additional muscle in order to make an arrest. Or arrests.'

Fabien nodded. 'Makes sense. So is there an ETA from France Telecom on the data?'

'This morning, but that could mean anything from now till one p.m. Can you ask Gabrielle if her contacts are working any faster, or if they're even working together? Wouldn't surprise me if we have two separate requests cancelling each other out.'

A few taps on the screen of his phone, a short buzz, and Fabien looked up. 'You're both working with the same people, but she was told in a couple of hours, in theory.'

Ninety-five minutes later Fabien's phone buzzed with an incoming message.

'Gabrielle's got the location data through from France Telecom.'

Bruno checked his emails. 'So do we. So now what? She's going to run it through her programme and get back to us?'

'Yes. And while we wait for however long that takes, we'll start going through it here. I thought about getting Annette to help out.'

'Good call. I'll get Yveline to send her up.'

It only took a few minutes before the three of them were assembled in Fabien's temporary office.

'Right, what we're looking for is regular occurrences of any one of these numbers pinging off these three towers between seven and nine in the morning, and between five and nine in the evening during the two weeks before Easter. Annette, can you go through the list of numbers that pinged the towers closest to Pamela's in the two-hour window around the murder and see if any of the crew mobiles appear.'

'*Oui, chef.*'

Bruno wrote down the phone numbers and tower IDs on the whiteboard in large print, and then divided the France Telecom printouts into three piles. 'There's a fresh pack of highlighters for you to use there.' Annette reached out to grab a pen, and something on her wrist caught his attention.

'Annette, is that a smartwatch you're wearing?'

'*Oui, chef.*'

'And it tracks what? Your workouts, your steps?'

She nodded. 'And my running routes, my personal bests, all sorts of data. On the app it even compiles monthly reports so I can monitor my progress.'

'Do you have to connect it to your phone, or would it store the data anyway?'

Annette shrugged. 'I'm not sure. But I can Google it?'

Bruno was pleased to note that Fabien was already on the phone to Gabrielle. 'Yup, any associated devices. Smartwatches, pedometers, wireless earbuds. Maybe those AirTag things people put on their keys or their luggage. Anything that has ever been connected to an account linked to an email address used by anyone in the data you just sent over.' A pause. 'Thanks.' He looked up at Bruno. 'Gabrielle's on it. Nothing for us to do but get back to work.'

About twenty minutes into their grunt work and Bruno's eyes were starting to swim. When Fabien's phone buzzed it made for a welcome distraction. 'It's Gabrielle. Maybe she's found something. Gabrielle, *salut*,' he went on. 'Okay, hang on – I'm going to put you on speaker.' Bruno and Annette stopped what they were doing to listen.

'So the short version,' said Gabrielle, 'is that my programme looks like it's working. I've been able to use my code to strip out the phones that pinged alone from those numbers that pinged in groups. All the phones linked to the names you've told me are the location scouts have set off practically every cell tower in the Dordogne, but most of those data points occur in groups of seven or more. So it looks to me like those will be genuine scouting trips, team meetings, that sort of thing, and I'm discounting them for the moment. But when I stripped out the phones that had only pinged those towers alone, we're down to six numbers.'

'Which six?' asked Bruno, notebook at the ready.

'I've got three from production: Marion Perrin, Odelie Marchant and Sébastien Gosselin. Two from security: Séverin Leclair and Roul Beauchêne. The last number belongs to the assistant director, Fleur Parris.'

'So if I understand your programme––'

'If my programme is working correctly, a big if!' Gabrielle interrupted. 'This is the first time I've tested the code on a data set, I'm not sure these results would hold up in court.'

'Okay, but if I've understood your programme and if it's working as intended, we have six people whose location data shows them to have regularly been near the retirement home in St Denis, and near Pamela's riding school, in the morning and evening windows we are interested in, correct?'

'Correct.'

'And each of these six people appears to have been within

range of the relevant cell towers while they were alone, unaccompanied by other members of the cast and crew.'

'Correct. None of their phones pinged a tower within the same fifteen-minute window as any other.'

'Thank you, Gabrielle. But please could you double-check your data, just to be sure we're not being misled by it.'

'Of course, Bruno. Any doubts and I'll be in touch. I'm working as fast as I can to get the connected device data Fabien requested, prioritizing these six names. It'll be with you the moment I have it.'

Fabien ended the call. 'Sounds like it's time to call our six friends into the station for more formal interviews.'

19

The interview suite at St Denis police station was much like every interview suite in every police station anywhere in the world, in that it was almost entirely featureless. The room had no windows and was lit by the harsh blueish buzz of overhead fluorescent lighting, giving everyone a consumptive air whatever their natural complexion. There were several red eyes of CCTV cameras placed about the room to record what was going on.

The walls might once have been described as vanilla, but these days they were more a greige network of scuffs and smudges, the only decor a small poster directing people to the nearest exits in the event of fire. Bruno and Fabien sat at one side of the lightweight aluminium table, bolted to the floor, on which stood a small recording device. On the other side of the table, on a stool that was also secured in place, sat Roul Beauchêne.

Bruno recognized him as the giant who had directed them to a parking space during their first visit to the set. 'Roul. Thank you for coming in.'

'I wasn't aware I had much of a choice.' His tone was friendlier than his words.

'Roul,' Bruno continued, 'we have data that puts your phone at or near several places we're interested in, at times we're interested in, and I was hoping you could answer some questions about your movements on specific days?'

'Would it be all right if I used my phone to remind me? I've got a terrible memory, but it's all on here somewhere.'

'Of course.' As Roul reached into his pocket, Bruno took out his notebook, scribbled quickly, and tore off the top sheet, folding it in half. He pressed a button in the middle of the table, and seconds later an officer was at the door.

'You rang, chief?' Bruno held out the note, and the officer took it, leaving the room.

'To begin with, when did you first come down here to start work for the current season?'

'About a week before filming began. I had to make security arrangements, do risk assessments of any outside sets, that sort of thing.'

'So, since the beginning of April?'

'Sounds about right. Could have been the tail end of March, but around then. Would you like me to check?'

'In a minute. And what's your role on the production? I know you're head of security, what does that mean?'

'It means I manage the team of security guards who work to keep the sets safe, clear from fans or members of the public wandering through shots. From a management perspective it's the same as any team – scheduling, disputes, that sort of thing. And then I'm also responsible for conducting security assessments of the exterior sets, making sure we can keep our cast and crew safe while they're working.'

Bruno nodded. 'And how much of this role takes you off site?'

'Oh, that very much depends where I'm needed. I'd say I spend ninety per cent of my time wherever we're filming, and maybe ten per cent doing recces of outdoor locations before we film there, helping the location crew decide between potential sites.'

'Have you been doing much of that on this project?'

Roul shrugged. 'Some. There's been a bit more than you'd expect over the past two or three weeks; they've had a few late dropouts to deal with, so I've been dividing the work with my assistant, Séverin Leclair.' Bruno nodded, Leclair was next on the list to be interviewed.

'Three evenings in a row we have noted your phone pinging in the vicinity of a riding school near the town of St Denis. This would be the first week in April, so two weeks before Easter. Any idea what you might have been doing up there?'

Roul shook his head. 'Not off the top of my head, no. What dates would we be looking at?' He tapped away at his phone and looked up expectantly.

'The fifth, sixth and seventh of April, after five o'clock.'

'I was doing security runs.'

'Security runs?'

'One of the leads on the show decided she wanted to stay in a farmhouse up in the hills, rather than at the hotel with the rest of the cast.' He raised an eyebrow. 'Little miss popular she isn't. Anyway, before the production could okay it with insurance, I had to run an assessment of the property, check out the surrounding area at different times.' He held out his phone. 'If you look at my timeline history, I ran the same route a dozen more times that week at various times of the day and night.'

*

While they waited for Séverin Leclair to arrive, Fabien asked Bruno what had been in the note he'd delivered at the start of their interview with Beauchêne.

'I've initiated a request for a judge's order so that we can subpoena Google and Apple for all their maps data, in case any of them don't want to hand it over willingly. I know it can be a slow process getting permission, so I thought that the sooner we got it under way, the better.'

Fabien nodded. 'Let's hope they're all as free and easy with their phones as Beauchêne was.'

'He clearly felt that he had nothing to hide. It'll be interesting to see if that holds.'

At that moment the door to the interview suite opened and Séverin Leclair was escorted into the room. Like his boss, the security guard had a physique built for action, and a face that had taken more than a few knocks. Bruno would not be surprised to learn that Monsieur Leclair had served in the military at some point. He smiled, exposing a top row of teeth constructed entirely from what looked like gold. 'I hope I've not kept you waiting long.' He leaned across the table extending his hand, and Bruno saw no harm in shaking it. 'Séverin Leclair.'

'Bruno Courrèges, and this is my partner, Fabien Panton. Please take a seat. Now, Monsieur Leclair—'

'Please, call me Séverin.'

'Very well, Séverin. Your phone has connected you with a few locations we're interested in. We've asked you here so that you can explain what you were doing.'

Séverin nodded. 'Anything to help.'

'You work under Roul on the security team, correct?' A nod. 'Aloud for the tape, please.'

'Correct.'

'And what are your duties?'

'I'm on-site lead. Whenever Roul is off-set, I'm in charge of the security team, and if he needs help with scheduling or whatever, I'm back-up.'

'So your duties don't take you off the main set?'

'Not typically, no.'

'Then could you please explain why we have a nightly record of your phone pinging cell towers in our area of interest for a period of more than two weeks?'

Bruno hadn't expected the man in front of them to laugh but laugh he did.

'I'm seeing Fanny's PA.'

'Fanny La Fey?' Fabien asked.

'Yes. Fanny's been staying away from the cast and crew at a farmhouse up in the hills, and my girlfriend is living with her in one of the cottages. I'm up there pretty much every night, back at the crew hotel as the sun's coming up.'

'And your girlfriend will vouch for you?'

'She will. And so will my phone. I don't know what search window you've been looking at, but I was up there last night, and the night before.'

Bruno wrote another note and rang the buzzer. This time it was Jules who came to the door. 'Could you follow up on this with the tech team?'

Séverin answered their questions without any fuss and shared his maps data for further corroboration. Ten minutes later

Gabrielle Teyssier confirmed that his pings had continued long past the Taun murder, and he was being escorted back out the door.

Bruno hadn't had any particular preconceptions about the sort of woman that assistant director Fleur Parris would turn out to be, but the person sitting before him certainly wasn't what he'd expected. She was tiny, one-forty-five centimetres at most, with a shock of thick auburn hair cut in a style not unlike Fabien's. She beamed at him as she took her seat, grabbing her fringe with her fist. 'Twins!' A collection of plastic bracelets in a riot of colours, some chunky and others thin as wire, clattered at her wrist with the movement.

Fabien gave a tight smile in response. 'Twins.'

Even sitting still, the woman in front of them crackled with suppressed energy. Bruno thought she must be a force to be reckoned with on set, someone more than capable of keeping many balls in the air at once. He repeated his spiel about her phone having linked her with sites they were interested in, and she launched into a long speech about the many and varied duties of an assistant director, which seemed to involve an awful lot more assisting than it did any sort of directing.

By her own account, Mademoiselle Parris had been sent here, there and everywhere at all hours of the day and night, dropping off dry-cleaning and picking up prescriptions, collecting special lunches from the area's top restaurants – lunches that often went uneaten, and were never offered to her. From the sounds of it, Bruno didn't think she would have had the time to stalk Joséphine Taun, unless the director added it to her list of duties, in which case he had no doubt that Fleur Parris would have found a way to do whatever was required.

But he persisted with the interview nonetheless. Parris appeared to have a sharp memory and answered his questions with an ease that did not strike Bruno as practised. While the location data from her phone, which she willingly handed over, would no doubt have its own stories to tell, for the moment his gut instinct was that Fleur Parris was not the killer they were looking for. If nothing else, she was far too short to have inflicted the fatal blows.

For the second time, Bruno let Fabien take the lead when it came to interviewing Marion Perrin, lest his liking for the young woman prejudice their investigation in any way. She handed over her mobile phone without argument, and Fabien gave it to a tech officer to strip off the relevant data for Gabrielle. It was a fairly quick process, and Marion's phone would be back with her before the interview was complete, barring anything unforeseen.

So far the interview had been progressing not well exactly, but not – technically – badly. Every question had been responded to with a non-answer, nothing to say she was being deliberately obstructive, but nothing of substance either.

To Bruno, she somehow seemed too at ease. Marion Perrin was as relaxed in the interview suite as she had been on Fauquet's sun-soaked terrace, and that alone gave him pause for thought. Police interview suites were designed to be stressful environments, and almost everyone who walked through the door, no matter how innocent, tended to react to the room in some way. But not Marion.

Whereas Fleur Parris had answered their questions with a fluidity that seemed entirely natural, there was a silky sheen to Marion's replies, a polish that didn't quite ring true.

'And the regular early mornings in St Denis?' asked Fabien. 'Can you explain those?'

She shrugged, examining a cuticle. 'I like to have a little time to myself before the day begins, a few moments of calm before the chaos of a long shift.' She put her hands to her shoulders and rolled them, and whether it was studied insouciance or a genuine need to move, Bruno couldn't tell.

'And did you used to stop anywhere, buy a coffee, perhaps?'

She shook her head. 'Just rode around, took in the scenery, let the wind rush through my brain. I'm sure you know what it's like.'

Fabien nodded. 'Our data sets clearly have you stopping at several points around town. Would you like to tell us what they were, or would you like to wait until we get the information from your phone before carrying on this conversation?'

'That's fine. I'm happy to wait.'

Odelie Marchant smiled grimly at the two officers as she sat down, smoothing out the fabric of her skirt to avoid wrinkles. 'I know you've got to keep up appearances, but was it really necessary to haul me into the station for a formal interview?'

'Yes, Odelie, I'm afraid it is.' She slouched back in her chair, the wind taken out of her sails. 'Your phone data has confirmed you as a person of interest, and we're going to need you to justify your movements for the periods in question.'

She sat up straight again, eye contact unbroken. 'But surely you can't think that I had anything to do with it. Do I need a lawyer?'

'I'm not allowed to advise you on that front, but I can offer you the services of a lawyer if you'd like one. We'd have to postpone the interview till their arrival, if you don't mind waiting?'

She shook her head. 'May as well get this over with, I've not done anything wrong anyway. What is it that you need to know?'

Sébastien Gosselin was no less arrogant on a second meeting, and Bruno hoped to be able to get the interview over and done with quickly. But he hadn't accounted for Gosselin's flair for drama – the man's talents were clearly wasted in accounts if the way he huffed and puffed through a series of simple questions was any indication.

He took his time confirming his name and profession and claimed not to remember anything of his movements over the past few weeks beyond saying his life had been an endless circle between the site office and the hotel, each day blurring into one incoherent mass. Which may well have been the case; Bruno's army days meant he was all too familiar with the drudgery of routine.

It didn't surprise Bruno in the least that Gosselin was the only one to refuse to hand over his phone without a subpoena. The young man flounced – there was no other word for it – out of the interview suite muttering things like 'EU' and 'data protection' and 'helping with your inquiries, *putain*.' Bruno didn't think he was the killer, although he really rather hoped he was, just so he could have the pleasure of locking him up for a night or two.

20

By the time Saturday night rolled around Bruno was more than ready to spend a few hours away from the case with Laura. During the day he kept checking his phone in case she'd messaged him to cancel, but around seven p.m. he received a text saying she was on her way to the restaurant and couldn't wait to see him.

They were meeting at a spot Bruno knew well: an old converted farmhouse roughly halfway between their two homes, which was owned by an artist and self-taught chef who spent considerably more time on the audacious sculptures decorating his business and garden than he did the food on the plates. But it was a romantic spot if one chose the right table, twinkling fairy lights wrapped around an orchard of trees, through which peeked the artist/chef's other-worldly sculptures.

Bruno arrived before Laura, and ordered a bottle of sparkling water for their table. With both of them driving tonight, it was only right that he wait for his date to arrive before deciding on wine for the meal. There was no menu to speak of; the owner, Arthur, cooked what he felt like making on the day and that was what you had. His repertoire consisted of simple but well-executed dishes; slow-cooked stews and casseroles in the winter, and grilled fare in the summer. Bruno had never eaten here in the spring and wasn't sure what to expect.

'You beat me!' Laura arrived, a faint waft of perfume in her wake. 'I was sure I'd get here first, but then I got stuck behind a tractor.'

Bruno rose to give her a kiss. 'You look marvellous.' In truth he hadn't taken in what she was wearing; the glow in her eyes and the warmth of her smile were all it took to convince him he was dining with the most beautiful woman in the world.

They took their seats, and Arthur came over with their water. 'Any wine for you this evening?'

Bruno cocked his head at Laura, who nodded. 'What's on the menu tonight?' he asked Arthur.

'To start, a vichyssoise. Then grilled black bass, caught in the Dordogne this morning and served with herbed new potatoes. For dessert, I have a selection of cheeses and a *tarte aux pommes*.'

'Sounds like we'll be drinking white. What have you got?'

Arthur reeled off a list of bottles, from which Bruno chose the 2023 Château Le Raz, which he knew to have won several awards. The vineyard's Ter'Raz red was a particular favourite, and he was curious to branch out into their other wines. Laura nodded her assent.

Once Arthur had departed for the kitchen, Bruno asked after George Sand, Laura's basset, and he hoped a future breeding partner for Balzac.

'She's the only thing that's been keeping me sane these past few weeks. I can't even begin to explain what it's been like at work.' Laura sat back in her chair and sighed. 'I know she's probably better off in a garden than she is in the office with me, but the respite I get when I take her out for a short stroll is the only thing between me and meltdown.'

'Does it have to be so stressful? Can't you hand over some of the work to one of the other partners?'

A brittle laugh. 'If only. It feels like I spend half my time refereeing power struggles among the team. Deciding where to move offices ignited a civil war. Or an uncivil war, more like. If I assigned some of my clients to someone else it would be viewed as favouritism and set off another skirmish.

'And then there are the clients. Losing Monique was a blow in so many ways – she had a knack for the personal touch, and I'm sure our clients can feel the difference. And if we're not offering the same level of service we did, is this even the right time to think about new offices, about expanding?' She looked Bruno in the eye. 'You can see I've got a lot on my plate.'

'Do you want to vent, or do you want suggestions? I can do my best to provide either.'

She smiled. 'That's very sweet of you, Bruno. I suppose I'm mostly venting, but if you happen to have any bright ideas, I'm all ears.'

Arthur turned up bearing a tray loaded with their soups, their wine, and an ice bucket, which bought Bruno some thinking time before he replied.

'The problem as I see it isn't the running of the business. Everything you can control, you have under control. And all of the random incidents, from burst pipes to arranging last-minute anniversary dinners, you can't plan for but have to respond to. But even there, you've got your systems in place: you're as covered as you can be. The two areas causing the most trouble are client care and managing the team, correct?'

'Go on,' said Laura.

'Maybe the solution lies in hiring someone to take on the managerial and client work that Monique used to do. You were always the one doing the behind-the-scenes heavy lifting, not the front-facing work. Perhaps trying to do both is a bit much?'

Bruno felt the mood shift before he'd even realized he'd erred. Across the table, Laura's eyes narrowed and her shoulders shifted back a degree as she straightened her spine. 'Are you suggesting I'm not up to the task?' Her voice chilled Bruno's wine.

'Not at all! I'm—'

'Because not only am I *perfectly capable*, but I owe it to Monique to ensure the continued success of her business. Her legacy.'

'Of course, and I didn't mean to imply otherwise. I just thought it would help your work–life balance to bring in an expert—' This time Bruno knew he'd said the wrong thing before he'd finished the sentence, and he was cut off.

'An *expert*?' Laura got to her feet and put her napkin down on the table. 'You have no idea how hard it was to carve out this evening with you, how early I had to be in the office this morning to make sure we could spend time together, especially after the other night. You're important to me, Bruno, but so is my business and it's been a part of my life considerably longer than you have. I will not waste my precious free time listening to you disrespect me.'

She turned to leave, and Bruno grabbed her arm. 'Laura, please sit. I didn't mean to upset you or disrespect you. I was just trying to think of ways of making this transition easier on you. And on me. I don't like spending my suppers alone, waking up in an empty bed.' He stood up, hoping to see a softening in her eyes.

'And what about me? Do you think I've not considered the possibilities of life as the partner of a policeman? Of the nights when you're out working and I won't know if you're safe until you're lying in bed beside me? I've seen your scars, Bruno. I was there when the man with the gun attacked you in your garden. You might lose me to my work in the figurative sense, but I could lose you in a very literal sense!' By the end of this speech, her cheeks were flushed and her nostrils flaring.

Bruno took a step forward, hoping to reassure her, but she drew back. 'Please don't!' She turned on her heel and began to walk away, before looking over her shoulder to say, 'Don't phone me. I will call you when I'm good and ready.'

Bruno was thoroughly depressed about the way things had ended – for good? – with Laura on Saturday night. Sensing his master's low mood, Balzac had scarcely left Bruno's side since he returned downhearted from his date. Having spent Sunday morning moping, in the afternoon he made for the riding school, where he hoped to get Hector out on his own for a gallop, leaving Balzac to nose around in the horse's stall.

It was not to be – as soon as he got out of the car he was accosted by Miranda's two children, who demanded he join them in the swimming pool. There was nothing for it but to go with the flow, so Bruno changed into a spare pair of trunks he kept at Pamela's for this very purpose and hoped that the children's company would provide a distraction from his woes. While he was able to turn his thoughts away from Laura to some degree, simply being in the children's presence was causing Bruno no small degree of pain, their every laugh a pointed question as to the likelihood of having his own one day.

After, he tried to distract himself by telling Pamela all about the market shunning and Stéphane's subsequent warning that the old guard were feeling hard done by, but if Bruno was expecting tea and sympathy he had turned to the wrong friend.

'I don't mean to be harsh, dear Bruno, but are you really surprised?' He furrowed his brow, and she went on. 'This is exactly what happened with Xavier and Mirabelle. You spotted a problem in their marriage and decided to solve it, charging in without asking those involved if it was what they wanted.' She sighed. '*Surely* you see the similarities?'

Bruno was forced to concede that he did and drove home in a reflective mood. In the early evening he decided there was nothing for it but to go for a long run. Time to blow out the cobwebs and get his blood moving, because even if it didn't make his heart feel any better it would certainly do his body good.

After a quick stretching session on the *potager* wall, he whistled for Balzac and set off for the forest at a light jog, enjoying the sensation of his toes pushing the ground backwards as he pressed on upwards. It took a few hundred metres before he found his stride, and he began to accelerate, feet pounding and heart pumping as the incline grew steeper. After a kilometre, most of it uphill, he could feel his muscles start to flood with increased blood flow, and he concentrated on breathing efficiently, inhaling through his nose and pushing the air out from his lungs.

At the ridgeline, the path forked left and right, and he chose to take the road more travelled, where the forest thinned out and gave way to some of the most glorious views the Périgord had to offer. He could hear Balzac's paws thudding on the soil behind him, and he slowed his pace slightly. Below, on the edges of the river, he could see workers at the holiday camp laying out canoes on the grass. From somewhere, he caught a quick waft of barbecue that disappeared on the wind. Bruno soaked in the view, delighting equally in the evening sun warming his skin and the light breeze keeping him just the right side of hot.

He ran on, and his mind kept turning to Laura. When would she call? *Would* she call? He knew he'd mis-stepped the night before. But however he looked at it, her reaction was extreme. He'd apologized, she'd marched out. And now there was nothing he could do but be patient. Perhaps this was another case of right woman, wrong time. He stopped, and at his feet Balzac dropped to the ground in his shade, panting heavily.

Bruno sat on the ground beside his dog, arranging himself in such a way that the basset still lay in his shade. Ruffling Balzac's velvety ears, he started murmuring to the creature, telling him what a fabulous runner he'd been, that his love was the purest. And then Bruno sat up with a jerk as, suddenly, a thought came to mind.

'Was it revenge, or was it *love*? Or perhaps a mixture of the two? Balzac, *allez*. I need to get back to my phone.' The dog leapt to his feet, his earlier performative panting forgotten, and the two raced back to the house as fast as Balzac's short legs allowed. Bruno was in for a long night of research. There was more to be found in the family tree, he was sure of it.

*

Throwing himself into his work had always proved ample distraction from personal problems in the past, and so on Monday morning Bruno had decided to go in early to pursue the hunch he'd had the previous day. He met Fabien in the gendarmerie a little after seven, where a skeleton staff of overnight officers shuffled through the final moments of their shift. Bruno was sitting at a corner of Fabien's desk that he'd claimed as his own, marking his territory with his police-issue laptop and reading back over the statements from Friday's interviews, when a cry from his fellow officer attracted his attention.

'We've missed something critical.' Fabien lifted his head from his own police-issue laptop. 'The timeline. Why did you choose April the first as the start date for Gabrielle's research? The location scouts have all been here for months. A couple of them never actually left after season three wrapped just before Christmas. We've got more interviews to conduct, more potential stalkers.'

Bruno was distracted, his mind on the research that had occupied his Sunday evening, although he wasn't ready to throw his theory into the ring just yet. 'Sorry, what was that?'

'Our timeline. It's all wrong. We've been trying to place people on the wrong dates. What about the eight members of the production team responsible for location scouting – if our killer works for this show I think it must be one of them.'

'That's not an assumption we can make,' said Bruno. 'Don't forget, Joséphine Taun had only been in the Périgord since early March. Whether or not the crew were around since December is irrelevant.'

'Do we know when her job offer was made?'

'No, but we can find out with a single phone call. Give me a minute.' Bruno rang the retirement home and asked to be put through to the head of nursing. A few questions, and the call was over. 'She was offered the position on the third of March, accepted immediately, and started two weeks later, on the seventeenth.'

'So at least we have a slightly shorter window to work with. Do we know where she was staying between starting at the home and moving in with Pamela?'

'I wasn't involved during the early legwork,' said Bruno. 'You were leading the investigation.'

'True, of course. Annette Fournet will know, I'm sure. I'll get her to dig it out of the case notes.' He rang the detective and explained what he needed. 'She'll check the files and send me the address.'

Bruno nodded. 'With any luck, we'll find a crossover between one of our location scouts and the location in question.'

Fabien raised an eyebrow. 'You put an awful lot of faith in luck.'

Bruno smiled. 'Experience. Luck is as crucial to an investigation as sheer hard work.' He flicked through the pages of his notebook, turning back and forth between two sets of scrawled notes. 'Our final six. Only the three from production are also on the list of location scouts, correct?'

'Correct.'

'And how are you feeling about the others?'

Fabien leaned back in his chair, hands in prayer position under his chin. 'It's only a gut feeling, but I'm reasonably confident we can eliminate both of the security guys, Leclair and Beauchêne.'

Bruno nodded. 'Agreed. They're both far too tall and broad to have been the biker we've got on CCTV, although that doesn't stop either of them from driving the Peugeot.'

'But hadn't we come to the conclusion that our killer was working alone?'

'I think you're right. But we still have to allow for it as a possibility, at least until we can prove otherwise.'

'And Gabrielle's programme isn't good enough for that?'

'Not yet, not where potential burner phones could be involved. What we do know from the France Telecom data is that none of our possible suspects were communicating with each other using their official phones if they were stalking. None of them were communicating at all during our window of time, which is strange, don't you think?'

'How so?'

Bruno gestured at the stacks of highlighted papers on the desk. 'Have you seen how many emails, texts, WhatsApps, phone calls these guys receive in a normal hour? Enough to restock the library at Alexandria. So the silence is suspicious.'

'I see what you mean.'

'I'm rather hoping for some form of *deus ex machina* intervention, a eureka moment in which it all becomes clear. But until that happens, we've still got work to do.'

Fabien grinned. 'Don't you mean *data ex machina*?'

Bruno groaned and shook his head. 'We can't be too reliant on the data – it's not the answer to everything. We still need to rely on old-fashioned police work, on our impressions from the interviews, go over their statements with a fine-toothed comb.'

'I don't disagree. But in this particular case, I think the location data is going to lead us to our killer.'

'I hope you're right,' Bruno said, turning back to his laptop screen, and Fabien did the same.

A quarter of an hour later Bruno raised his head and broke the silence. 'What do you think of Odelie Marchant?'

Fabien looked up. 'She's been very helpful.'

'Too helpful? Should we be suspicious?'

'Isn't our job to always be suspicious?' He shrugged. 'My gut feeling is that she's trustworthy – I don't get the impression that she's playing games, stringing us along.'

'And she was very surprised when we called her in as part of the final six.' A knock at the door revealed Annette Fournet.

'I've come back to help you with the rest of that data, chief,' she said. 'Is this a good time?' Bruno nodded and waved her into the room.

'I'd say more annoyed than surprised,' Fabien responded to Bruno's comment.

Bruno chuckled. 'Initially annoyed but definitely surprised. I'm with you but my gut is telling me she's one of our less likely options, though we can't discount her entirely.'

'Agreed. Fleur Parris. What about her?'

Bruno shook his head. 'I'm convinced it's not her. Where would she find the time? And she's so short.'

'I agree.'

'Which leaves us with Marion Perrin and Sébastien Gosselin. I'd love it to be Gosselin, but I'm not inclined to put him in the frame as the murderer, however much of an ass he comes across.'

'I'd love it to be him too, he's such a prick. But I don't think he could so much as sneeze without boasting about it.' He shook his head. 'And then there was one. Perrin. I know you like her, but what are your policeman's instincts telling you?'

Bruno let out a puff of air before responding.

'Her location data puts her in the frame for both the stalking and the killing. And she's the right height. But I still have my doubts.' He made a face. 'What mainly makes me suspect her is the way she behaved in the interview suite.'

'Too calm by far,' Fabien agreed. 'What did her background check bring up? Has she got a criminal record of any kind, been hauled in after protests or anything?'

Bruno turned to his screen for a few seconds, then shook his head. 'Nothing of the sort. As far as I can tell, that's the first time she's been brought in for an interview.' His eyes returned to the screen.

The internal line rang, and Fabien stood to answer it. He listened in silence for a moment, then, 'Gabrielle, really? You've got to be kidding me. Hold on one second.' He fiddled with the phone. 'I've got you on speaker. You're on the line with me, Bruno, and Annette Fournet, an officer at the gendarmerie here. Could you please repeat what you just told me?'

'Marion Perrin's maiden name is Ventou. My bots finally traced it back from Perrin, via Deschamps and Milau.'

Bruno jumped up from his seat. 'A relative. She's much younger, but could she be Matthieu Ventou's sister?'

'Got it in one,' Gabrielle replied. 'Our records show she's the baby of the family. I'll send over everything I've got on the Ventous to your email.'

Bruno shook his head. 'Marion Perrin. I should have known. Balzac wasn't remotely interested in her attentions.'

Fabien smiled grimly. 'I'm not sure we could put him on the stand as a character witness, don't beat yourself up for missing his signs.'

'Thank you very much for all your support on this case, Gabrielle,' said Bruno. 'I don't think we could have done it without you.' He looked at Fabien. 'We'll need an arrest warrant from the judge.' Turning to Annette, he asked her to round up a team – two cars, to maximize attention. He wanted Marion Perrin to know that this time it would be rather more than helping them with their inquiries.

21

Once again, Marion Perrin was unusually calm for someone who had been picked up by a police officer in a marked vehicle and driven down to the station for questioning. Bruno watched her on the CCTV feed from the interview suite. He had deliberately left her there for more than half an hour with no explanation in order to see how she would react. So far she had been staring, unmoving, at the same blank patch of wall, a neutral expression on her face and her posture apparently relaxed. There was no fidgeting, no nail-biting, no hand-twisting, just an outward sense of composure.

When the half hour was up, Bruno and Fabien joined her in the interview suite. After making the necessary statements about time, place, and the recording devices in use in the room, Bruno settled himself in his seat while Fabien poured all of them glasses of water in paper cups.

Once Fabien was seated, Bruno began. He looked down at his notebook, and then up at Marion. 'Mademoiselle Perrin, we have brought you in today as a suspect in the murder of Joséphine Taun. You are under arrest, and face formal charges. We are required to offer you legal representation, and have a lawyer on standby should you not have one. Would you like a lawyer?'

She shook her head.

'Out loud, please, for the audio recording.'

'No, thank you.'

'You're sure?'

'Very.' She shuffled around in her seat and somehow found an extra few centimetres in her already erect spine. 'I assume that one of the reasons I'm here is that you've managed to establish my maiden name?'

Bruno nodded. 'You didn't make it easy for us, not with three marriages under your belt by your thirties.'

Across the table, Marion raised an eyebrow. 'Which has nothing to do with this case, officer.'

'Understood. It just took us rather longer to work our way back through the records than it would have had you never married.' Bruno flicked through his notebook. 'You're still sharing an apartment with Monsieur Perrin up in Paris, but you're in the process of divorcing?'

She looked taken aback. 'Not that I was aware of.'

'Ah. I had assumed that you had initiated proceedings to be with Monsieur Gosselin, but that's not the case?'

'Sébastien? Sébastien Gosselin? What does any of this have to do with him?'

Bruno looked at her, he thought it was obvious. 'You two are lovers, no?'

She laughed. 'Not in that sense, no. We fuck from time to time when we're on set, have done for years, but that's all there is to it.'

'Not just on set, we have the pair of you sharing a room at Le Moulin du Roc just before filming began on the current series.'

A shrug. 'It was the weekend before filming started. As far as I'm concerned that's all part of the season. But we weren't dating. It was casual, usually – but not always – around work. *C'est tout.*'

'So you're saying that Sébastien Gosselin knows nothing of your possible involvement in the death of Joséphine Taun?'

'I'm not convinced he even knows much about my involvement in the show we're working on.' She laughed. 'He couldn't be less interested in anything that's not about him.' Bruno was pleased to hear his opinion of the man confirmed, and had to suppress a small smile. The woman before him might be an accomplice to murder, but it didn't stop her having a sense of humour.

'On what evidence do you arrest me this morning?'

'We are in possession of location data from both your work and personal phones that puts you at the scene of the murder of Joséphine Taun, in the weeks preceding it and on the night of the murder. Have you anything to say in your defence?'

She shook her head. 'Nothing.'

'Do you admit that it was you?'

'I do.' Bruno hadn't expected it to be anything like this simple.

'You do?'

'I do.' Marion paused, and Bruno could see the seconds tick by on her face as she plotted her next move. She leaned her arms on the table and bent forward, inviting them to lean in. The invitation was ignored by both officers. 'There's simply no point in trying to hide it any more, is there? You would hardly have arrested me without plenty of evidence to back your case. Besides, if I'm cooperative now it should help me earn a reduced sentence later. Isn't that how these things usually go?' She looked at Bruno across the table and smiled.

'If you don't mind me saying, you don't seem to show either guilt or remorse at your actions.'

At that she barked a laugh. 'Is that because I was raised Catholic, condemned to be plagued by guilt whatever I do?'

'More because you've just confessed to killing a woman in cold blood.'

Marion raised her eyebrows. 'I didn't realise policemen were allowed to be sarcastic.' She sat upright in the chair and spread her arms wide for a stretch, rolling her shoulders. 'Do I feel guilty? No. I had a plan, and I executed it perfectly. Pun unintended. Actually, I'm a little bit proud of pulling it off.'

'Proud?'

'Well for one thing, I wasn't sure if I was going to be able to go through with it. Thinking about killing someone is very different from actually doing it, and it's only in the heat of the moment that you learn whether or not you're capable. I was.' At this she sat up a little straighter.

'And why did you kill Joséphine Taun?'

'Why don't you tell me why you think I did it, and I'll tell you how right or wrong you are?' She leaned back in her chair, presumably a more comfortable posture. 'I'm interested to know what you think you have on me, where it is that I slipped up.'

'Slipped up? You can't have thought you were going to get away with it forever.'

She shrugged. 'Unlikely, but still possible – people do get away with murder, from time to time. I've been planning this for years. Believe me, I weighed up the pluses and minuses before going ahead, and even taking into account the strong likelihood of getting caught, I couldn't come up with an answer that didn't make killing her worth it in the end.'

Bruno was repelled by the young woman before him, so calculating and rational in the face of both murder and a prison sentence. She was clearly playing a game, and he was confident he knew what it was.

'You seem very relaxed about being here.'

Another shrug. 'I always expected it would end like this, eventually. I killed a woman, and whatever precautions I may have taken to cover my traces, with the technology you people have access to I knew it was likely that it would be a matter of time before I got caught – even the coldest case can be reopened when the technology progresses. So whether it was now or in forty years' time, I'd made my peace with the notion of getting caught. I committed a crime, and it's only reasonable that I pay the price.'

Bruno nodded his head, slowly. 'I think I understand.'

'What made you narrow it down to me? Was it the location data on our phones? I thought I'd disabled mine.'

'Actually, it came down to a FitBit.'

She pulled a face. 'What FitBit? I don't wear one.'

'No. But your sister does.' Across the table Marion went white. It was Bruno's turn to lean forward, close the gap between them.

'Your older sister Céline? The data from the FitBit she wears – the FitBit you bought for her – puts her at the scene of the Taun murder. Not only that, but it registered a spike in heart rate around the time of death. As we speak, my colleagues in Marseille have rounded up your sister and charged her with the murder of Joséphine Taun. You are being charged as an accessory to the crime.

'For at least the last three years, Madame Perrin, that FitBit has been recording all of your sister's daily movements, and posting the results to their website. During the window of our inquiries, her FitBit data and your mobile phone location data shared a lot of overlap. We can match your movements with the CCTV footage from both the riding school and the centre of town. We know you two were watching Joséphine Taun. Would you like to tell me why you were interested in this woman in particular?'

Marion smirked. 'Surely knowing her real name, knowing who she really is, what she did. Isn't all that reason enough to want her gone?'

Bruno raised his eyebrows. 'I couldn't possibly comment.' A long pause. 'So you knew the victim?'

She scoffed. 'Victim. No, I never met her, and I don't think Céline did either, unless you count the night she killed her. I'd never even laid eyes on her till earlier this year.'

Bruno tilted his head to one side. 'And where were you that night?'

Marion looked at him as though he were an idiot. 'Can't your precious location data answer that?'

'Madame Perrin, you are not doing yourself any favours. You have confessed to a murder you didn't commit, and we can add wasting police time to the list of charges you face. A little cooperation here, a little explanation, could go a long way when it comes to trial.' He stood up and motioned for Fabien to join him. 'We'll give you a few minutes to think about it.'

Out in the hall, Fabien's face was stiff.

'Bruno, we're supposed to be on the same team,' he said. 'And I'm still the one officially leading this investigation, don't forget. I'm impressed, but you still need to keep me informed.'

'I'm sorry, but I couldn't tell you in case it changed the atmosphere in the room. I needed her to think we'd bought the picture she'd been painting for us. It occurred to me on my run yesterday that she could have been covering up for someone, that love was mixed up in it as well as revenge. And when I saw that Matthieu had a twin—'

'A twin?' Fabien shook his head, then looked to the floor and took a few deep breaths. 'That's got to have upped the trauma. How did we not make that connection earlier?'

'By the time we got onto the Taun identity we were swept up in the Netflix vehicle link.' He shrugged. 'That shouldn't have happened but it did. The important thing is we got there eventually. Let's see if Madame Perrin has decided to play ball.'

Marion was waiting for them, her hands clasped together on the tabletop. 'Céline has been arrested and charged already?' she asked.

Bruno looked at his watch. 'About ninety minutes ago.'

She nodded. 'Okay. I'd like to change my statement.'

'For the benefit of the recording, we're restarting this interview at 15:23 on Monday the twenty-fifth of April. Present are myself, Bruno Courrèges, Officer Fabien Panton, and Madame Marion Perrin. Madame, could you please confirm for the recording that you've been offered and have refused legal counsel?'

Marion cleared her throat. 'I have.'

'You would like to alter your statement, is that correct?'

'It is. I didn't kill Joséphine Taun, my sister did. Céline and I had been following her and I wanted to scare her, getting too close on my motorbike when she was walking down the street, being a bit of a threat. I didn't want her to feel safe now that she was out of prison. She didn't have the right to a comfortable old age, not after what she did.'

'And when did it turn from stalking to murder?'

'Stalking? I suppose you would call it that. For us it was more about monitoring our prey.' A pause. 'Which, I guess, is the dictionary definition of stalking, so there you go.' She shook her head. 'I'd not ever thought of myself as a stalker. It's just such grubby behaviour.'

Bruno raised an eyebrow but said nothing.

'I don't know what happened that day, I wasn't even there. Céline never said anything about killing her, not until after it was done.'

'And yet it was a determined and brutal assault. Did you know that your sister continued to strike her when she was already dead? The coroner's report confirmed that the bulk of the blows were issued post-mortem.'

'What of it? She was dead. I might not have done it, but I do think she deserved it.'

'And that's why you were happy to help cover up your sister's crime?'

'I wouldn't call it much of a cover-up, leaving the body where it fell.'

Bruno had never encountered such defiance in someone so ready to offer their confession and wasn't sure what to make of it. He looked at Fabien, and the younger officer gave the smallest shake of his head, equally puzzled. Marion pursed her lips and stared off into the distance behind his left shoulder. Bruno knew better than to say anything, and he hoped Fabien would follow his lead.

It took a long minute, but then she was ready to speak.

'Joséphine Taun destroyed my family. She had to be made to pay for what she did.' She looked at Bruno and at Fabien, making eye contact with each of them separately.

He nodded. 'Your brother was Matthieu Ventou.' It was a statement, not a question.

'He was.' She smiled broadly at the mention of him. 'Matthieu was my oldest brother, and I loved him like no one else in the world. So did Céline.'

'It must have been terrible for you when he died,' said Bruno.

'When he was murdered, you mean. I used to dream of avenging his death.'

'But you would have been a small child when he died, no? Around eight or nine?'

'I was eight. And I can assure you that your childhood comes to a fairly sharp end when you suffer a loss like I did.'

Bruno nodded. 'I was raised in an orphanage. It's not the same but I can understand what you mean.' He looked back down at his notebook, although there was nothing written there he hadn't already committed to memory. 'So you've been planning this for the best part of thirty years?'

'Yes and no. Yes, in that I fantasized about killing her from the moment we got the news about Matthieu. But I was, as you said, a small child. I imagined putting a bomb in her car, like you see in the movies, or pushing her off a cliff. They were just revenge fantasies, really.'

'But your stalking became reality. How did that happen?'

'When we realized that she would be coming up for parole. As family members of her victim, we are required by law to be notified in the event of her release, and of any court proceedings that might accelerate her release.' She readjusted herself in her seat and leaned forward.

'Obviously I took an interest in her hearings, we all did. When we got the news – I guess it would have been around six or seven years ago now? – that she was coming up for early release, I made it my business to keep an eye on where she went, what she was doing with her life.'

'There's a very big step missing between monitoring her movements and following her to and from work, harassing her,' said Fabien.

'There is. But I had to monitor her movements if I was going to be able to take advantage of any opportunities that presented themselves to make her life miserable. I got her fired from several care homes with anonymous reports before she landed on her feet down in Menton. Then it transpired that she was coming to work on my turf. It felt almost too good to be true – I could make her life very uncomfortable indeed. But I wasn't planning to kill her.'

'And Céline? Where does she fit into all this?'

'Céline was even more affected by Matthieu's death than I was. Her behaviour became extremely erratic and she was diagnosed with schizophrenia a couple of years later. She's been on medication ever since, heavy stuff. They never seemed to get the balance right, she was always veering between catatonic and manic. I might have been younger, but I always felt I had to look after her. The two of them were inseparable, in the way some twins are. So immersed in their own little world that they didn't need friends. Not till Matthieu was sent off to boarding school, anyway. Celine came out of her shell a little more when that happened.'

She stopped. Her demeanour had changed, become more thoughtful.

'You'll have to ask her what happened on the day itself. When she went to the house, she intended to confront Madame Taun, shock her, give her a bit of a scare. But things must have got out of hand. Céline could turn violent sometimes. All I know is that she turned up, soaking and dirty, in the car park of the crew hotel where we all stayed and I had to get her away as quickly as possible.'

'Soaking?'

'She'd showered at one of the campsites, I don't know where. She'd had the idea of using mud to cover the blood stains and she looked a complete mess. I took her a set of clean clothes and dropped her off at the station.'

'And why did you decide to cover for her?'

'I've *told* you. She's my big sister. Matthieu's death may have broken me, but it shattered her. It destroyed her mental equilibrium, and she hasn't been right since.' She looked at Bruno. The old defiance was back.

'Frankly, I'm much tougher than she is. I have to protect her, and I thought I'd have a better time of it in prison than she would.'

22

The St Denis Tuesday market was absolutely buzzing, and Bruno didn't see the Mayor until he bumped right into him, the two men briefly held together by the press of the crowd. Around them, customers were queueing impatiently for Lorraine's organic vegetables, for Stéphane's cheeses, for the fish that Guillaume drove in from the coast long before dawn.

'The longer I've known you, dear Bruno, the more convinced I am that you were born under a lucky star.' Bruno was rather taken aback – his life had hardly been a cakewalk, he felt.

'A lucky star? I'm afraid I don't follow.'

'Who else would manage to have a murder investigation all sewn up the day before the world's media descended on our little town to experience the delights of our revitalized market? That show you put on yesterday, lights and sirens and a convoy to the station? It would have killed any hope we had of making our market a story.' The Mayor clapped Bruno on the back. 'Your timing is impeccable.'

Bruno laughed. 'It's hardly the world's media, not like when you had all those dignitaries here after the discovery of the Resistance grave last autumn. The region's media, I'll give you.' Despite the tireless efforts of Colette Cantagnac, Bruno had to admit that he too had been surprised by the level of media attention afforded their market stars project – Philippe Delaron's piece for *Sud-Ouest* had hit something of a nerve, and colour pieces about the plucky small town trying new ways to breathe life back into its historic market had abounded on the airwaves of the Périgord, led by the formidable Marie-Do of Radio France Bleu.

That was without getting into any of the circus surrounding the Joséphine Taun murder and successful investigation. Once the victim's real identity had become known, the story had dominated the national news despite endless statements from the police asking that people not speculate lest they risk prejudicing an ongoing investigation.

Among those here to film the opening day of the three winning stalls was the Périgord branch of the TF1 news team, who would no doubt put the most attractive of the eloquent vox-poppers on at the end of that evening's local segment, the feel-good human-interest story to round out an hour of global tragedies. Privately, Bruno's money was on Marianne Mentier and Aurélie Marcelin getting rather more screen time than Javier Arnoux with his broken rugby nose, for such was still the way of the world, even in the twenty-first century.

Colette Cantagnac had arranged for Bruno to give the TV crew a tour of the market and had promised the broadcaster an on-camera interview with the man whose ingenuity was breathing new life into a once stagnating town. Although no stranger to the camera's glare, Bruno had to admit he was far more comfortable talking about progress in St Denis than he ever was speaking out in the hope of soliciting information from the public, whose appetite for the details of crime often bordered on ghoulish. As if conjured up by his thoughts, Colette appeared in front of him, plucked at the shoulders of his dress shirt, and smoothed down what Bruno assumed was a flyaway tuft of hair.

She nodded. 'You're looking presentable. Ready for the cameras?' Without waiting for a reply, she turned on her heel and marched towards the winning stalls, clearly expecting that Bruno would follow in her wake. At the stall of Aurélie Marcelin, he stopped. Apparently Aurélie was very talented at cross-stitch, her stock made up of a variety of hand-sewn interpretations of the more intimate aspects of the female anatomy. Behind the cameraman, Bruno could see Colette suppressing a smile, and he determined not to let anything faze him lest he really give her something to smile about.

'Chief Courrèges,' the presenter began, 'thank you for taking the time to talk to us, and congratulations on the success of your market revitalization scheme.'

'Any time, and thank you.' He cleared his throat. 'We're really happy to be able to show off the diverse array of talent found across the *département* – every month will see three new stallholders taking part, and it's a real opportunity to jumpstart a local business.'

'You said diverse,' the presenter went on. 'How would you categorize the display behind us? Pornographic?'

Bruno shook his head. 'What is Western art if not a multi-century celebration of the female form? Almost every one of the prehistoric caves in the Perigord has an engraving of the female vulva, and yet the male sexual organ is extremely rare. Mademoiselle Marcelin's work is but one example of a long classical tradition, although I suspect others might see it otherwise.'

Bruno raised his eyebrow at the presenter, who pulled an over-the-top chastened face for the cameras before wrapping up the segment with a reminder that St Denis market had been held every Tuesday morning for more than seven hundred years.

Interview duty completed and a potential trip hazard deftly swerved, Bruno began to make his rounds of the market, starting with a quick check of the stock on offer at the stalls of Marianne Mentier (wallets and purses made out of wasted stock from fast fashion brands that would otherwise be sent to landfill) and Javier Arnoux (beautiful hand-carved salad bowls, forks and spoons made from fallen chestnut trees in the surrounding countryside). After the cross-stitch surprise, he wanted to know what else St Denis was putting its promotional efforts behind.

'Bruno!' He felt a tap on his shoulder and turned to see an abashed-looking Lorraine. 'I owe you an apology. That wasn't kind, how we treated you.'

He shook his head. 'Maybe not. But I've been reliably informed that I need to spend more time asking people what they want, and less time doing things on their behalf. Apology accepted, but only if you accept mine. I didn't see you at my meeting last week, or I would have asked your forgiveness then.'

The old farmer beamed. 'You're a good boy at heart, Bruno. A little too impetuous, but decent. We're lucky to have you.' She leaned forward and squeezed Bruno's upper arm. 'As Stéphane took great pains to remind me.'

His spirits lifted, Bruno moved on. If Lorraine was back on side it was only a matter of time before the rest of the old guard thawed. While completing his tour he kept half an eye open for a glimpse of the elusive Laura. He hoped that she might be leading clients around the market, however unlikely a prospect that may be, but there had been no sign of her so far. He did however see Fat Jeanne, who approached him with a grin.

'I like these two new slots. They're bringing in a lot of money but not giving me any extra work.' She chuckled. 'I think I might even be able to charge a premium to be the stall next to one of these freebies – look at the foot traffic.'

There were certainly long lines at all three of the new stalls, although how many people were just looking he couldn't tell from this distance. 'Foot traffic doesn't mean money spent, Jeanne. Don't go counting your chickens . . .'

She spat on the ground at their feet and then beamed at him. 'As if a woman my age needs lessons from a boy of yours!' An eye roll, and she was back off into the throng. And a throng it was – Bruno wasn't sure whether to credit human curiosity, the social media promotion done by Vincent and Claudine, or Colette Cantagnac's assault on the more traditional forms of press and broadcast, but St Denis was as full as he could remember seeing it. There could be no denying that the first week of the market stall trials was a resounding success. The question was, could it be sustained throughout the summer?

Bruno knew that the answer to that question would depend on the people around him, on their willingness to carry on supporting the market once the initial burst of enthusiasm had worn off and the media spotlight grown cold. He had no doubt that the residents of St Denis would continue to rely on it as they always had done, but he needed to do more to keep people coming in from further afield.

It was time to put into action Massimo's suggestion of sponsored shuttle buses.

Epilogue

One month later

As Bruno carefully steered his faithful Land Rover through the narrow lanes of tightly packed vehicles he thought to himself that he'd never before been so happy to find it so hard to park in St Denis. The slots along the back wall had all been taken by news vans with satellite dishes on their roofs, stickered sides identifying them as belonging to France3, FranceInfo, even TF1. The Netflix team – what was left of it – looked to have made the journey across from St Christophe, although whether their outing was for business or pleasure Bruno did not yet know. The revitalization of the St Denis *marché nocturne* was big news, it seemed.

Giving up on the idea of parking in the official town lot, Bruno turned left onto the main road and immediately indicated right, turning into the small road that ran behind the *boulangerie* and towards the funeral parlour. It would mean a ten-minute walk back to the car at the end of the night, but he could live with that.

Bruno was still a few hundred metres from the night market when the sound of people having a good time reached him. He could hear laughter, shouting and the clinking of glasses and cutlery, accompanied by strains of music and the tantalizing scent of hot fat dripping onto charcoal. As he drew closer, he could see the size of the crowd that had made it so difficult to park – there must have been a couple of hundred people queueing for food, jostling for space at the picnic tables, lining up on the temporary stage that Colette Cantagnac had insisted would be the perfect dance floor.

'But will people dance?' Bruno remembered asking. Colette had laughed in response.

'You're serious?' she asked. Bruno nodded. 'I take it you've never been on a Club Med holiday?'

'Club Med?' He laughed. 'Never.' Colette was full of surprises.

'Let me assure you, Bruno, that there's nothing we French like more than organized dancing. Unless it's organized dancing accompanied by good food and wine, of course.'

As the strains of 'Le Madison' burst from the loudspeakers – with only a little squawking feedback – there was a stampede towards the stage, a hundred or more visitors of every age sticking out their arms and hips in sync, before jumping a quarter turn and repeating the process. There were grandmothers and toddlers, cool yet self-conscious teenagers giving it their all. Bruno spied Miranda's children dancing in a circle with Florence's twins, Patsy in the centre. In the corner, Claudine Jaboullier and Delphine Mausans were in a fit of giggles, Claudine filming the show with her phone. He was surprised to see a familiar shock of hair bouncing near the middle of the packed dance floor, a grin splitting Fabien's face from ear to ear. Bruno raised a hand in a half wave, unsure if he'd been seen.

Fabien's returning wave answered that question. A few seconds later he made his way through the dancers and over to Bruno, a light sheen of sweat on his brow. Bruno offered his hand to help him down, forgetting that a man in his late twenties still had knees that absorbed a jump.

'*Salut*, Bruno – *ça va*? Can you believe how many people have turned out? I think you've got representatives from every hamlet in the Dordogne!'

Bruno nodded, smiling. 'I couldn't be more pleased.'

'Come this way, I've got us set up at a table with everyone, next to the *pommes sarladaises*.'

The two men weaved their way through the bustling crowd, stopping what felt like every metre to bestow a *bonsoir* or a kiss hello, soaking up congratulations for a job well done. Bruno kept his eyes peeled for Laura, hoping that she might have cleared some space in her busy schedule for his big night, although he wasn't optimistic.

As they passed the beer stall Bruno stopped to say hello to Massimo, and found himself buried in the Italian giant's chest. It was a hug which at that moment he very much needed. '*Bravo*, Bruno, *bravo*. Your plans have worked a treat. Let me pour you each a glass of La Nocturne – the first one is on the house.'

'Business is better, then?'

'Business is booming.' Seconds later Bruno and Fabien were clutching cold glasses of an Indian pale ale, its scent hoppy and bitter. 'You'll have to come to Le Cromlech for a drink, I'll introduce you to my new staff.' With that, Massimo turned back to the queue of thirsty beer drinkers, and Bruno and Fabien continued their slow weave through the bustling crowd. When they finally reached the table Bruno saw it was filled with most of his favourite people – Pamela and Florence were deep in conversation, a cold bottle of Bergerac sec between them, with Jack and Miranda alongside. Opposite, J-J sat in a huddle with Jérôme, Marcel and the Baron, the four men sharing a huge platter of *confit de canard* and *pommes sarladaises* while Gabrielle Teyssier toyed awkwardly with a glass of red wine.

On spotting Bruno, the four men made as if to get up, but Bruno bade them stay seated. 'J-J, what a surprise! I wasn't convinced that you'd make it tonight.'

Further along the table Bruno spied Colette Cantagnac sitting with a gaggle of administrative staff he recognized from the regional council offices in Le Croiseau and raised a hand in salute. Gaston sat awkwardly among them, and for a moment Bruno was puzzled, but then he saw the adoring look on the print shop owner's face as he gazed at the smiling assistant. Colette mouthed the words 'well done' across the gap, while Agnès showed her youth with a double thumbs up. Despite his own aching heart, Bruno smiled; it pleased him to see how their hard work had brought so many people together.

Pamela and Florence finally noticed Bruno's arrival and broke away from their chat to give him kisses. 'Bruno! At last! For a minute there I thought you were going to miss the fruits of your labours.'

'As if,' he said. 'I can't believe you doubted me. I saw Patsy dancing with Daniel and Dora, so I imagine Kirk and Cassandra must be somewhere nearby?'

'Queueing for food with Fabiola; I'm sure they'll all be back soon,' Pamela explained. 'We'll have to budge up a bit when they come, we're starting to run out of space.'

'Don't forget Horst and Clothilde,' added Florence. 'I had a message from her a couple of hours ago; they've got a cocktail party at the museum this evening but will be along from Les Eyzies before nine.' She looked around. 'We might have to get them some food before it sells out.'

J-J affected a stern voice and drew the group's attention. 'I need to have words with you, Bruno. I simply can't have your lot poaching my best officers like this.' But then his face broke into a smile, and he half stood, leaning across the table to clap Fabien on the shoulder, where the young officer had found a seat next to Gabrielle. 'Bravo, young man. I think you've made a good decision.'

Fabien nodded. 'I think it was the right time for me to come home.' With some shuffling along the benches, room was made for Bruno and Fabien to sit down, and the younger man turned to his old boss. 'I wanted to thank you for everything you've done for me, both personally and professionally. I don't want you to think me ungrateful – I know you invested both time and money in me, in my career.'

'Both incredibly well spent, my boy. My job was to make an excellent officer out of you, not to put you on a path that wasn't right. As far as I'm concerned, good job done.' Fabien coloured slightly, a small smile on his face, and J-J went on. 'Besides, if I'm going to blame anyone for the loss of one of my most promising officers, it's Gabrielle Teyssier, and I can't fault her for being so damn good at her job. This case has allowed you to put a few old ghosts to rest, has it not?'

'Perhaps not to rest, not entirely. But it has made me confront a lot about myself, my past.' Bruno noticed Gabrielle giving Fabien's arm an affectionate pat.

Across the other side of the market Bruno caught a glimpse of Laura's profile. He was halfway out of his seat in pursuit when he was brought back to earth by J-J hoisting his glass in the air. 'Cheers to that!' As he raised his glass in answer, Bruno thought to himself that it was hardly the most appropriate response, but J-J would always be J-J.

'What are we cheersing?' Pamela and Florence again broke away from their conversation and focused their attention on the group. Laura had disappeared into the crowd, and Bruno scanned the faces in vain.

'Fabien, and his new role as *chef de service* at the *police municipale*, Le Buisson,' J-J boomed; the glass of wine in his hand clearly not his first.

At that moment a pair of hands covered Bruno's eyes and he caught a whiff of scent that he recognized.

'Guess who?'

Author's Note

This novel is dedicated to the memory of Fabien, a young man who died tragically early. He was the son of two dear friends, Gabrielle and Michael, the first chums Julia and I made in 1980 as a couple of newly-weds in London. Michael, a teacher and journalist, had been a foreign correspondent in the Lebanese civil war. Gabrielle, a translator, was to put my novels into French. When they moved to France they invited us to their new home in the Périgord, the old farmhouse at La Dinanderie. It was here in 1982 that our newborn daughter Kate played with theirs, Olivia, and then with their two slightly older children, Fabien and Laura, who were then all joined by our second daughter Fanny. When we were based in Moscow and later in Washington, we came back each year to our Périgord friends, to the food and wine, the medieval castles and the prehistoric caves, the markets and rivers and stately chateaux that make this region the most beguiling in France.

The original idea for this novel, for the threats that modern life, from supermarkets to women with full-time jobs, represent for the old village life of home cooking and open-air markets, was not mine. It came from our elder daughter, Kate. She is my co-author. As such, she invented the character of Fabien, named for her childhood friend and Bruno's new ally in law enforcement, along with his nickname of Sonic the Hedgehog from his unusual haircut. Kate made her name as a journalist specialising in Formula One motor sports, and her work appeared in the *New York Times* and the *Financial Times*. More lately she has become a food-loving travel writer who can direct you to the best *gyoza* in Tokyo, Mexico's finest *chilaquiles*, tacos and more, and the tastiest seafood in Costa Rica, along with the best cocktails in Cambodia and across South East Asia. I strongly recommend her food, drink and travel columns on Substack, https://substack.com/@thekateadventure.

While working on this book, Kate also drew my attention to the powerful and deeply disturbing report of the Independent Commission on Sexual Abuse in the French Church. Established by French bishops, the report found that an estimated 216,000 children were abused by priests, deacons, monks, or nuns from 1950 to 2020. That is more than 3,000 a year. It added that when abuse by other Church workers was also taken into account, 'the estimated number of child victims rises to 330,000 for the whole of the period.'

Like Kate, my wife Julia really deserves to be honoured as a co-author since almost all that I know about food and cooking I have learned from her. Julia has written on food for the *Sunday Times* and *Observer* in London, the *Washington Post* and *Gourmet* magazine in the USA. And her mimeographed column on food and what was to be found in the Moscow markets of the 1980s, initially intended for the foreign media and diplomatic community, became so well known that the Kremlin used to send a limo around to pick up a copy for the Politburo wives. As co-author of the Bruno cookbook, Julia was the one who really deserved the prize awarded to us by Gourmand International for the World's Best French Cookbook of the last twenty years. I mainly wrote the jolly bits and the history and the wines that came between the recipes. You can keep up with her weekly column on food and its fascinating history via juliawatson.substack.com

One of the aspects of writing novels that I find the most intriguing is the way that as an author I sometimes feel I am not in charge of the story. In this instance, it was the unexpected determination of Bruno and Laura to keep their love affair going, despite the stresses of work and conflicting schedules, the broken dinner dates and difficulties in communication.

As always when one novel is finished, a new one beckons and I am still waiting for the various characters to tell me what comes next. And now I have also to consider another couple in this relationship, the basset hounds Balzac and the beautiful George Sand. And what of Fabien's romantic future with the cyber-queen of the police commissariat? And who will be the new stallholders in the bustling market of St Denis? The future, tantalising and mysterious, lies in wait.

Martin Walker,
Perigord, 2025

RAISING READERS
Books Build Bright Futures

Dear Reader,

We'd love your attention for one more page to tell you about the crisis in children's reading, and what we can all do.

Studies have shown that reading for fun is the **single biggest predictor of a child's future life chances** – more than family circumstance, parents' educational background or income. It improves academic results, mental health, wealth, communication skills, ambition and happiness.[1]

The number of children reading for fun is in rapid decline. Young people have a lot of competition for their time. In 2024, 1 in 10 children and young people in the UK aged 5 to 18 did not own a single book at home.[2]

Hachette works extensively with schools, libraries and literacy charities, but here are some ways we can all raise more readers:

- Reading to children for just 10 minutes a day makes a difference
- Don't give up if children aren't regular readers – there will be books for them!
- Visit bookshops and libraries to get recommendations
- Encourage them to listen to audiobooks
- Support school libraries
- Give books as gifts

There's a lot more information about how to encourage children to read on our website: **www.RaisingReaders.co.uk**

Thank you for reading.

hachette UK

[1] OECD, '21st-Century Readers: Developing Literacy Skills in a Digital World', 2021, https://www.oecd.org/en/publications/21st-century-readers_a83d84cb-en.html

[2] National Literacy Trust, 'Book Ownership in 2024', November 2024, https://literacytrust.org.uk/research-services/research-reports/book-ownership-in-2024